"I CAN MAKE LOVE ONLY WITH WORDS."

Mischa's voice was seductively soft. "Shall I tell you how I would touch your hair, your lips, your full young breasts? Shall I describe what we would have together if the world were different?"

Laddy said breathlessly, "Mischa.... "

He glanced at the art exhibited around them. "Look at this painting by my friend," he commanded. "This is a woman in love body and soul, as you will someday be, but not with me. If I were the one, how could I keep from touching you? When I am next in prison," he continued, "I will remember this moment as though I had touched your flesh, as though we had become one."

Laddy felt sudden tears at the thought of the years stretching ahead, desolate and loveless, while she waited for this man, the man who could never come to her....

AND NOW...

SUPERROMANCES

Worldwide Library is proud to present a
sensational new series of modern love stories—
SUPERROMANCES.

Written by masters of the genre, these longer,
sensual and dramatic novels are truly in keeping
with today's changing life-styles. Full of intriguing
conflicts, the heartaches and delights of true love,
SUPERROMANCES are absorbing stories—
satisfying and sophisticated reading that lovers
of romance fiction have long been waiting for.

SUPERROMANCES
Contemporary love stories for the woman of today!

ALEXANDRA
SELLERS

CAPTIVE
OF DESIRE

A SUPERROMANCE FROM
WORLDWIDE
TORONTO · LONDON · NEW YORK · SYDNEY

This book is dedicated
to prisoners everywhere
and to you.

———————————◆———————————

Published, February 1982

First printing October 1981

ISBN 0-373-70013-X

PROLOGUE

THE JET stood at some distance from the terminal building, engines quiet, its door open on the steps that ran down to the tarmac. Near it, on the runway exit ramp, was parked a long black car. The two machines had been standing in these positions for half an hour, while men walked back and forth at intervals between them. Throughout there had been an unnatural silence; no one ran, no one shouted; if they spoke, their voices did not carry.

A moment before, a gray-haired man in a nondescript coat had come out of the plane and rejoined two that stood waiting by the car.

"This is it," he said quietly, and his two companions, in similar dress, turned to open the rear door of the car.

Now the first whisper of excitement breathed across the scene, for the man who got out of the back seat of the long car was not in the mold of the other three. As he stood beside them, short, thin and wiry, his tension was palpable. Beside the nondescript coats of his companions his leather jacket and creased trousers seemed incongruous, as did his obvious emotion.

His three escorts surrounded him, and at the aircraft four men appeared at the top of the steps. As though at a signal, these two groups started silently forward, across the tarmac and down the steps, and so measured was their motion that an alien being might have watched, fascinated, for this elaborate ritual of the coming together of eight to produce, perhaps, a ninth.

Simultaneously, at a distance of about five yards from each other, both parties stopped, and it then became obvious that a fourth man in the group from the plane also did not fit the mold of his three protectors. He was easily the tallest of all and very thin; his broad gaunt frame was covered by a badly fitting suit, and his hair was shaved close like a convict's. His eyes searched hungrily over the heads of his escort, though there was nothing to see in the fading light save grass and tarmac and, in the near distance, the large terminal building. In the far distance there were the lights of tall buildings, but it was impossible to say whether it was at these that he gazed.

Without apparent signal, the two waiting groups parted within themselves to allow each odd fourth man, slowly and hesitantly, to walk toward the center of that empty space between them. The short man walked easily, his well-knit, wiry muscles giving him a smooth gait, but the big man held himself rigidly and walked stiffly, as though he saved himself from stumbling only by an effort of will.

There was no sign of salute as the two passed

each other and moved toward the opposing groups without pause.

In that moment there was not a whisper, a breath of movement, from the waiting six. The motion of the two men, one jaunty, the other painstaking, seemed to require all the concentration of the watchers, until each group had been joined by a new fourth man.

Then a sudden burst of emotion electrified the atmosphere. Each group received its newcomer protectively, joyously, like a mother bear or a lioness with her lost cub, and drew him, quickly now, back to each respective den.

The blast of noise of the jet engines drowned out that of the car, and within moments the only evidence that the scene had taken place was their departing roar.

CHAPTER ONE

"YOU WHAT?" asked Harry Waller, his manner preoccupied, as he looked up at the girl leaning intently over his desk on the back bench of the newsroom of the *London Evening Herald*.

He was not surprised to see Laddy Penreith waving the last edition of that evening's paper practically under his nose, because Harry Waller had been the news editor of the *Herald* for nearly seven years now and very little had the power to surprise him anymore. But he was interested, because he was always interested in the things that got particular people going, especially Laddy. In her three years on the paper he had grown used to her appearing in front of his desk every now and then, passionately demanding that something be said about an injustice or asking to be assigned to cover a story that interested her.

"What is it this time?" he began, and then he realized, and he smiled at the memory of how the story had broken just in time to catch the last edition.

"BUSNETSKY RELEASED" was the headline

she was pointing to, all right, and he waited to hear why.

Laddy's name on her birth certificate and her by-line was Lucy Laedelia Penreith, but she had been Laddy as long as she could remember. It had suited her in the days when she had looked more like a boy than a girl, when she had worn torn shirts and grubby trousers, and raced along fences and climbed trees with the best of them. But she didn't look like a boy anymore. Now, at twenty-five, she was very much a woman—slim and full breasted, with "the longest legs in the newsroom"—and there were times when her dark eyes and full mouth made her almost beautiful.

This was not one of those times. When her "conscience was up," nobody noticed whether Laddy was beautiful or not. They only saw that her eyes were alight with the fires of passion and truth and that it seemed as though she would be consumed by them.

"Harry," she said, as he knew she would, "I've got to go on this story. You've got to let me cover Mischa Busnetsky's arrival." Her low voice had a faint transatlantic accent, and Harry Waller was conscious of being soothed by it. But he couldn't resist his little gibe. He threw down his pencil, leaned back and regarded her with the amused look she knew so well.

"You know, my love, when you get to be as old and jaded as I am, it's a great pleasure to see the young ones running around caring about Issues.

Now why, I ask myself, has this one got our Laddy so concerned? Mmm?''

Laddy laughed. ''What a liar you are, Harry. A less jaded man in this newsroom I do not know, but you say what you like. And you know perfectly well that I'm always interested in dissidents.''

That was certainly true, but Mischa Busnetsky was much more than a dissident in Laddy's mind. Harry could not have said how he knew that, but he was as certain as if she'd said it aloud.

''Dear girl,'' he said, ''as far as I can make out, you are interested in everything.'' Certainly, she had dedication, but Harry was trying to see if he could lead her off the topic, and Laddy laughed.

''Come on, Harry, someone's got to do it, with Brian away,'' she pressed, and her dark eyes lost their smile and willed him to say yes.

Harry Waller added this information to his mental file of what made Laddy Penreith tick. ''Brian may be back in time,'' he said, for no other reason than to see her face fall.

''But he's bound to be in Brussels till tomorrow, isn't he?'' she protested. ''When is Busnetsky arriving?''

''We don't know,'' said Harry.

Laddy burst out, ''Harry, you must have a very good idea!''

Of course, she would realize that he had read the national press-release bulletin and even that he had been the one to dash off the front-page story that afternoon, and he always had some information that was not going to be printed.

Abruptly Harry tired of his game. "He'll be staying the night in Zurich," he told her, "but the word's out he's flying straight on to London tomorrow. I'll call you when I get the word."

"Tomorrow!" Laddy breathed. "Thanks, Harry."

There was too much relief in her voice, and Harry's curiosity, already aroused, heightened.

"What—" he began, but she had already left him to go back to her own desk, and Harry shelved his curiosity and went back to the overnight report that he would be leaving for the night-duty reporter.

Harry blessed the powers that be for the timing of Busnetsky's release. The news had broken in time for the last edition of the evening papers, and now the morning papers would be scrambling for a new angle on what would otherwise be stale news. With luck, Busnetsky would arrive in England tomorrow, in time for the early-afternoon edition of the *Herald*. Unless the newly free man came up with something very newsworthy tomorrow evening, the mornings would be making do with "in-depth analyses" and backup stories again on Saturday.

Harry Waller checked the overnight report with a smile on his face and thought about Laddy Penreith's interest in Mikhail Busnetsky. He might have assigned her to cover the story without her asking, he reflected; it had been in his mind. With her strong background of involvement in her late father's interests, she was a natural choice.

Laddy had expressed an interest in Soviet affairs when she had been hired into the *Herald* newsroom from a smaller paper three years earlier. But the Russians were Brian March's exclusive domain, and he was not about to move over for the dark-eyed dedicated young woman who was a good enough reporter to be a threat to anyone—including, Harry reflected, himself.

Laddy had had to be satisfied with being among the general run of news gatherers for two and a half years, until Harry, recognizing that her brain and her nose for research were being wasted, had asked her to act as the paper's London expert on Israel.

But of course she still routinely covered other stories, and now Brian March was in Brussels covering the latest SALT talks impasse, and he could hardly complain—although he would, bitterly—if Laddy were assigned to cover an area that she had been so intimately involved with all her life.

Harry Waller threw the overnight list into his drawer and decided to go home. Brian March would be filing a backup story from Brussels tonight on the political inside of the Busnetsky release, and Harry would decide tomorrow where that would go, depending on how interesting it was to the man in the street. The rather uneducated man in the street, he amended mentally, and grimaced. In older days the full text of Brian's report would have gone on page two regardless, but stiff competition from what Harry called the "yellow" papers was inexorably forcing down the intellectual tone of what used to be an evening paper he was proud of. With passing contempt he cursed the *Herald*'s editor for his shortsightedness.

Harry put on his jacket in the empty, echoing newsroom. Tonight the paper seemed more to have died than to have been put to bed. But that was just his mood: he had been thinking of the lowered tone of the *Herald*.

The light in the library was still on, so Laddy must be in there, researching Busnetsky's background. That was interesting. He would have thought her father's own papers would have been far more valuable than the library clippings of the last eight or ten years. Extremely interesting, unless she was looking for some particular piece of information.... Harry crossed to the library door.

A long tattered gray envelope lay on the desk, and he could read the upside-down "Busnetsky" scrawled in red across the back of it. Laddy's head was bent intently over the tiny pile of newsprint, her dark curls glossy in the yellow light.

"Slim pickings," Harry said, indicating the pile, and she looked up, her hand resting almost caressingly on the tiny column-wide piece of newsprint she was reading. It was from the *Times*, he could tell from the type style: the *Herald* library, like that of all newspapers, kept clippings from every London paper in its files.

"Very slim," she agreed, smiling at him, but she

was preoccupied, her brown eyes were distant, and Harry filed away the information in his capacious brain that this story meant very much indeed to Laddy Penreith. Now, what special connection had her father had with Mikhail Busnetsky? As far as Harry knew, very little of Busnetsky's work had ever seen the light of day in the West, though it was a known fact that he was a writer.

"Don't work all night," he said, in a fatherly tone that was most unlike Harry Waller, but his brain was ticking over so rapidly he didn't notice.

"On this?" Laddy laughed, indicating the scanty pile of clippings that she had yet to read. "Another ten minutes at most." And she bent her head again, unconsciously dismissing him.

His footsteps thudded hollowly on the wooden floor and the rattle of his car keys in his hand was lost in the silence as he crossed the dimly lighted newsroom. Harry Waller's chin sank into the collar of his old mac as he let himself out.

Very curious. He hoped the SALT talks would keep Brian in Brussels over the weekend. He would like to be able to leave Laddy on the story for a while. He would like to learn what this was all about.

LADDY SIGHED, stuffing all the clippings back into the gray envelope, and threw it into the filing tray for the librarian to put away in the morning. There was nothing there she didn't already know. This had served no purpose except to bring back all the memories, all the pain.

Laddy rested her forehead on her palm and glanced at the wristwatch on her other arm. She had better get home; she couldn't stay here all night, although if unconsciousness had descended on her here and now she would have welcomed it.

John was coming for dinner tonight, she suddenly remembered. Of all nights! John, who had something special to tell her, something she knew she wanted to hear. But not tonight. Tonight she wanted to crawl into her bed and cry herself to sleep.

Well, she couldn't. It was the first time she had invited him to dinner at home, and John would not understand a last minute put-off.

Wearily she got to her feet and left the library, thinking about the evening as she had originally planned it. She should have had the meal halfway cooked by now and had time to dress herself carefully, beautifully, and been relaxed and smiling when John came in.

Relaxed and smiling and ready to hear, when he told her, that he loved her. That was what she was sure he was going to say, and that was what she wanted to hear.

But now she would be rushed and unhappy, and all she would want to do would be to put her head on his broad chest and weep and have him tell her that it didn't matter.

Laddy gathered up her coat and ran through the

door, down the stairs and out into the warm spring evening.

If the sun had not actually set, it had certainly gone down behind the tall buildings of the Fleet Street area, and Laddy walked down the laneway to the small red car that sat, alone now, by the pavement. Well, at least the rush-hour traffic would be long since over; she would make good time home.

She tried to push Mischa Busnetsky's face out of her mind as she drove, and her father's, too, but it was impossible. She tried to think of John, to conjure up his smiling handsome face to drive away her pain, but his magic was impotent against this. Everything took a back seat to this, even the face of the man she was sure she loved.

Laddy parked her car behind a dark green one in the old, tree-lined street and breathed deeply in the scented spring air as she moved up the front path to her house.

Margaret and Ben Smiley were home upstairs, and if she had had time, she might have gone up for a cup of tea and a quiet, calming chat. That was one of the benefits she had not foreseen three years ago when she had rented out the upper story: that she always had friends on call.

But not tonight. Laddy unlocked her door and moved down the hallway to the kitchen at the back.

Laddy's kitchen was the prettiest room in the house, its soft yellow wallpaper with the tiny flowers giving it a warm glow all year round. But tonight it was too full of memories: she could not look at the unstained pine table without seeing her father sitting there, talking, listening, understanding.

Laddy dropped her bag and the paper onto the table and turned to the stove. Well, she had planned a simple menu, melon and beef Stroganoff and salad, and luckily she had stewed the beef last night. Now she turned it into a saucepan and pulled mushrooms from the refrigerator and began chopping them. Suddenly she put down her knife and crossed over to the table, staring down at the copy of the *Herald* that she had dropped there. Mischa Busnetsky's face filled half the front page under the blazing headline and she studied the picture intently.

A broad forehead, close-cropped hair, dark eyes full of a dedicated fire that were riveting in their intelligence. He would look older now; the photo had been taken almost eight years ago. Laddy had seen it countless times. It had been shot during one of his early trials, after he had already spent a year in Lefortovo prison. He wouldn't look like that now, she reflected grimly. Not after all those years of....

And tonight he was flying to freedom. What was he thinking now, she wondered, leaving the homeland he might never see again?

The hot oil in the saucepan spat loudly, and with an exclamation Laddy hurried to the stove to continue her preparations for the meal. Damn it! He was a job of work, a story assignment, that was all! She would think about him tomorrow.

After a moment she returned to the table and collected the paper, taking it back to set beside her on the counter. She gazed at Mischa Busnetsky from time to time as she worked.

Her father had first shown her the picture when she was seventeen and the man in the picture twenty-three. She had been mesmerized by him then and she was now, but now between her and those eyes was a barrier of pain. Personal pain, which, added to the long years of hatred she felt for Mischa Busnetsky's oppressors, became an intolerable knot in the pit of her stomach. A knot of anger and hatred for all the oppressors of the world, who sought out that intelligence and burning dedication in order to destroy it.

Laddy gazed at the picture. He had a wide and well-defined mouth that seemed to be almost smiling at the photographer, at his accusers, and in his eyes was the knowledge, the contemptuous acceptance, that the outcome of the trial was a foregone conclusion.

What had happened to that intelligence now? What would he look like now, after the long series of prisons and labor camps and, finally, confinement in psychiatric hospitals? What had happened to that burning intelligence under the onslaught of modern medical and psychiatric knowledge?

Laddy put the salad in the refrigerator, leaving the rice and the beef simmering on low heat, and went into the bedroom. John would be here in fifteen minutes; she would have time for a shower if she were quick.

But it was not the way she had intended it, she thought as she dried herself quickly and pulled over her head the beautiful wine-colored caftan embroidered in gold thread that her father had brought her back from one of his last trips. She had meant to laze in the bath, and dress and make up carefully.

She put on more makeup than usual, mechanically outlining her dark eyes and using mascara and a lipstick in a shade called raisin, which matched the caftan. Her black hair needed no special care. A quick brushing restored the natural fall of curls that clustered around her head and to her shoulders.

In the kitchen Laddy laid the table quickly, foregoing the flowers she had meant to cut from the garden for a centerpiece. She was ready, but it looked as though John were going to be late. Laddy sank into a chair and almost involuntarily picked up the paper again. . . .

"Another Soviet dissident on the ICF's list," her father had said, passing the picture to her across the desk in his study upstairs, now Margaret and Ben Smiley's sitting room. "I'll be traveling to Moscow soon, with a fair chance of meeting him."

Laddy had not been able to tear her eyes away from the face in the photo. "I wish I could go with you this time," she'd said. She had just entered university to study journalism, and it was the first time in seven years that her own interests would prevent her traveling with her father.

As one of the founders of the International Council on Freedom, Dr. Lewis Penreith had put his massive dedication behind the cause of dissident thinkers under totalitarian regimes the world over. His small publishing house in Covent Garden had published the works of these dissident thinkers, which Lewis Penreith had obtained secretly on his travels and had often smuggled out of various countries. The publication of such works in the West sometimes contributed to the release of the author from prison or internal exile, or to his expulsion to the West.

From the age of ten, ever since her mother had died, Laddy had traveled with him. Lewis Penreith had believed that travel was the best education she could have, and her warmest childhood memories were of lying on his study floor, poring over an atlas while her father described the people, culture, language and history of the country they were about to visit.

Although they had traveled as far afield as Hong Kong and Argentina, Lewis Penreith had been a Russian scholar, and the Soviet dissidents had been closest to his heart. Their cause he had made his personal one.

He had taken up Mikhail Busnetsky's cause after publishing a powerful exposé of the Soviet treatment of political dissidents that Busnetsky had written in Lefortovo Prison. Lewis Penreith had decided to go to Moscow to try to meet him.

"I wish I could go with you this time," Laddy

had said again, looking into the searching eyes in the photograph and feeling somewhere inside her that she knew the man as deeply as though he were herself. But Laddy was seventeen then and starting on her own career, and her years of traveling with her father were over. She was excited by the future work she had chosen—her goal even then had been to work as a newspaper reporter—but now she was seeing the price of it for the first time, and it caught her a deep blow somewhere in behind her ribs: because of her choice, because of the timing, this was a man she was destined never to meet. She had looked at her father sadly.

"Well, it's only a five-day trip," Lewis Penreith said easily. "Why don't you come? Make it our last jaunt together. It'll be worthwhile."

Laddy read Busnetsky's *Details of Oppression* that night, and she knew that if there was the faintest chance of meeting the author, she had to go with her father. The next morning she told him she would make one last trip with him—to Moscow.

It was an end for her, she thought, and somehow also a beginning.

CHAPTER TWO

Moscow was stark, cold, gray, dirty and impressive, as always, and although she had been here before with her father, as always it took her breath away.

But there was little time for tourist pursuits. They had contacts to make, people to seek out—in secret. Pushkin Square, Red Square, the Kremlin; all were seen with craned neck through the dirty window of a taxi.

The rules she had learned on past visits came quickly back to Laddy: never talk about anything but the weather in your hotel room; ignore the fact that you are being followed; never carry the address of any Russian contact with you; and don't bother to get upset over mild inefficiencies like a lack of toilet paper in the hotel.

Mischa Busnetsky, who had been out of prison only three months, had organized a showing of the works of an underground artist—a showing that had no official sanction. It was at this exhibition that Lewis Penreith hoped to meet him. In those days in Moscow there was another "thaw," and foreign correspondents were allowed almost uninhibited access to certain dissident intellectuals who had been published in the West. These men and women, holding court in small overcrowded apartments, were taking all the advantage they could of their sudden immunity from the secret police, for they were felt to be too well known in the West to be sent to internal exile or prison.

It was in one of those small apartments that Mischa Busnetsky had organized the art showing, and as they approached the large stark apartment building, Laddy's heart had leaped in a kind of fear she had never known before on such trips. No meeting with a dissident, famous or obscure, had ever caused such turmoil in her.

The building was large enough that no secret follower could be certain of which apartment was being visited, and as she and her father climbed the stairs to the fourth floor they heard no step on the stairs behind them; nevertheless, a tight band had formed itself around Laddy's ribs so that it was almost impossible to breathe.

The apartment was packed to the rafters. The exhibition had been running for six days, and people knew that it would not be allowed to run much longer.

The forbidden paintings were all nudes. Sensuous, erotic, compelling, and the glow from the skin tones seemed to suffuse that small, over-furnished, overcrowded apartment with a wave of sexual warmth that touched her, washed her from the moment Laddy walked through the door.

At seventeen, Laddy had never even had a boy-friend. Her father's work and her life of travel had cut her off from conventional friendships, but she had never missed such things, her life was so full.

The paintings—some softly, some harshly seductive—made Laddy suddenly, and for the first time, aware that she was a woman. She had stood motionless, gazing at the nudes, scarcely able to breathe, until her father had softly called her name.

And she had turned, and her father was standing beside the man in the photograph.

Laddy had watched her body's changes over the past few years, had watched herself becoming a woman, with an air almost of detachment: her breasts had filled out, her legs had suddenly been long and well shaped. She was, after all, a female. But it had not touched her. She had begun to wear more adult clothing because the salesgirls had led her to those racks.

Now, in the moment that she and Mischa Busnetsky looked at each other for the first time, what she felt was, oh God, what it is to be a woman! And it was a prayer of the deepest, the most delighted gratitude, and the most profound discovery suffused her, earthshaking, as significant to her as "I think, therefore I am."

He was tall, taller than her father, taller than anyone in the vicinity, and he was thin and his hair was jet black. And those eyes that even in the photograph had seemed to see so much, saw everything there was to see about Laddy Penreith—heart and body and soul. Over Mischa Busnetsky's shoulder, the painting of a naked woman on her knees, her back arched and her hair dangling down her back, cast its golden glow over her mood, and she had a light-headed, drunken feeling that she knew the entire meaning of life.

He took her hand and said her name, and his warm hard strength seemed to issue equally from his deep voice and from the touch of that roughened palm. From him directly she recovered the strength to speak, and what she said, softly, gently, was, "Don't go to prison again."

An indecipherable look, like a mixture of regret, resignation and sacrifice crossed his face, and his eyes were momentarily darker. He smiled down at her, a slow, understanding smile, and that, too, touched her physically, in a way she had never before experienced and only instinctively now understood. "I do not want to go to prison again," he said, "but this is a choice that is not mine to make."

She understood that he intended to continue his battle, whatever the result might be, and something deep within her cried out for her to tell him to give it up, to give in, to tell him that nothing was as important as what she felt in that moment—not freedom or right or truth. But she held back the cry as a betrayal, and she smiled at him in her turn. In that moment she knew all the agony of a woman who sees her man off to battle knowing that nothing in life is as important as what they have together— nothing—but letting him go to make the world right, knowing that the world can never be right for her if he does not come back.

Mischa Busnetsky and her father talked quietly for a long time about important things—of which Laddy heard not a word. Afterward she could not even remember whether they had spoken in Russian or English. She was learning a whole new language—the song her body sang. She understood that the red velvet of her dress over the soft fullness of her breast was an unmatchable eroticism, that the brush of red velvet on her thigh was also the touch of black denim on Mischa Busnetsky's; that she and this dark man were, at one and the same time, one complete being and its two composite, opposite halves.

When her father's attention was claimed by someone else and he moved away from them, Laddy and Mischa Busnetsky stared at each other in the crowded room, buffeted by the milling crowd, but untouched by anything except what they saw in each other's eyes.

"Have you looked at my friend Vaclav's paintings?" he asked her at last. And when Laddy shook her head, he said, "Come. I will show you." And the electricity between them was so powerful, she knew that his putting an arm round her waist, light as the touch was, was an involuntary movement; she knew with a direct, certain knowledge that he could not prevent himself from touching her in that moment, any more than she could stop her own body's moving toward him so that her hip and leg brushed his as they walked.

He paused in front of the painting of a woman who stood in a simple pose, facing the viewer, waiting. That was all, except somehow one sensed the woman was watching the approach of her lover. Her eyes and part of her golden body were in shadow, but Laddy knew that the woman was looking at a man she loved passionately, and in every line of that naked body was evidence of a battle she was fighting with herself to wait, to wait and make him come to her.

Laddy drew in her breath through opened lips and felt Mischa Busnetsky glance down at her. They said nothing, and he guided her gently but firmly to the next painting.

A woman on her knees, her arms up and her lips parted, but this time the shadow falling on her was in the shape of a man's leg and hip, and when she realized the significance of it, Laddy felt her insides turn over. For a moment she closed her eyes.

"You are young," his deep voice came from over her head. "How old are you?"

"Seventeen," she breathed, her whole body aware of the contact between them at leg and hip, and his hand, burningly strong at her waist.

"In the West that is old enough to have learned about love," he said quietly. Laddy caught her breath.

"Have you learned about love?" he asked, quietly, gently.

She whispered, "No."

"It will not be long before someone will wish to teach you," he said. "You are so beautiful, so alive." There was quiet regret, resignation in his tone. "I would like to teach you about love," he said, and Laddy felt as though she had been struck in the stomach. She looked up at him; he was looking down at her, the same quiet regret in his eyes as she heard in his voice.

"But these things are not to be," he continued, his voice now causing a warmth to flow through her body, his voice caressing her and her body responding.

Her eyes, wide, gazed into his, and she felt that he must kiss her. "Look at the picture," he commanded quietly, doing so himself, and she looked at the picture of the enraptured woman with parted lips.

"This is a look I will never see on your face," he said. "But this is how you would look for me if I taught you about love."

No one around them in the crowded apartment was taking the least notice of them, and Laddy realized, with a kind of drunken joy, that what he was saying to her, in English, could not be understood by anyone in the room except her father, who stood by another wall engrossed in conversation.

"Here I can make love to you only with words," Mischa said. "Shall I do this? Shall I tell you how my mouth would touch your hair, your soft lips, your full young breasts? Shall I tell you what we would have together if the world were not what it is at this moment?''

She murmured, ''Mischa—''

''Look at the painting of my friend Vaclav,'' he commanded again. ''This is a woman who is in love with a man body and soul, as you will someday be, but not for me. But if it were I, if you looked at me like this, how would I keep from touching your lips?'' And he reached out and his fingers lightly touched the oil-on-canvas lips of the woman kneeling in the golden glow and the shadow.

Laddy's mouth burned as though it were her lips that he touched. His hand dropped to his side.

''When I am next in prison,'' he said, ''I will remember this as though it were your own flesh I had touched, and I will remember you looking at me with a face such as this, and then I will wish that life had been different.'' He looked down at her again.

''You do not yet know about love, but I know how you have looked when my hand is on your breast, I know what you have said to me when I touch your thighs, your long legs. Everything I know about you, even how you have made me tremble.''

Laddy already could hardly speak, could hardly stand, but the thought of what it would do to her to know she had made this man tremble, made her head reel. She swallowed, licking her lips.

"I would like to make you tremble," she whispered, hardly knowing what she said.

She saw that she had reached him by the sudden breath that he took, the involuntary tightening of the clasp of his hand on her hip.

"I trembled the first moment I saw you," he said roughly. "These other things will never be, but— you have made me tremble."

Suddenly she felt tears in her eyes. "Tell me," she said, fighting back the tears, for in that moment it was as though all the years stretched out ahead of her, desolate, empty and loveless, while she waited for this man, the man who could never come to her. And instinctively she wanted all the memories that he could give her, to store up against the future emptiness that she saw so clearly. "Tell me how it would have been," she repeated, and in her voice was a plea against the loneliness, and she knew that he heard and understood.

They walked around the whole room then, looking at the paintings, and all the time his deep quiet voice, rough with passion, was making love to her, slow, incredible, passionate love to her, and her body responded fanatically, drunkenly, to every word until, when he said that she would moan his name aloud, she did so.

"Mischa," she breathed.

He said, roughly, "Lady," for in his deep, full-voweled accent her name was changed.

She looked into his dark face and thought she could feel her heart breaking, and Mischa Busnetsky touched a tear from her cheek with a gentle finger and smiled down at her.

"The world is not as we would make it," he said quietly.

She saw her father coming toward them over Mischa Busnetsky's shoulder, and her heart was chill. She looked up at him while her father helped her into her coat, and she saw in Mischa's eyes that she looked at him for the last time, and it was a pain worse than dying. He caught her hand and their fingers clung, as though through a barred gate—a gate that would never be unlocked.

Holding her hand, Mischa saw Laddy and her father to the door and then down the ill-lighted hallway to the top of the stairs. Her father started down, but with a foot on the first step, Laddy turned and gazed in anguish at the man looming so darkly above her.

"I love you," she whispered, her stomach hollow and knotted with pain. Mischa Busnetsky breathed as though he had been struck and silently bent to bury his mouth in her trembling palm.

The sound of a stifled cough several floors below traveled clearly in the silence. The secret shadow, their watchdog, was waiting in the warmth for his quarry to reappear.

Mischa raised his head and caught her gaze. "Not as we would make it," he repeated, and he smiled at her as he might have smiled at his own death.

She would not protest at what could not be changed. Smiling back at him in salute and farewell

Laddy took her hand from his and turned and walked slowly down the stairs to her waiting father.

The next day the art exhibition was closed by the secret police.

A month later Mischa Busnetsky was in prison again, for "possession of anti-Soviet propaganda."

CHAPTER THREE

LADDY GAZED unseeingly at the newspaper that had slipped off her lap and lay on the floor beside the hem of her dress. The heavy burgundy silk was a deeper hue than the red velvet from eight years ago, as though the color had mellowed and aged. Laddy shook her head to clear it.

Her memories had not mellowed and aged. She had locked them away, long ago, and now when she took off the lock, she might have expected them to have less immediacy, less power—but no. Eight long years had passed, but when she thought of Mischa Busnetsky she might have seen his face yesterday.

Laddy bit her lip and dropped her forehead into her hand. That he should have been released today, of all days! That she should be sitting here tonight, of all nights, remembering the scene that had destroyed her, remembering the man whose face came between her and every man who wanted her!

In eight long years, John Bentinck had been the only man who had kissed her without her tasting betrayal on his lips—betrayal not of Mischa Busnetsky, but of her own knowledge of what love should be.

Tonight, after two months of gentle courtship, he was going to tell her he loved her—and Laddy had allowed those memories out. What were her chances now of being made to forget them forever, by John?

The doorbell had rung three times before it filtered through to her conscious mind. With a smothered gasp, Laddy jumped up, hurled the paper with Mischa Busnetsky's picture onto the counter and ran down the hall to the door.

At the sight of the handsome golden-haired man on her doorstep, Laddy resolutely pushed her memories down. "Hello," she smiled, and John Bentinck smiled at her in a way that turned her heart over, and she willed him to have the power to make her forget.

"Hello, yourself!" he said, his deep northern voice warm and his smile broadening in appreciation as he looked at her.

John had joined the staff of the *Herald* two months ago as a news photographer, coming from a small paper up north, and Laddy had liked him the moment she had seen him.

He was a very good photographer, she had discovered during the many assignments they had covered together, with a sensitive eye for the unusual in a scene.

He was twenty-seven, and he lived for the moment when one good picture was picked up by the wire services and used in newspapers around the world, and his name was made.

Laddy knew it would happen; she had confidence in him. And she was nearly sure she could love him.

"Well!" John exclaimed. "You are something, aren't you? Come here!" He drew her to him slowly, smilingly, and kissed her, and she wanted to be in love with him.

She reached her arms up around his neck; in response, his kiss became more ardent. "Well, well, well, my love," he said when they drew apart. He touched her chin with a forefinger and smiled down at her.

Her heart racing pleasantly, she hung up his coat and led him down the softly lighted hallway to the kitchen, where he sniffed appreciatively before looking around. "Very nice," he murmured, as his glance fell on the table. He smiled again. "I do hope," he said, "that the kitchen is where you feed your special friends."

Laddy laughed. John could always make her laugh.

"But of course."

"It's not where you feed the men you're keeping at bay?" he pressed with mock worry.

"I don't feed the men I'm keeping at bay at all," she responded gravely.

He smiled meaningfully at her. "You have just made a very damaging admission."

Laddy laughed again as the truth of this struck

her. "And you," she said accusingly, "tricked me into it!"

They laughed together. They laughed all through the meal that was, in spite of the kitchen background, intimate, with the soft lamp lighting the table and the plants around the darkened window creating a cozy world for them. Laddy almost succeeded in banishing any other thought than that John was with her and that she was fond of him.

"This meal was really something," John said, as he finished the last bite and pushed his plate away. "I can see why you don't feed the men you're keeping at bay."

"Thank you for those kind words," Laddy said wryly. John blinked, then a rueful smile spread over his face.

"That does it," he said. "I am going to get my mother to teach me how to compliment a lady!"

When she had poured their coffee, John said, "Let's move out of these chairs to somewhere more comfortable." Laddy followed him into the sitting room with her coffee cup in her hand and sat down obediently beside him on the sofa where he patted it with his free hand.

"Remember I told you I had something to tell you?" he said, when he had put one arm around her and pulled her closer. He felt her nod against his side. "Well—" he said, leaning forward to set his cup and saucer down on the small table in front of them and turning to face her "—I've got my holiday time. I had to fight Richard for it, but I got it."

He paused significantly. "Starting two weeks Monday."

"That's when mine are," said Laddy, in surprise.

"I know," John said smiling. "I do know. How would you—" he bent and kissed her lightly on the lips "—how would you like to come to Greece with me?"

Laddy jerked her head from his chest and blinked up into his slightly apprehensive eyes.

"Greece?" she repeated stupidly, taken completely by surprise.

"Warm sun, golden sand, rosy sunsets, soft nights and sea," John said softly. "And me."

And him. The man she wanted to love, the man she had thought—hoped—was going to tell her tonight that he loved her.

He wanted her to go away with him, he wanted to start an affair with her.

Laddy breathed deeply and sighed.

"I would have to think about that," she said quietly.

She wanted to say yes. She wanted to forget Mischa Busnetsky and the effect he had had on her. She wanted to forget her unrealistic dreams and take what was offered her, wanted to fall in love with warm, safe John Bentinck and be loved by him. And yet. . . .

"Are you thinking about it?" he asked from above her head, his voice resonating in his chest under her ear and breaking into her confused thoughts.

"Oh, yes," she said, smiling as she lay in the comfortable curve of his arm.

"And what's the result?" he pressed. She could hear that he was smiling as he said it, and underneath the smile, she could hear—hurt. He had expected her to say yes immediately.

She knew with a sudden painful clarity that if she said no, she would lose him.

In the two months of their almost platonic relationship, he had never pushed, never demanded anything of her. He had kissed her good-night, he had sometimes held her as he was holding her now—but she had never had an uncomfortable moment with him, had never seen impatience in his eyes. It was as though he had understood her private, inexplicable pain, as though he had known that the way to help her was never to demand more than she could volunteer.

She did not want to lose him.

Greece, she thought, conjuring up in her thoughts a vision of what was being offered her. She was sitting with her head on John's shoulder, his arm around her, her arm around his chest. She felt physically comfortable with him. She felt warm and close and. . . loved. Suppose they were lying on a warm beach in this posture, her cheek resting on his naked, sea-damp chest; suppose she knew that when they got up they would be returning to a shared hotel room?

She passed her hand nervously over his chest, and he ran his free hand up her arm to her shoulder and then, tilting her head back, he bent to kiss her.

A gentle *frisson* of passion touched her spine, and she welcomed it. Surely it would grow?

"Why?" she queried softly when he lifted his head.

"Why?" John repeated in surprise.

"Why did you work so hard to get your holidays? Why are you asking me to go with you?"

"My sweet, modest woman, because I adore you—" he kissed her lightly "—and love you—" another kiss "—and I fancy you like mad," he said. He wrapped both arms around her and held her tightly to him. "Come with me, love," he whispered.

"I have to—" she began.

He interrupted in an urgent tone, "Don't think, Laddy. Don't *think*!" He began to kiss her, urgency mounting in his hands and his mouth, as though a tight rein he had held on himself had suddenly broken.

His urgency fanned the pale spark of her passion, so that she did not resist, and he kissed her throat and eyes and then her mouth again—

The phone rang.

John swore, lifting his mouth from hers. "Let it ring," he said thickly, as she struggled out of his arms.

"I can't!" said Laddy. "It's probably Harry!" Suddenly the thought that she might be seeing, talking to Mischa Busnetsky tomorrow, made her stomach turn over. She was almost afraid.

She ran to the kitchen to the phone.

"Hello, dear girl," Harry Waller's voice said in her ear. "Were you busy?"

"No," Laddy replied. "What's the word?"

"Ten o'clock in the morning at Heathrow," he said, and added other details. "He's all yours. Have a good time with it," he ended, mocking her a little as he hung up.

Laddy turned back to the sitting room, but the phone rang again. This time it was Richard Snapes, the pictures editor, and he asked for John.

"Yes, he's here," she said, surprised. "What made you think of trying here?"

"Only the fact that he left me your number as where he'd be available tonight," Richard's dry voice responded.

Laddy turned to the doorway to call John. "It's Richard," she said. She watched him curiously as he came down the hallway toward her and crossed to the phone. "Tonight," Richard had said. Well, tonight was an ambiguous word. It could mean merely the evening—or it could mean all night.

Laddy moved into the sitting room. Richard Snapes had expected her to answer the phone. He'd greeted her hello with "Hello, Laddy." But there was no way Richard Snapes would be that familiar with her telephone number—or her voice. He was the pictures editor; he organized the assignments of the photographers and had little to do with reporters.

Which could only mean that John had said, "I'll

be at Laddy Penreith's tonight, here's her number." Of course, he had to leave a number where he could be reached if he was expecting an assignment call to come through, but why had he made a point of saying it was her number? And had he really said "tonight" and not "this evening"?

Perhaps he had been very confident that he would be staying the night?

No, she wouldn't believe that. Not of John. John, who never pushed her an inch farther than she was prepared to go. . . .

Yet a few moments ago she had known that he wanted, intended to make love to her. She had felt the sudden breaking of his restraint, as though for the first time he had lost a control she had not even been aware he was using. But if he had already told Richard that he would be here "tonight," what did that make it? Calculated passion?

Laddy suppressed an irritated exclamation. She was responding like a teenager, reading far too much into too few facts.

John came back into the room and walked up to her, putting his arms around her waist. "Now, where were we?" he asked.

"You were talking to Richard," she said. "Was that tomorrow's assignment?"

"Yes," John said, making a face. "Airport, ten o'clock."

"Yes, me, too," she said, hugging him. "I'm glad we'll be covering it together." John was a very good photographer, and they worked well together.

And she was a fool to have any doubts about him. Nevertheless, when he had kissed her again, she found herself saying, "You have to go now. I want to be on my toes for Busnetsky tomorrow. There's going to be a crush."

John drew back, almost angry. "Aren't you taking devotion to duty a little too far?" he asked. "It's not even eleven o'clock."

But suddenly she could think of nothing but Mischa Busnetsky, and she was afraid; it was something she did not understand. She drew away from him, and John looked down into her eyes and saw the fear.

"All right, Laddy," he sighed. She knew that he thought she was afraid of *him*. "Go to bed—but dream of me."

He kissed her again and chatted a little as he took his coat and found his keys—but she did not hear what he was saying. She smiled at him when he smiled at her, laughed a little because he did, and said goodbye but in her thoughts she was miles away from him.

Tomorrow she would see Mischa Busnetsky for the first time in eight years. And now that the meeting was almost upon her, she realized that she was utterly terrified of it.

Laddy gazed unseeingly around her comfortable living room and shook her head as if to clear it. But Mischa Busnetsky would not so easily be banished.

She had thought about him almost constantly in the first years after her last trip with her father. She had written him in prison, letters she could never be sure he would receive, letters Mischa had never answered.

His memory had stayed strong in her because the promise he had made her, of what her experience of love would be, had been false. She had never felt that drunken joy again; no man's kiss had shaken her the way the sight of Mischa's hand caressing the lips of a woman in an oil painting had shaken her.

She had never understood what had happened to her that night, but she had learned, with a resigned disappointment, that it had been a myth. One day she had realized that that one false memory was in danger of destroying her life. She had resolutely pushed all thought of Mischa Busnetsky from her mind from that day.

She was appalled at her discovery that the memory had as much power over her, after years of her deliberately repressing it, as it ever had. Because now was not the time to remember private dreams. Her connection now with Mischa Busnetsky was entirely business—publicly, the *Herald*'s business; privately, her father's.

Lewis Penreith had had unfinished business with Mischa when he had died three years ago, but Laddy had not known of it then. She had never connected his death or his last activities with Mischa.

Three years ago her father had been killed by a hit-and-run driver, but no one in the International Council on Freedom, and no one close to Laddy, had accepted that it was an accident. There were too many governments in the world that would have been interested in the cessation of Lewis Penreith's activities, and it was an eventuality that her father had prepared her to accept long before.

She had expected it, had understood it, but she was nevertheless unprepared for the anguish and anger that had consumed her. She was unprepared, too, for the terrifying need to know why. Why now? But Laddy had been a journalist then; she had just left a smaller paper to join the newsroom of the *Herald*, and it had been a long time since she had worked closely enough with her father to know what cause had been consuming him then and had last sent him abroad.

Only three months ago had she learned what Lewis Penreith's last mission had been. It was for that reason, and not for any personal one, that she had begged Harry to let her cover Mischa Busnetsky's arrival in England.

Laddy stared down at the pile of multicolored cushions that she had added to the living room one by one over the years, till she had achieved this air of casual comfort and warmth. There was no way out. She owed it not only to Mischa Busnetsky, but also to her father. She had to see Mischa again no matter how much that thought terrified her.

Three years ago, shortly after her father's death, Laddy had come home to a house that had seemed somehow changed. As though. . . as though someone had been in the house and disturbed only the air. She told herself she was imagining it; the house seemed changed because her father was no longer there—but still she took a weekend to go through his papers to see what there was that someone might have wanted.

She found nothing. If the house had been searched, either they had found and taken what they wanted—or her father never had it.

She did not learn how wrong she was for nearly three years.

She shivered now, remembering the day three months ago when Margaret had rung down to her from the flat upstairs, an odd note in her voice: "Can you come upstairs for a minute, Laddy? Something I think you should see."

Laddy had run up the stairs, expecting to find evidence of mice or termites, to meet a flushed-looking Margaret waiting for her at the top. "Ben's asleep," she'd said. "I don't want him to wake." And she had led the way to her sitting room, the room that had been Lewis Penreith's study.

The room had, no doubt, originally been designed as the master bedroom of the house; it had a large walk-in closet in which her father had kept his filing cabinets. The door to the closet stood open, a bucket of soapy water beside it and a bottle of lemon oil.

"I've been giving the woodwork a good scrub-down," Margaret said, closing the door to the hall as she spoke. Then she walked over to the closet door. "It's the oddest thing."

She bent down to the edge of the door toward the

bottom. "Look at this," she said. "Did you know it was here?"

It was a solid oak door, like all the doors in this magnificent old house—or so Laddy had always thought. She watched, riveted, as Margaret ran her hand up the bottom few inches of the edge and a portion of the edge slid up, exposing a hollow. Laddy gasped and crouched down near the door. The gap was eight or nine inches high, and ran in for what seemed an inch or two.

"No, I've never seen it before," Laddy exclaimed. "How extraordinary!"

Margaret looked at her for a moment. "There's something in there," she said.

Suddenly Laddy's heart was thumping as though she had run the four-minute mile. She looked closer and almost fainted. The bottom of the door must be completely hollow, for what she saw was the edge of a dusty oilskin envelope that was as familiar to her as her own face.

With the help of a knife and some ice tongs, they had eventually pulled out two oilskin-wrapped packages of the kind she had seen her father pack into his case in foreign hotel rooms the world over. She knew without looking what they contained, but mesmerized, she had opened them there on the floor, surrounded by the bucket and lemon oil, the knife and the ice tongs.

"What language is that?" Margaret had asked, her shrewd, lined face alert as the manuscripts were exposed.

Laddy had lied, "I don't know. I suppose it's some manuscripts my father never had translated." She spoke lightly, ignoring the powerful thumping of her heart, the fear that suffused her. She jumped up. "Well, isn't that fascinating. I never knew dad had that hidey-hole! I guess I'd better turn these over to someone."

She had laughed as though it were unimportant, but by the time she got downstairs she was shaking almost uncontrollaby. She had locked herself in the sitting room and sat down to open the packages again.

The language was Russian. Lewis Penreith had seen to it that his daughter had been able to speak and write some of that language, although she had never become fluent, as he had. One glance at the top page of that dirty, much-handled manuscript had told her the name of the author: M. Busnetsky.

She was looking at her father's death warrant. *This* was the reason for the last trip he had taken. To get these manuscripts, so that one day Mischa Busnetsky would be free.

It was as though lightning struck her. Clutching the packages to her chest, almost sobbing, she had rushed to her bedroom, where her father's filing cabinets still stood, and pulled open the top drawer. Feverishly, she had searched the *B*'s, once, twice, three times. Then she had gone through all the drawers, with a desperate cold precision.

It was twenty minutes before she closed the last drawer, and then cold chills began in her spine. The file on Mischa Busnetsky was missing. They had found the file, three years ago, but they had not found the manuscripts.

Now she knew the cold truth, and slowly she was filled with a pain and anger unlike anything she had known before. Now she could put a name to those nameless people who had killed her father; now the suspicion was a fact. A deep, burning hatred for those who had taken the life of the most dedicated, intelligent man she had ever known flamed through her.

It was only with the sharpest edge of reason that she had prevented herself from also hating the man for whose future freedom her father had traded his life.

The next day she had requested a copy of the picture of Mischa Busnetsky from the *Herald* picture library and had put it in her father's filing cabinet. But she had never looked at it again. She was afraid to.

Laddy reached deep under the pile of cushions she sat on and felt for two near the bottom. Yes, they were still there; if she squeezed hard enough she could feel the resistance in the center of the cushions.

She should have given the manuscripts to the ICF three months ago. There were other publishers in her father's field who would have jumped at the chance to publish them. Her father would have wanted that.

Instead, she had hidden them in the only place

she could think of—she had cut open two of her foam-filled cushions and had stitched them up again with the manuscripts inside. And every day she had told herself she must speak to someone about the manuscripts, get them into safe hands.

They were her last link with her father. She had not been able to let them go. She did not let herself feel that they were also her last link with Mischa Busnetsky.

But now she would put them into Mischa Busnetsky's own hands, and perhaps she would be able to stop thinking of her father and the fact that he had died for the sake of the papers stitched up in her sitting-room pillows.

And perhaps, seeing Mischa Busnetsky again, she would be free of him, perhaps the memory of that night would lose its potency. . . .

Laddy sighed and got up, picked up the coffee cups she and John had left and moved into the kitchen. The sink and table were still piled with dishes, and she tied an old faded full-front apron over her beautiful burgundy caftan and set to work.

Well, there was one thing you could say about washing dishes, Laddy thought as she filled the sink with hot soapy water, it didn't require brainpower. It was a great time for thinking about other things.

John, for instance. She was so concerned with Mischa Busnetsky that she had forgotten John. Tonight she had thought he might tell her that he loved her. Instead he. . . . Laddy froze, her hands in the warm water.

But he *had* told her he loved her. He had said, "I adore you and love you and I fancy you like mad." And that declaration had gone by her as though he had said it was going to rain tomorrow. Why? Why had it seemed unimportant, when it was something she had been waiting and hoping to hear?

She knew why. It had seemed unimportant because she had been thinking of Mischa Busnetsky.

John Bentinck had no more power to move her than any of the others.

CHAPTER FOUR

LADDY WAS MET with a chorus of greetings as she entered the arrivals area of the airport at nine o'clock the next morning and walked over to the corner the press seemed to be commandeering. She returned their greetings and sat with a smile. Many of those present were reporters and photographers she knew well from similar occasions, and everyone was cheerful and friendly. She looked around. It was a very large group, for all the wire services and several foreign papers and television networks were represented, but even so, it would grow. In the next hour, before the flight arrived, the ranks would swell significantly, so it looked as though Mischa Busnetsky might have a small army to greet him.

Her heart sank. She would not get anywhere near him this morning. Of course, that in itself was not important. She couldn't, in any case, have talked to him privately. But she must make very sure she knew where he was intending to go so that she could get in touch with him later.

"Does anybody know where he might be going?" she asked Larry Hague, a reporter from one of the morning papers whom she knew well and with whom she often traded information.

Someone picked it up on her other side. "If so, no one is saying." Well, that was nothing new. She ought to have done some phoning last night.

The talk among the reporters covered a variety of the topics in the news but mostly centered on dissidents and exiles. Several people here, some of whom knew Brian March much better than they knew Laddy since they tended to specialize in Soviet subjects, were talking about the progress of the SALT talks and discussing the likelihood of success with varying degrees of cynicism.

Laddy left them to it after a few minutes and strolled around the airport, looking for the signs that would tell her which exit had been marked out for Busnetsky's use. She found it without trouble, cordoned off, with a number of security men and others, casually dressed, who were obviously plain-clothesmen.

Laddy approached one of the men standing near the rope barrier that had been set up.

"Laddy Penreith, *Evening Herald*," she introduced herself to the young man with close-cropped hair. "You're waiting for Mischa Busnetsky?"

"Yes, we are." He was friendly, if taciturn.

"Do you know if the flight is on time?" she asked.

"So far we haven't heard anything to the contrary."

"Who is accompanying Mr. Busnetsky on the flight?" Her questions might not be answered, but she had to ask.

"Well, of course there will be security people," the man said, which meant Secret Service, and he excused himself as his communicator bleeped. He listened and talked for a moment but did not use this as an excuse to leave the rope where she was standing, so when he had restored the little machine to his belt, she tried again.

"What is his final destination in England?"

"I couldn't say, miss."

"Do you know if he has any friends, anyone from England, traveling with him?"

"I couldn't say, I'm sure."

Which didn't mean he didn't know. Laddy chatted casually with the man, hoping he might inadvertently drop some information, until John Bentinck came up to her. He had a large leather shoulder bag and a camera slung around his neck.

"I think I've spotted the pickup car," he said in her ear. "Want to come and look?"

Laddy checked the time. Still half an hour till ten o'clock, and she didn't seem to be getting anything out of the security man. "Yes," she said. She had to get some lead in case Mischa Busnetsky's destination was not revealed.

John pointed out the car in the parking lot as they stood at a distance and pretended to be deep in conversation.

A man sat at the wheel and smoked, while

another hovered in the background, wandering around the cars in the vicinity and giving them what appeared to be casual glances but were more likely solid appraisals. He surreptitiously spoke into a walkie-talkie from time to time.

It looked as though John had found the car that Mischa Busnetsky would be taking from the airport.

"Did you get the license number?" Laddy asked.

"Haven't been close enough."

Laddy took out her notebook and wrote down the make and color and other details of the car, but it was going to be difficult to get close enough to see the license plate.

"John, could you get a telephoto picture?" she asked. The signs were that Busnetsky was going to try to avoid the press, that he would jump into this car and disappear. If Laddy and John were too obvious now, it was quite possible someone might come and escort them back to the arrivals area. They would have to work quickly and quietly.

"I can try," John said. "Stand in front of me."

The problem was that the long telephoto lens would be very obvious. Protected from sight of the occupant of the car by another parked car and by Laddy, John fitted the lens to the body, then dropped the camera into his shoulder bag, the cord still wrapped around his wrist. Talking together, they walked till John had found a direct angle to the car that did not block their view of the license plate. He kneeled and rested the bag on the asphalt, pulled out the camera holding it at chest level, and shot several photos, adjusting the focus fractionally between shots.

It took him less than the time it would take to tie a shoelace. He dropped the camera back into the bag and stood up. "Are you pretty sure you got it?" Laddy asked.

"Pretty sure," he replied. "Do you want to try moving closer?"

But it was nearly ten. Planes were landing all the time; there was no way of knowing whether the Zurich flight had come in. "Let's get back," she said.

By the time they got back to the arrivals area where the media people had been sitting, the area was deserted. "Let's go," said John, and they set out at a trot for the cordoned corridor Laddy had found earlier.

The corridor was packed with people, all obviously from the media. Television and still cameras jostled for position with tape recorders and notebooks, and a loud hubbub filled their ears. There would be no getting near Mischa Busnetsky this morning.

She was warned of his imminent arrival by the sudden increase in the noise and activity in the corridor; people around her began pushing to get closer to the ropes.

Her heart in her mouth suddenly, she craned to see past the moving heads and caught sight of a close-cropped head above them, and then Mischa Busnetsky came into her line of vision.

He was absolutely gaunt. Totally unrecognizable as the man in the photo, the man of her memory. His facial bones were almost painfully prominent, his cheeks hollow and his eyes burning, even from that distance. He was very tall, and a new overcoat of obviously Western origin hung on his gaunt frame.

People crowded at the ropes, and those closest to Busnetsky began to call out questions. "Mr. Busnetsky, how does it feel to be free?" "Mr. Busnetsky, Mr. Busnetsky, how many political prisoners would you estimate there are in the Soviet Union?" "Do you plan to make your home in England, Mr. Busnetsky?" The hubbub became cacophony.

Mikhail Busnetsky stared at them all with the pained horror of a man who had seen them all before, behind other faces, in other guises; then for a moment he was terrifyingly like that old picture, for the same look of cynical acceptance of the power of fools crossed his features. Instantly he shut their presence out of his mind and continued his painstaking progress along the cordoned-off passageway, ignoring them all.

At that moment a television cameraman dodged the security man near him and ducked under the rope in front of Busnetsky for an unrestricted shot, and suddenly everyone was surging forward, under and over the ropes. As Busnetsky went down the staircase that led outside, the body of press people followed. They surrounded him now, pushing mikes and cameras into his tortured face.

Laddy and John were swept up in the crowd; they could not have stopped their forward motion.

"Are you getting this?" asked Laddy, who had never seen anything quite like it.

John, who had not stopped shooting since the first man had broken through the cordon, was turning his camera in all directions. He knew exactly what she meant. Not pictures of Busnetsky, but of his welcome. Pictures of a sick man being given no more quarter by the newshounds than he had been by his oppressors.

The force of the crowd carried Laddy much closer to Busnetsky when they reached the pavement, and here he turned as though at bay. His face was tortured, ill, but suddenly she saw in it some remnant of the man she had met that evening in Moscow, and in that moment Laddy knew with sickening clarity that if she spent her whole life pushing that face out of her mind, she could never forget him. She was seized with a desperate urgency to touch him, to speak to him, to learn whether this dreadfully sick man still had the power to remember her face and a night that had changed her forever, and she began to push her way through the crowd like an animal fighting for survival, until she stood on the pavement next to him.

His watchful eyes followed her progress in the few seconds that it took her to reach him, and when she looked up at him it was as though she had run into a brick wall. His look was wary, accusing, condemning, like that of a trapped animal facing its captor.

"Mischa," she whispered, but in the cacophony that assailed his ears, he could not possibly have heard her cry.

"Please leave me alone," he said in weary torment, and he was looking right at her, speaking to her, and there was no recognition in his eyes. Laddy knew in a blinding flash of pain that there never would be.

A car was waiting by the curb behind him, and Mikhail Busnetsky turned and climbed through the open door into the back seat. Laddy watched as though her eyes were glued to him, immobile in the sea of humanity that surged and swelled around her. Half a dozen reporters were sprinting for their cars parked nearby, and Laddy, who had parked her own car very close to this point in preparation, knew somewhere in the dim, still-functioning recesses of her mind that she ought to be doing the same. No word had been given out of Busnetsky's destination, and that certainly meant that he was going into hiding.

But she could not move, and so it was that the blond woman who had remained unnoticed in the mad rush to Busnetsky had to brush past Laddy to get into the car after him. She wore a white coat and sunglasses, and she muttered a low "Excuse me," as she passed; then the door was slammed shut and the gray car pulled away. As it roared down the road toward an underpass, several cars moved out in pursuit, and Laddy watched as the television cameraman who had begun the whole thing, dedicated to the last, leaped into the road to film the progress of the speeding car.

By the narrow underpass another car pulled smoothly out as Busnetsky's car passed, then stalled for a moment, blocking the way. To a chorus of irate honking, the driver started the car again, but the few moments of delay, whether deliberate or not, gave the nondescript gray car the time it needed to disappear. Watching, Laddy wondered whether any of the pursuers would think to follow the car that had blocked the road.

"Who was that blonde?" several people asked at once. No one had got a word out of the obviously sick man—no one except Laddy—and some of the reporters were mildly cursing Busnetsky for being "uncooperative."

No one knew who the blond woman was, and no more time was wasted in talking. The few security people about were assailed with questions, while large numbers of journalists dashed back inside the arrivals building to the telephones.

Laddy stood on the pavement without moving. Her mind was churning. *She* knew who the blond woman was, she was sure of it. Somewhere deep in her mind that quick glimpse of the face behind dark sunglasses had touched a chord. She had met that woman somewhere in the past. But she could not remember where or who she was.

While she sought an unoccupied phone booth,

John pulled the film from his camera and looked around for the messenger that was waiting to take it back to the *Herald*. With luck they might make the deadline for the early-afternoon edition, so when he found the orange-helmeted young motorcycle driver, he thrust the film into the boy's pouch and pushed him into a run.

"Get going!" he said, and the young man, who was new on the job, thought that this was just like a movie and that he had a photographic scoop in his keeping. He dashed down the stairs and out to his cycle.

Inside the phone booth, Laddy, who had been composing her story in her head from the moment Mischa Busnetsky had said, "Please leave me alone," dialed the number she knew best and began dictating as soon as the *Herald* copy taker was on the phone. Her shame and disgust at the way she had contributed to a sick man's pain in that undisciplined crowd still suffused her and gave her imagination wings.

"'Someone has got to say, "I will not trample the daffodils,"' Alexander Solzhenitsyn once said," she began, "but Soviet dissident Mikhail Busnetsky's reception at Heathrow Airport this morning proved, if anyone doubted it, that the press of this city is not going to refuse to tread on the daffodils when a news story is breaking. The gaunt, obviously sick man who arrived into freedom today after nine years in Soviet prisons, labor camps and psychiatric hospitals must have thought he had gone from nightmare...."

Knowing she had been part of the nightmare and knowing that it was not the press she condemned but herself, Laddy dictated quickly, covering Busnetsky's career and discovery by the West with professional clarity, but emphasizing his illness and the press's reception of him.

When she had finished, she asked to be connected to Harry Waller. "He's come and gone, Harry," she said. "No leads and no statement. The films are on the way."

Harry grunted absentmindedly, and she knew he was reading the story she had just filed. He would have received it page by page as it came from the copy taker's typewriter, and it would be obvious from the very first page what she had done.

"What the Sam Hill is this, Laddy?" Harry said.

Laddy cut in, "Harry, that's the way it was, it was—"

"No doubt," Harry said dryly. "Would you like to take two minutes to collect your thoughts, dear girl, and file this again?"

Rewrite the story, he meant, and Laddy, sensible, professional Laddy, whose hurt and shame overcame the knowledge that a slam like that on her profession and colleagues should never have been written, said, "Harry, that's the way it happened, and that's my story."

Harry sighed. "All right, dear girl," he said, "any leads?"

"We think we got the license number of the car on John's photos," she said. "Have you got anything?"

She had a job and a responsibility to the paper to get a story no matter how she felt about it, but she was not going to tell Harry about the blond woman, not right now.

"Nothing here, dear girl," said Harry. "You'd better come back in."

Harry Waller hung up the phone and flicked an exasperated finger at the pages of copy that were Laddy's story. "Get me the agency copy on Busnetsky!" he hollered, to no one in particular.

•

JOHN CAME OUT of the phone booth next to Laddy, where he had put in a call to Richard Snapes. "Going back in?" he asked, and Laddy nodded. "Richard wants me over on some picket line, but I'm not hurrying," he said. "Let's have a coffee away from everyone, Laddy." Laddy nodded again. At this moment she needed coffee.

They found seats in a back corner of the coffee bar, where they might avoid being seen by any wandering reporter looking for someone to sit and talk with.

"I got some great pictures of that bunch," John began. "At the end there, when he turned around, he was surrounded by screaming faces. Looked tortured." He grunted. "Good picture, that."

"I know," said Laddy, somehow exhausted. The faces of the blond woman and Mischa Busnetsky were emblazoned on her mind—his accusing stare, and her somehow familiar features. In spite of herself, Laddy could not help her mind's frantic search through her past to where she might have met that woman. She realized John was speaking to her.

"It would be wonderful to get away," he said. He was talking about Greece. Laddy wondered if the terrible exhaustion she suddenly felt could be of long standing. She felt as though she had been waiting ten years for a vacation.

"I've heard that Kos is very beautiful," John said. "Laddy...."

"Yes," she said. "Look, I've got to get back and see if I can get a trace on where he's gone. See you." She bent and kissed him lightly and walked out, wondering how she managed to put one foot in front of the other.

THERE REALLY WAS PRECIOUS LITTLE in the clippings library, considering that the battle to free Mischa Busnetsky had been going on for so many years, but Laddy dutifully skimmed it all for the second time in two days, looking for leads. Her father was mentioned in some of the early accounts, but few other people were mentioned by name. Laddy realized with resignation that it was going to be a long haul. There would be no easy road to Mischa Busnetsky unless she had some rare luck.

In the end, her leads consisted of the name of the president of the Committee for the Liberation of

Mikhail Busnetsky—which Laddy knew was partly composed of ICF people, and the names signed to a letter to the editor of the *Times*—a group of prominent literary citizens condemning the "reprehensible detention of Soviet thinker Mikhail Busnetsky." His name had cropped up, of course, in the Amnesty International lists of prisoners of conscience and again in the Campaign Against Psychiatric Abuse.

She saw the gaunt and tortured face of Mischa Busnetsky again as she read, and now the words of his oppressors took on a special, personal significance that they had not held for her since before her father died. "It is no secret to anyone that you can have schizophrenia without schizophrenia," a powerful Soviet psychiatrist had said to justify the practice of declaring dissidents schizophrenic and committing them to institutions. Laddy turned the clipping over on the pile.

"Arrested, stripped, searched, interrogated and detained twenty-four hours," someone described the state's early methods of harassment, "the prisoners experience systematic underfeeding and receive a hot meal only once every two days." Well, she had always known that. "It is spiritual murder."

Laddy stopped reading and rested her forehead on her hand. "It is spiritual murder." The words ripped at her. Not him, she prayed. Don't let it have killed him; let him not have submitted to spiritual murder.

She handed the gray envelope back to the librarian and returned to her desk in the newsroom. For all the names and various committees she had extracted from the clippings, she found phone numbers, some in her own contacts book, which yielded other names of people who might be helpful. She called every one.

Either no one knew where he might be or no one was telling. Even the old friends of her father's who had been involved with him in the International Council on Freedom could or would tell her nothing about Busnetsky's whereabouts. She was her father's daughter, but she was also a journalist.

She told none of them that she wanted to know his whereabouts as a private person, for a private reason. She was not a private person in this search. This was work for the *Herald*.

"I can't tell you the whereabouts of Mikhail Busnetsky," someone from the offices of a freedom-fighting committee said to her. "But I can tell you where Anatol Alexei Kolakowski is—in a labor camp in Siberia. And Ludmila Rinkovitch is in a psychiatric hospital undergoing 'treatment.' And—"

"All right," Laddy interrupted. "Point taken."

"I wish it were a case of point taken," the man said. "Why is it you people are only interested in someone after he's released? Where's the coverage for the thousands still over there?"

"I don't know," was all Laddy could say.

"He's a sick man. Leave him alone," the man said, and hung up.

"Were you asking for these?" a voice said to her, and Laddy turned to see Salvatore, the *Herald*'s copyboy, waving some photographic prints at her.

"Oh yes, Sally, thanks." She reached out and took them from his extended hand. Sally didn't leave. His bright enthusiastic gaze was fixed on her.

"You working on Busnetsky?" he asked with interest. Laddy was not surprised. Salvatore unfailingly knew the story that each reporter was covering each day.

"Yes," she said.

"He got away from you all, dinnee?" he said with relish. "Wish I'd abeen there." Sally had yearnings to be an investigative reporter.

"No, you don't," said Laddy. "It was awful, and useless, too."

"Well, that's the way it is, sometimes, innit?" Sally said philosophically, and left her.

There were two good shots of the license plate. A London license, she found, but her telephone search led to what was probably a dead end: the plate was the number of a rented car. Laddy sighed. The only possibility now was to get to the car-rental office and try to convince someone to let her look at the record of the transaction.

Laddy pushed her chair back and crossed the office to get a cup of coffee, then came back to her desk for a re-thinking. There must be something she had missed.

Sally had long since delivered the early-afternoon edition of the *Herald* to her desk, but she had not looked at it. She reached out to pull it toward her. Richard, the pictures editor, had used a picture that John must have caught just before Busnetsky got into the car, when he had turned to look at the reporters. At her. But the photo had been cropped. A tired, haggard man with accusing eyes looked just to the left of the camera, but his face filled the whole picture. No one appeared beside him.

Laddy checked through the pile of prints that Sally had brought to her. Yes, there they were in the original photo, pushing microphones and cameras at him. Incredibly, most of her colleagues in the photo were smiling, though one man whom she did not recognize looked almost satanic, his mouth open, his eyes scrunched up, like an animal going in for the kill.

Well, the picture had been cropped. John wouldn't like that. Laddy returned to the paper, her eye glancing over the copy. "BUSNETSKY IN ENGLAND!" screamed the headline and, underneath, "Lucy Laedelia Penreith, Staff Reporter."

Mikhail Busnetsky, the well-known dissident who has spent much of the past nine years in Soviet prisons, labor camps and psychiatric hospitals, looked tired and ill, but nevertheless happy to be free today, when he arrived at Heathrow Airport....

Harry Waller had rewritten her story! Damn him! Anger began to burn in her stomach as Laddy flipped the page to the continuation of the story, looking for some remnant of what she had written. But there was none. Harry had taken what she said about Mischa Busnetsky's background, all the factual information, and had left out all the facts of his experience at the airport. It was all mindless pap, the kind of copy that anyone, whether at the scene or not, could have produced.

For the second time in two days Laddy stood over the back bench waving a newspaper under Harry Waller's nose.

"Why didn't you let my story stand?" she demanded, and when Harry looked up his eyes were unfamiliarly cool.

"Because, dear girl, it doesn't do to knock the profession," he said. "I might as easily ask you what the hell you think you're doing filing that kind of trash."

"Did you or did you not look at John's pictures?" she demanded. "Do you have any idea what that scene was like?"

"Yes, I think I have a very good idea," Harry said. "If that is the first time you have run into something of the sort, you are either fortunate or blind. We have, in this country, a moderately free press. It should be freer. We do not need stories like the one you filed this morning to add ammunition to the guns of people who think otherwise." He didn't say "grow up," but it was in the tone of his voice. He sat looking up at her, waiting for her to speak or to leave.

"A free press means—ought to mean—a self-governed, responsible press," Laddy returned. "And that lot out there this morning wasn't either." She took a breath. "And I wish to hell you hadn't used my by-line on it!"

When he did not answer, she stalked away.

THE GRAY CAR had been rented by the president of the Committee for the Liberation of Mikhail Busnetsky, but he was no more willing to talk the second time she phoned him than he had been the first. In the phone booth outside the car-rental office, Laddy phoned Harry with what she knew and told him she was going home.

It was five-thirty Friday afternoon. Laddy had never been so glad of an approaching weekend in her life.

A weekend, of course, did not mean she could turn her brain off. Her thoughts were filled with the problem of how to find Mischa Busnetsky as she drove home, so that afterward she never remembered making the trip.

But as she unlocked her front door and wearily hung up her coat, the alternatives were clear: either she had to stake out the home of the man who had rented the car, or she had to remember who the blond woman was.

Laddy walked down the hall to the kitchen, filled the kettle and lighted the gas, her mind far removed from the mechanical motions of her hands. Who was the blond woman? Someone from the long ago past, her faint memory told her, which logically meant a friend of her father's.

"This is my daughter, Laddy," she suddenly heard her father's voice saying.

The woman, smiling and shaking her hand in a grown-up way that had flattered Laddy at the time, had said, "She's very like you, Lewis."

Laddy looked down. The kettle had boiled and she made tea. She carried the pot and a cup and a pitcher of milk to the table and sat down.

"She's very like you." That at least placed it in time. As a young skinny child Laddy had looked like a boyish version of her father, but at the age of fourteen she had begun to change, becoming more and more like the picture of her beautiful mother that still occupied a corner of the mirror on her bedroom dresser. After the age of fourteen or fifteen no one had ever again remarked on her resemblance to Lewis Penreith. "You're your mother all over again," her father had said to her one day, and she had been torn between the delight of knowing he thought her like the womanly beauty of the photograph and heartbreak at the sound of pain in his voice. . . .

So she had met the blond woman at least ten years ago.

More than ten years and less than fifteen, because if her mother had been alive, she would have been with them.

That left a five-year period. Laddy sighed. In those five years she and her father had done a great deal of traveling; she could have met that woman almost anywhere.

Still, she had something to go on. The woman was a friend of her father's whom she had met sometime between age ten and age fifteen. The fact that she had accompanied Busnetsky—probably from Zurich and certainly from Heathrow—meant that she was involved in the civil-liberties movement now and probably had been then. This, added to Laddy's certainty that English was the woman's native language, was at least a start.

The massive filing cabinets in her bedroom that held all her father's papers from over the years were rather daunting, considering she was looking for one name, but starting with her father's book of contacts, Laddy went through it, hoping that some face or phrase or name would spark that faint memory into flame.

When she was finished she had a pile of papers to look through more closely, and it was time for the News at Ten.

Mikhail Busnetsky was the headline story, and the newscast began with his gaunt face staring out from behind the anchorwoman's shoulder, then cut to the film clip of his arrival that morning. The cameraman had been close to Busnetsky throughout his painful progress, and though Laddy's own approach to him had not been captured on film, the reporter had been close enough to catch his "Please leave me alone."

Laddy was surprised at how quickly after that the blond woman made her appearance, for it had seemed to her that she had stood frozen on the pavement for a lifetime after hearing those words, seeing that accusing face. But suddenly there she was, climbing into the back seat. The film froze for a few seconds at the end of the report while the woman, one leg still on the pavement and her head out of the car, reached out to close the door, and Laddy sat up with a stifled gasp.

She knew who the woman was.

CHAPTER FIVE

"I CAN still remember the first time I told you I loved you," the harsh-gentle voice sang into the intimate closeness of Laddy's little car as she drove through the black velvet of the country at night, and she swallowed suddenly. How many memories could be evoked by a song heard in the small hours!

The headlights tried to pierce the night, but they seemed a feeble resistance to the enclosing darkness. On the sparsely traveled road, Laddy suddenly caught sight of the pale red glow of the taillights of a car some distance ahead of her and they gave her some direction.

She relaxed and let the masculine voice touch her, seduce her into memory. "Now and then I find myself thinking of the days..." the singer told her, but when he went on to remember a mid-July Alabama rain, Laddy slipped back to a Moscow evening wet with early snow....

"Richard Digby, Tymawr House, Trefelin, Pembrokeshire, South Wales," was the address she had found in her father's contacts book, and suddenly she had been in the grip of a compulsion; nothing could have prevented her setting out to drive to the

place where Mischa Busnetsky might possibly be...
certainly not the fact that she would be driving
through the night. She was no longer in control: she
was on automatic pilot, like a salmon returning
upstream, or a homing pigeon....

"I'm always thinking of you and sad that you're
not there...." The radio station seemed to be
devoting what it called "the midnight hours" to the
subject of lost love, Laddy thought with a wry
smile, and every song had a special significance for
her—though perhaps it was in the nature of love
songs to have a significance for people who had
loved.

Laddy pulled out to pass a large truck, its familiar roar and numerous lights a comforting sign of
another intelligence in the lonely night.

There was no guarantee that Mischa Busnetsky
would be at her destination. In the years since
Laddy had spent a faintly remembered, quiet two
weeks with Richard and Helen Digby in their house
in Wales, that house might have been sold. Or
perhaps Helen Digby had taken Mischa Busnetsky
somewhere else and not to their own home at
all....

But Laddy could not have phoned them so late at
night, and she could not have waited until morning,
and besides, if she had given the Digbys advance
warning of her intention, they might have put her
off.

Helen Digby was an artist, Laddy remembered; it
was her husband, Richard, an old friend of her

father's, who was involved with the ICF. Was that why Helen had met Mischa Busnetsky at the airport? Because Richard Digby would have been recognized by the press and it would have been more difficult to keep his destination secret?

Very likely; and Laddy's sixth sense told her that Mischa Busnetsky was at this moment lying asleep in Tymawr House in the village of Trefelin on the beautiful southwest coast of Wales. And that in a few hours—she glanced down at the cushions resting on the seat beside her—she would be handing him the manuscripts that her father had paid for with his life.

Would he remember her? In the more relaxed environment, when she told him about her father, would he remember that once in Moscow her father had been accompanied by his daughter? Would he remember the woman to whom he had said, "I will remember this as though it were your lips I had touched"? Laddy thought of all the times in those prisons and hospitals when the naked necessity to survive must have driven dreams into oblivion, and the certainty that he would not remember clawed at her.

"But I always thought that I'd see you, one more time again," yet another masculine voice was singing, and with an exasperated rejection of self-pity and fear she reached out and snapped the radio off. But the words stayed with her, echoing endlessly in her head: "one more time again."

She could not hope that after all this time,

Mischa Busnetsky would imagine himself in love with a woman he had spoken to for one hour eight years ago. Or that she herself would, on meeting him, talking to him, find in him the man that she had carried in her memory—almost unconsciously—for all that time.

She was not in love with Mischa Busnetsky, the man. She was in love with the memory of an incredible, drunken moment that had occurred at a crucial time in her life, when she was on the threshold of womanhood. She was in love with the memory of the first promise of sexual fulfillment, which had been irrevocably linked in her mind with a man with whom she could not explore it and who, for arbitrary and external reasons, had been destined to remain a dream lover.

But she had always thought she would see him one more time again, and it was of the utmost importance that she do so, Laddy thought grimly, as she gripped the steering wheel a little more tightly and slowed down to pass through a sleeping town. Because she had to be cured of this insane commitment to a dark and unknown stranger; she had to exorcise the ghost of Mischa Busnetsky from her memory so that she could begin to live an ordinary, normal, fulfilled life.

The real, live Mischa Busnetsky must drive the dream Mischa from her memory. "Hair of the dog!" she said suddenly aloud, and laughed into the shattered silence of the car.

Her mood lifted then, and at length the black of

night faded into the early gray of dawn. Laddy reached forward to switch on the radio; the announcer's voice was the cheerful voice of morning. There would be no more songs of lost love played now. The world was beginning afresh with the new day, and it was time to wake up and shake off the dreams of night.

THE VILLAGE of Trefelin lay on the coast a few miles south of Fishguard, according to the small road map Laddy had bought after breakfast in a cheerful café in Fishguard Town and was consulting from time to time as she drove. It was not long before she had to leave the main south road for a narrow paved side road that meandered back toward the sea through green rolling farmland that looked damp and fertile in the spring sun.

She was tired. She had driven all night and then had spent a long hour over her breakfast and coffee so that she would arrive at Tymawr House at a civilized hour. Nevertheless, what she felt most now was not fatigue but the pervasive grip of tension, of fear. And when the road curved down a green hill toward a cluster of houses that spread across a tiny valley and up the side of the far hill, when the small black-and-white sign on the side of the road told her she had reached Trefelin, what she felt was a cowardly impulse that told her to turn around and drive back to London.

Shaken by that and a host of sudden emotions, Laddy pulled the car off the road and got out, then breathed in the scent of the spring air, the ocean, the greenery. There were sheep on the hillsides all around, and off in the distance, on a cliff behind the village that must overlook the sea, a white horse was poised against the horizon. As she watched, the horse was suddenly sparked by joy and the spring wind, and he exploded in a gallop along the cliff, his long tangled tail streaming out behind him.

Whatever was in the wind reached Laddy in the next moment, lifting her hair from her shoulders and forehead and making her suddenly wish she could sing. She laughed aloud instead, stretched her arms above her head and felt the knot of tension in her stomach easing.

The through road was met by two smaller streets in the center of the small village. Laddy stopped again, in front of a house whose front room had been converted into a shop, and went in.

Four women, all of them small, thick and dark, stood or sat chatting in the small room, and conversation died as the stranger entered and they turned to stare at her.

Any old-world flavor was confined to their presence, Laddy saw, for the shop itself had more modern appointments than her corner co-op in London. A glass-fronted chrome-and-enamel meat cooler sat beside the Formica counter, and a small freezer stood against the wall. The shelves were covered with a variety of canned and packaged goods.

"Good morning," Laddy said, smiling a little

awkwardly around at them. Then she looked toward the woman behind the counter. "I wonder if you could tell me how to find Tymawr House?"

At this, one of the seated women looked at Laddy even more sharply, her black eyes under the sharply inverted V's of her black eyebrows good-natured but intent.

"Tymawr you're wanting, now?" the shopkeeper asked, then exchanged a quick glance with the dark-eyed woman. "That's out Aberdraig way." She moved to the large window that looked over the road, which ran straight out beside the shop and through the village. She pointed down the road. "Follow the road out past the church, and when you've passed the Mill Path take the next road on the right." She turned back to the strong-featured young woman who seemed so interested in the conversation, and said, "Are they here, then, Mairi?"

Laddy shifted her gaze and smiled expectantly at Mairi. In a place this size it was unlikely that the whole village would not know whether the Digbys were in residence, so Mairi had been brought into this conversation for a reason, and Laddy was curious to know what it was.

Mairi Davies said placidly that Mr. and Mrs. Digby and a guest had arrived yesterday evening and, with an open friendliness, mentioned that her sister Brigit "did" for them. In return she managed to elicit from Laddy a good deal of information about who she was and where she was from and even the fact that her own forebears had been Welsh on her father's side.

This admission was practically inspired, Laddy saw, for the atmosphere in the shop became markedly warmer, and before she got away she had even learned that the Digbys and their guest would be getting their own breakfast this morning. Brigit had not been asked to come until later in the day.

To break Mischa Busnetsky in to new faces slowly, Laddy wondered as she drove, or to gain time to disguise evidence of his identity in case someone should be interested in notifying the press?

Whatever the reason, there was no doubt now that in a very short time she would be face to face with Mischa Busnetsky for the third time in her life, and tension knotted Laddy's stomach so tightly that she could hardly breathe.

The Mill Path, she noted fleetingly, led down to a stony beach. The next path on the right was a narrow dirt track signposted "Tymawr" and "Coastal Path," and on higher ground in the near distance she could see the big white house with outbuildings that was her destination.

Laddy drove more quickly than the rough track deserved, suddenly feeling as though she were driving to her doom, suddenly enormously fearful, but gritting her teeth and jolting on.

The white house sat on top of the cliff, overlooking the sea. It was of indeterminate age, with a low roof and trellised windows, its two small outbuildings at a distance. The three buildings were well ensconced in the budding green of bushes and trees.

At some distance from the house, a navy car was parked beside a white barred gate. Laddy pulled up beside the car, collected her handbag and the two brightly patterned cushions, walked up to the white gate, took a deep breath and pushed it open.

As she walked across the green grass and up the flagstone path, Laddy saw that the house was actually quite old and not as big as she had first thought. It was more like a very large cottage, which seemed to have been redecorated at some expense. It had an idyllic simplicity that nowadays only money could impart.

As she knocked on the door there was a step on the flagstones behind her, and she glanced around. And before she had time to breathe, Laddy was seeing Mischa Busnetsky one more time again.

He wore a thick, dark-blue cotton shirt and corduroy trousers and a blue quilted jacket that disguised the gauntness of his broad frame, but nothing disguised the bone structure of his face.

It was broad and rough, like a clay head sculpted by a fine impatient talent, and it was still lighted from within by the burning intelligence in his dark, square-browed eyes.

There was recognition in those dark eyes, too, Laddy saw, and washed by an almost unaccountable joy, she smiled up at him. "It is spiritual murder," a man had said, but she knew with certainty they had not succeeded in murdering Mischa Busnetsky's spirit.

"Hello again," she said softly, and he pressed his lips together and his eyes blazed with what looked like anger, but that could not be. As he opened his mouth to speak, the door behind Laddy opened, and both of them looked around.

"Good morning," said Richard Digby on a startled, questioning note, as he took in the fact that a strange woman was standing on his doorstep with Mischa Busnetsky; but then his gaze fixed on her and she knew Richard Digby would recognize her in a moment. She had not changed so much in the three years since Richard had come to her father's funeral.

"Good morning, Richard," she said. "How have you been keeping?"

Before he could answer, Mischa Busnetsky's harsh voice broke in on them. "Please do not invite her in," he said to Richard. "She was at the airport yesterday. She is a reporter. I do not want to speak to reporters now."

With a gasp, Laddy whirled to face him again, and his last words he directed at her with a cold, spaced emphasis.

That was the recognition she had seen in his eyes! He was remembering the journalist of yesterday, not her father's daughter of eight years ago. Laddy bit her lip.

"Yes, I was at the airport, but that's not. . ." she

began, but he interrupted her even more harshly, staring down at the burden she carried.

"Why do you carry these pillows? What is in them?" he demanded harshly, angrily. "Do Western reporters copy the police of Russia and carry hidden cameras and microphones? Did you plan to place these in this house to spy on us?"

At that, Richard Digby, looking pale and shocked, stepped out of the house and closed the door firmly behind him.

"What *is* all this?" he said to Laddy coldly, Mischa Busnetsky's accusations and the strange fact that she was carrying cushions making him forget that he had nearly recognized her.

"It's not what you think!" Laddy exclaimed desperately to them both.

"Do you have surveillance equipment in those cushions?" Richard Digby asked quietly, coolly.

She exclaimed, *"No!"*

"Your feet! Look at your feet!" Mischa Busnetsky exclaimed in sudden horror. Taken completely by surprise, and with a strange sensation that there was a snake crawling over her ankles, Laddy looked down.

She had time to see that there was no snake on her foot and to realize that Mischa Busnetsky's horrified instruction had been spoken in Russian, and then the full weight of his attacking body was upon her. With a stifled scream, Laddy staggered backward off the flagstone path and, cushions and handbag scattering, went down under him.

He might be thin, but he was very big. Laddy lay winded beneath the length of his body and did not resist as he wrenched her arms up over her head and held them against the grass with thin strong hands.

"Or maybe you are not a mere blameless, Russian-speaking reporter, eh?" he questioned with quiet menace. "Maybe it is not a story you come after, but something more—perhaps even a life?"

Eight years ago he had touched her on waist and hip, eight years ago he had kissed her palm—but his body had never lain on hers, though she knew it had been meant to, and his dark face had never been so close to her own as it was now. Laddy had spent eight years wanting to be held by the man who now held her. She licked her lips and looked up at him, and at the look in her eyes his anger was unsettled and uncertainty crept in.

"I...uh...uh...." Laddy could not think rationally, and besides, she was still winded. Suddenly she felt a stirring awareness of her in Mischa Busnetsky's body—an awareness that took him, it seemed, by surprise.

Then, as though his body had recognized her before his brain did, he frowned down at her and cried out, "Who *are* you?" But he knew, he knew.

Laddy quoted softly, "Everything I know about you—even how you have made me tremble."

Recognition and passion together blazed in his eyes, and Laddy's body sang with joy, and her lips parted as she waited for the inevitability of his kiss.

"Lady," said Mischa Busnetsky, and his hands

gripped her wrists more tightly in passion than they had in anger, and his chest came down against her breasts as he lowered his mouth toward hers.

"I don't think she can be what you think, Mischa," Richard's apologetic voice broke through the silence that encircled them. Startled, Laddy turned her head to see Richard crouching over her handbag, its contents on the flagstones and her wallet open in his hand. He was reading her name from her press card. "She is...someone I know quite well. She's the daughter of an old friend of mine." He coughed. "Actually, she's the daughter of the man who published your papers over here. Hello, Laddy," he said, as Mischa lifted himself away from her. "It's been a long time. Sorry about all this."

Laddy laughed, feeling slightly drunk. "Don't apologize, Richard," she said. "I should have known better than to come without warning, especially with two cushions under my arm."

"Why did you bring the cushions?" Mischa asked, as with his broad strong hands he helped her to her feet and brushed her down, gently removing bits of grass from her hair.

"I was bringing you something important, and I thought that would be good camouflage in case—" She broke off and looked around. "The cushions!" she exclaimed. "Where are they?"

Richard was putting the last of her cosmetics and papers back into her bag. He stood up and gave it to her. "Well, I thought I'd better get them out of the

way, just in case they contained something nasty,"
he said, smiling. "So I dropped them down the old
cold cellar. Best I could think of at a moment's
notice."

He moved to pull open the squeaky wooden door
of an ancient little stone structure that had been
some Welsh housewife's refrigerator in days gone
by. He bent over and reached down deep inside and
pulled up the cushions.

"They are safe, I presume?" Richard said, getting up and dusting his hands. "They really are not
going to explode on us?"

"Well, I must say I've no idea how explosive
they may be," Laddy said with a slow smile.
"Mischa is the one to tell us that—the cushions
contain two of his manuscripts. As far as I
know, the last manuscripts my father ever obtained." She turned to him. "Are they terribly important ones?" she asked, a sudden urgency in her
tone.

"Good God, and I nearly pitched them over the
cliff!" exclaimed Richard in horror.

Mischa Busnetsky was staring at her in amazement. "They might be, depending on what they are.
One of the possibilities could certainly upset people," he said, weighing the word "upset" with a
touch of irony. He was watching her face. "Why?"
he asked.

Because I think my father died for them, she
thought. *And I have to know if he died for something that mattered.* "The house was searched after

my father died. I wondered if they were looking for those manuscripts," she said instead.

Mischa Busnetsky said quietly, "Your father is dead? Dr. Penreith? I am most sorry. How—"

Richard, who had his own ideas about "how," glanced from one face to the other and interrupted very firmly, "I think before any more is said we ought to go into the house. Laddy certainly could use a cup of tea, and I know I want one. And this is obviously quite a story."

He was a man who was used to having his matter-of-fact commands obeyed, and they all turned toward the door.

Richard brought up the rear, carrying the cushions, and inside the door he laid them on a small table. "I'm quite sure Helen is working," he said. "If you two will hang up your coats I'll put the kettle on."

When they were left alone, Mischa turned to her. "When has your father died?" he asked, and she knew by his voice that he had considered her father a special man.

"Three years ago," she said, slipping out of her coat, and she told him a little of how he had died, but nothing of the possible "why."

He led her down the hallway over a floor of red ceramic tile to a large sitting room in the corner of the house. They sat opposite each other in wing chairs by the huge windows that looked out to the edge of the cliff nearly twenty yards away, and to the sea below and beyond. The morning sun glinted on the sea, and the windows were open to its faint roar.

They sat quietly looking at one another until a clatter of crockery announced Richard with the tea. He set the tray down on a small table near Laddy. "Would you pour for us, Laddy?" he asked, and she nodded, picking up the delicate teapot as though it were an artifact from another world. She felt oddly detached, as though she were seeing everything around her for the first time.

Under Richard's gentle questioning and Mischa Busnetsky's quiet gaze, she told them the history of the manuscripts as she knew it.

At the end Richard turned to Mischa. "Well, I must say this is a most unexpected bonus," he said. "Shall we have a look and see what we've got?" He went out and came back with Laddy's cushions, and again they sat in silence when alone.

"Perhaps you should spread some newspapers before you open them up," Laddy said. "Brigit won't thank you for a carpet covered with foam bits—they're the devil to clean up."

Richard looked at her in amazement. "Brigit?" he exclaimed. "How on earth do you know the name of our daily?"

Laddy laughed. "I had to stop in at the store to ask directions," she explained, and Richard rolled his eyes.

"I'm not sure a village was the best place to bring you for anonymity," he said to Mischa. "You'd be less likely to be noticed in Trafalgar Square!" He stood up. "And the Lord knows we'd better not have Brigit talking about bits of foam on the carpet."

Helping him spread yesterday's *Times* over the pale-blue carpet, Laddy wondered whether he was concerned that the press might hear about the guest at Tymawr House or that someone else might. Another stranger in the village of Trefelin, perhaps, who might have an undue interest in the doings at Tymawr House.

"I suppose a knife would do the trick," Richard said when he had laid the cushions in the center of the *Times*'s front page—right beside the old familiar picture of Soviet dissident Mikhail Busnetsky. Laddy gazed down at the ink-on-newsprint face and then up into the eyes of the real man, and it was as though in a single second she catapulted through the eight years between the two faces. "Or scissors, if I knew where they were..." Richard was saying, as he moved to the door.

"Where is the bag of valuables I brought with me?" Mischa Busnetsky asked suddenly, surprising them both, and then got up and left the room. Laddy and Richard blinked at each other.

When he returned, Mischa was carrying a tiny flat object wrapped in a bit of dirty paper, and he sat down in the chair and painstakingly unwrapped it. In a moment he held a small black object up to view. "One of the valuables they let me bring out of prison," he said softly.

It was a razor blade. Mischa Busnetsky regarded

it with a bemused air. "Two days ago," he said, "this could have been traded for some hot food—the equivalent of two weeks of life for someone. Now it is worth a few pence." He laughed wryly. "And it will serve to cut open a pair of cushions."

He dropped it gently onto Laddy's extended palm, and she looked down at it for a moment. Then slowly and deliberately she closed her fist over the blade, feeling the sharp edges slicing into her palm, and she smiled at Mischa with a small smile through the pain.

When he understood what she was doing, he made a sharp exclamation, leaned forward and grasped her wrist. His grip was cruelly strong; she would bruise.

"Let go!" he ordered harshly, and she opened her hand flat and stared at the bright droplets of blood against her flesh.

Mischa Busnetsky shook her hand so that the razor blade dropped onto the newsprint. Then he pressed his lips to her palm and she felt his mouth move over her wound.

After a moment he closed his eyes and Laddy gazed at his bent head, with its close-cropped, almost shaven hair, and suddenly, kneeling there on the floor with his dark head bent over her, she was trembling. It was a painful, aching trembling that choked off her breathing, and when she saw that he was trembling as much as she, she bit her lip against a moan.

Richard Digby looked at them like a swimmer in

the shallows vaguely recognizing that someone was diving to depths he scarcely knew existed, and at his awkward movement Mischa raised his head.

"Let us look at the manuscripts," he said calmly, and the razor blade that two days ago would have bought extra weeks of life for someone, sliced open the bright cheap cotton of two homemade cushions and then was dropped and lay useless on a day-old headline.

Moments later, two black oilskin-wrapped packages lay on the newsprint; Mischa's hand dusted the foam from one of them and brought it up on his lap to unwrap it.

"To Make Kafka Live," he translated the title page, then flipped the pages slowly under his thumb. "This one indeed they will not like to see in print," he said quietly, and she knew that someone might well have thought that the suppression of this manuscript was worth a life. Her father's life.

She swallowed. But it had been the way her father had chosen to live—constantly at risk—and she must not dishonor him now by laying his death at Mischa Busnetsky's door, even in her thoughts.

Mischa passed the manuscript across to Richard as though his interest would be somehow personal, and suddenly Laddy remembered that Richard Digby was a respected literary agent.

"Do you want to have a go at translating it yourself?" he asked. Mischa waved his hand as he bent to pick up the other package. "My English will not stretch to that, I think," he said.

He unwrapped the second package and stopped short as he read the title page. He laughed a little; his eyes flicked to Laddy and then into the distance, and he smiled at a memory.

"This one is not political, I am afraid," he said to Richard. "It is fiction. In fact, it is a love story. Odd that your father should have acquired this one," he said to Laddy. "Perhaps he took what he could get."

"What's the title of it?" she asked, for three months ago she had sewn the manuscripts up in her cushions without having the courage to more than glance at them.

His dark eyes held hers as though he wished to see the first reaction in her eyes.

"Love for a Lady," he said quietly, and she looked at him and knew that nothing would ever hurt her again.

CHAPTER SIX

RICHARD DIGBY took the manuscripts and went to his study to begin the work of finding publishers and translators for them. Already he was talking about simultaneous publication for the two very different works.

Mischa smiled at her slowly when Richard had gone. "He is very excited about this," he said. "He thought he would have to wait for me to write something, and here are two books ready and waiting."

"It amounts to a literary coup," Laddy said. "I should think he'll get a very good advance for you—perhaps he'll even put the books on auction. By this time next month you might be rich."

"Good," Mischa said, and smiled. He stopped for a moment and breathed deeply. "I am very tired," he said simply. "I tire easily."

It did not seem in the least odd that she should get up to stand beside him and stroke his forehead with a cool hand or that he should rest his head against her breast in fatigue, like a battle-weary warrior. It seemed fitting, like something that had been destined from before time.

After a moment she felt him take a long, deep breath, then he stood up and smiled down at her through what she now perceived was deep exhaustion.

"If I lie down here, you will stay?" he queried softly, and she nodded, unable to speak. Nothing and no one could have made her leave his side in that moment.

He lay on the long blue-flowered sofa in the shadowed part of the room, and she pulled a blanket over him, drew a chair up close and sat watch.

"Talk to me," he commanded quietly. "Tell me everything about your life that I have missed. Tell me about these past eight years." His voice began to grate with exhaustion. "I cannot speak to ask questions, so you must remember everything for me."

She told him then about university and her first job, the excitement of being a reporter, getting a job on the *Herald*, her father's death. She told him everything about herself, in a quiet, slow voice.

Everything—except the central fact of her existence; everything, except the fact that she had been in love with a memory through all those years— with the memory of a man of indomitable courage whom she had fully expected never to see again. She talked as though her only guiding light had been her work, her career. She told him only half a truth, because at twenty-five she no longer had the courage she had had at seventeen, the simple courage to touch his hand and say, "I love you," without knowing for certain whether he wanted that love or not.

She talked about learning of his release with only the faintest betrayal of emotion in her tone, talked about how Harry had rewritten her story, how she had worked to find him so that she could deliver his manuscripts to him.

But she did not tell him of the letters she had written him, all those years ago, the parcels she had sent—or the ache in her heart when she had finally stopped asking her father which prison he was in.

He might read those things between the lines, if he wanted to. Or if he asked her one question, she might have the courage to tell him all that she wanted to say.

But he was at the point of collapse. He did not speak at all; he listened, he heard every word. When she stopped speaking he said, "Your voice is like moving water," and turned his head and fell asleep.

"How LONG did you actually spend in prison?" Dr. Edmund Bear asked Mischa after dinner that evening.

"Of the past nine years," Mischa replied, "nearly six in prisons or camps."

While Laddy had slept that afternoon in the little blue-and-white bedroom that was prepared for her, Dr. Bear, a friend of Richard's and Helen's who practiced chiropractic and nutritional therapy, had come down from London to examine Mischa.

"Well," he said now, "I don't want to underestimate what you've been through, but you're in remarkable shape for someone who's suffered what you have for six years.

"Naturally, you'll have to take things slowly at first while you build up your health. But I've seen a number of exiles over the past few years, and I think you must have had the constitution of a horse to begin with."

Edmund Bear, a vital middle-aged man with warm brown skin and a strong Canadian accent, looked as though he had never suffered a day's poor health in his life. No doubt he knew about strong constitutions, Laddy thought, but she was remembering the sudden exhaustion she had seen in Mischa's eyes.

"That's not to say that you're not feeling hellishly weak right now, of course," Dr. Bear continued. "But with good food—Helen knows all about that—lots of rest and a little exercise, you'll start to recover, all right. There's no serious pathological damage. And the important thing to remember is patience. You can't recover nine years in a few weeks."

Laddy looked at Mischa Busnetsky sipping his coffee while he listened to Dr. Bear. Was he a patient man? She knew nothing about him—everything and nothing.

Richard laughed. "Are you feeling hellishly weak, Mischa? No one would have known it this morning!" He turned to his wife and Edmund Bear and smilingly explained, "If you can believe it, we were suspicious of Laddy here this morning, and while I was still wondering what to do, Mischa took her down in a flying tackle that would have done credit to—''

"What?" Helen stared at her husband in amazement while Laddy and Mischa exchanged a glance. For some reason Laddy felt herself blushing.

"Mischa held her down while I very tamely went through her handbag," Richard said, chuckling. "Fortunately, before too much damage was done, I found her name and remembered who she was."

Mischa held Laddy's eye. "Not before the damage was done," he said quietly, meaningfully, for her ears alone, and she remembered his body on hers and the way the grip of his hands had changed from anger to passion.... She could not look away.

"Well, there you are," said Edmund Bear. "The reserves of strength in the human body fool us every time. I would have said you couldn't easily have sustained such a shock."

And his glance flicked almost unconsciously between herself and Mischa, and Laddy understood with a little jolt that Dr. Edmund Bear had picked up on what was between them, while Helen—and perhaps even Richard—had not. She was at once intrigued by what had given him that sensitivity toward other people. Was it professional expertise or personal experience?

"You say you have treated other exiles?" Mischa asked him then, and Edmund Bear explained that he was a member of the ICF and usually looked after the treatment of the dissidents whose freedom the group had obtained.

"I would like to ask you about one or two people," Mischa said. "Perhaps tomorrow." Edmund Bear nodded.

"How long will you be able to stay with us, Ned?" Helen asked then.

"Just the night," he answered. "I'll have to get the train back tomorrow afternoon, I'm afraid."

"There's no afternoon train tomorrow. It's Sunday," Helen said. When she had first emerged from her studio before lunch, Helen had seemed rather remote to Laddy, as though she were seeing everything around her as a possible subject to paint. But Laddy had had to revise that opinion quickly. Helen Digby was an extremely practical and well-organized woman. "There's no train at all on Sunday. You'll have to stay till Monday."

Dr. Bear looked put out by this information. "I checked and double-checked with the railroad!" he said. "And I've got to get back before Monday."

"I'm going back tomorrow afternoon," Laddy said. "We can drive back together. It is London you're going to?"

Mischa Busnetsky was in the act of filling a pipe with tobacco. This quiet motion was arrested suddenly as he looked over at Laddy.

"You go back to your work—to your newspaper?" he asked, and he was as still as a cat.

"Yes," she answered. "Work again on Monday."

"Your last assignment, I think, was me," he said, still motionless.

Was it, she wondered. Yet it seemed as if an age had passed since she had asked Harry to let her cover Mischa Busnetsky's arrival in London. Two days. How many things could happen in two days! She gave vent to a surprised little laugh.

"Yes, that's right."

"And now you have found me," he said, an odd harshness threaded through his tone. "When you go back to your editor on Monday, will you tell him that?"

God help her, she hadn't even thought of that. Laddy's lips parted and she breathed through her mouth as she gazed at him.

"Oh, no!" she said, in dismay.

"You have quite a story here," Mischa pressed. He had everyone's undivided attention now; they were all watching him and shooting awkward glances at Laddy. "A Welsh hideaway, a literary agent, a doctor who is frequently consulted in the treatment of dissidents and two lost manuscripts that have a compelling story of their own." With his pipestem, he enumerated the points on the fingers of his left hand, his eyes calm, cool, and suddenly Laddy knew she was facing the man who had held his own against psychiatrists, investigators, prosecutors and KGB colonels; the calm patient power of his intellect was terrifying.

He didn't trust her. He could look at her the way he had looked at her, say what he had said—but he was as suspicious of her now as he had been when he had accused her of carrying electronically bugged cushions.

In the absolute silence that fell when he stopped speaking, he struck a match, and his eyes dropped to the flame while he lighted his pipe.

Inside Laddy's head the battle lines between the public and the private woman formed, and she was aghast at the speed with which she was suddenly at war with herself.

What a dry term "conflict of interest" was, she realized. It carried no emotional overtones at all. It made one think of a lawyer who had two opposing clients and cared about neither very much.

But she cared desperately about both her clients: Lucy Laedelia Penreith, staff reporter, who ought to file this story with Harry Waller; and Laddy Penreith, father's daughter, whose true love had come home against all odds, wanting peace and quiet after years of an unequal battle.

"How long would it be before you would be willing to talk to the press?" she asked tentatively.

Mischa, who had watched the battle beginning in her, said in that calm, cold, silent way, "No. I will not bargain for a few days or weeks of peace against an exclusive story. I have played enough games with my rights, my freedom, my life."

"But I could—"

"No," he said. "Not anymore. And not with you. Now I will live my life the way I wish to live, and other people will do the same with theirs. I have paid for my right to privacy and freedom. If you are going to take them from me now, you must make up your mind to steal them. They are not for sale."

She should have known he would be a no-bargains man—he had spent the past nine years refusing to compromise with the might of the Soviet government, and he would not begin with her. She *had* known it, had seen it in their first moments together in that crowded Moscow apartment: "I do not want to go to prison again," he had said, "but this is a choice that is not mine to make."

As far back as that she had wanted to beg him to give in, but his strength had been equal to spending five of the next eight years behind locked doors, and he was telling her now that it would be equal to anything she could do to him.

She knew if she could only tell Harry Waller that by keeping the lid on Mischa Busnetsky's whereabouts for two or three weeks they could have an excellent exclusive story at the end of it, Harry would agree. Of that she was certain...ninety percent certain, she amended.

But if she told him they were to keep the story quiet until Mischa Busnetsky decided to call a press conference—with no promise of advance warning as to when that would be? Of course Harry would not sit still for that. It would be a case of the story or her job.

She had two choices: say nothing to Harry Waller and hope that he would never find out that she had known anything at all about Mischa Busnetsky...

or file the story now and never hope to see in Mischa Busnetsky's eyes anything but the calm, cool look of a man whose rights were even more important to him than life.

She felt bruised, battered, torn. It would have been easier if he had asked her to die for him. She would not have required an instant's hesitation for that.

It was not merely a story. She could have let the story go by without a murmur. If he had asked the private Laddy Penreith, who loved him, to protect his privacy.... But he had deliberately confronted the professional woman. He had deliberately set his integrity against her own, and only one could survive. He had created an insurmountable problem out of nothing.

Which did she love—the memory or the man? If she loved the man, how was it he could not trust her, and why was she looking at him now through a blaze of anger and hurt and a desire to hurt back? Nothing made any sense.

"I will let you know my decision before I leave tomorrow," she said to them all, and saw in his eyes that he had already known it.

Laddy went to her room early, but not to sleep. Instead, confused, heartsick and weary, she paced up and down the small blue-and-white bedroom, trying to discover what she ought to do, trying to understand how so much could have happened to her in one day.

She looked down at her palm and with sudden

impatience ripped away the small bandage that covered it. She stared at the razor-thin cut across the skin at the base of her fingers and at the deeper cut near the thumb as though she might read some truth there that was now escaping her. Then, with an exclamation, she pressed the sticky tape back into place.

Her room faced out the back of the house, down toward the village, and one by one in the lonely hours of night she saw the lights going out, until it seemed as though she was alone in the world—alone with an impossible decision.

Sometime after midnight she dressed again, crept down the stairs and slipped out into the night.

The air was cold and damp, and as always, the smell of the sea seemed stronger on the night air. Stumbling a little, Laddy made her way to the edge of the cliff and in the light of the stars found a convenient rock to sit on.

She sat for a long time with the stars and the half-moon and the quiet sea, thoughts washing in and out of her head at random. The decision came to her slowly, on the wind, on the waves, and she listened carefully. When she understood it all, she returned to the house.

"GOOD MORNING," said a friendly Welsh voice amid a tinkle of crockery that woke Laddy up.

She rolled over and looked into a younger version of Mairi Davies's bright dark eyes and upside-down V eyebrows, and she said, smiling, "You must be Brigit."

Brigit smiled back. "So I am," she said. "And you would be the young woman from London who has people in Fishguard, would you?"

Laddy sat up, eyeing the tea tray with great favor as Brigit set it on the bed beside her, and laughed. "You might say that," she smiled. "My great-grandfather was born in Fishguard a hundred and fifty-odd years ago. I was born in Canada. And I haven't been served breakfast in bed since I was nine years old and had the measles."

"Not breakfast," Brigit corrected her. "Just tea. Breakfast will be downstairs. When I took Helen a cup of tea to her studio she said you might appreciate a cup, too."

Bless Helen, thought Laddy. When they were all staring at her last night waiting for her answer, she had felt as though she hadn't a friend in the world. But Helen had cared enough to fortify her with tea—and a sign of friendship—before Laddy had to go downstairs and face them all.

"Thank you, I do," said Laddy. "I feel as though I haven't slept at all. Is it late or early, please?"

Brigit laughed. "It's just after 8:30, and how could you not sleep well when you are escaping the horrible noises of the city?"

"Maybe I've been programmed so I can't sleep in silence," Laddy suggested, taking a deep drink of her tea.

"Programmed, is it? Well, if you stay here long, we'll have you de-programmed in no time. And you'll never want to see a city again!"

Laddy regarded her quizzically. "You sound as though you're speaking from experience," she said.

Brigit, who was a dark, almost gypsy-looking woman in her early twenties, put her hands on her hips and shook her head. "Three years I spent in London," she said, as though she ought to have known better. "No one could stop me, you see. I went to study art, and I said I would never come back to Trefelin."

"And?" Laddy prompted, rather fascinated by this recital.

She laughed. "And the city was big and sophisticated, but it was also noisy and dirty, and no one said hello to their neighbors. Three years was enough. I came back to Trefelin." She glanced at her watch. "I must go now, or breakfast will be late."

Laddy put her empty cup down on the table beside her bed. "But what about the art?" she asked.

Brigit smiled. "Ah—for art you do not need London! If you are staying, I will show you my work one day, if you like," and she disappeared out the door.

Getting out of bed, Laddy eyed with a grimace the blue jeans she had worn yesterday and wished she had brought a change of clothing in her overnight case. She had tossed in nightclothes, fresh underwear and cosmetics, but she had thought the jeans and red high-necked sweater would serve. Now she wanted nothing so much as a fresh shirt.

She put on eye makeup and a little lipstick, although normally she would not have bothered. Makeup might give her confidence, and this morning she needed confidence.

The door to Helen's studio was open, and as Laddy passed it on her way to the dining room, Helen called to her. "If you'll hang on a second, I'll go with you," she said, laying down her pencil and standing up. "I'm famished." She crossed casually to the door and Laddy had the feeling that Helen had been waiting for her to appear. Helen was going out of her way to give her moral support, and Laddy wondered just how badly Helen thought she needed it.

Mischa Busnetsky, in black trousers and a black sweater over a check shirt, was standing at the trellised window looking out over the sea. One hand was in his pocket and the other hand was holding the delicate white curtain aside, and he was staring at the cliff edge as though it held the answer to a question he was asking.

After a moment he turned around, and when he looked at Laddy, the question was still there in his eyes.

"Good morning," they all said together, and Helen, keeping up a polite conversation by asking him how he was sleeping, began to load a plate from the sideboard.

Laddy sank into a chair and poured herself a cup

of coffee. She needn't have bothered coming down to breakfast at all—she wasn't going to be able to eat, anyway.

"That glass," Helen was saying to Mischa, "contains Ned Bear's special protein-vitamin-mineral supplement and although it's quite pleasant when fresh, it does taste rather murky if it's been left to sit. So you had better have that first."

The glass she indicated was immediately opposite Laddy, and Mischa dropped into the chair and placed his large hand around the glass, looking at Laddy as he did so.

His hands were large and broad, but almost fleshless, and she watched the fingers curl round the glass with a detached, almost aesthetic pleasure as she stirred cream into her coffee.

With an abrupt gesture he lifted the glass to his mouth, and unconsciously following the motion of his hand, she suddenly met his eyes. His eyes were looking at her as though she had already betrayed him and he had accepted it.

She said, "Would you like to hear my decision?" Mischa breathed once and nodded, as Helen sat down beside them, at the head of the small table, with a plateful of bacon and eggs.

"I'm surprised you've been able to make a decision," said Helen, and then Richard and Ned Bear walked into the room, making her audience complete.

"I won't file the story yet," she told them when they were all settled. "And I won't tell my editor

I've got anything. I'll keep a lid on everything until Mr. Busnetsky—" she faltered a little over the use of his last name "—until Mr. Busnetsky decides that he is ready to talk to the press. And as soon as I hear that, I'll file a story. I'm not going to ask you again to let me have that information in advance. But neither am I going to wait in London and get the news at the same time as everyone else. I'm going to spend my holidays down here in Trefelin— I'll put up at a bed-and-breakfast—and as much extra time as I can get my editor to give me without telling him why." Finally she looked at Mischa Busnetsky, but his face was deliberately unreadable, his jaw clenched. "You've already said you won't accept any conditions for my silence, and I won't ask for special treatment. But I hope you'll give me equal treatment and notify me along with everyone else when and if you do decide to talk to the press."

And if I don't get my story filed a day before anyone else under those conditions, she added to herself, *I deserve to be fired.* She would check out some local photographers in Fishguard so that she would have them on call—in fact, she would bring back a camera from London—and while the members of the press were winging their way down to Trefelin or being drummed up in Fishguard or Cardiff, her first story would be on its way to Harry.

It sounded like the perfect solution, but in fact it posed several problems: how to get the extra vacation time from Harry, what to do if her time ran out and Mischa Busnetsky still had not come out of seclusion and what the hell she could say to Harry if the plan somehow backfired and he found out. Probably "goodbye," she thought, and snorted wryly. She looked at Mischa Busnetsky, who was no longer looking at her. Why was he doing this? It could all have been so simple. . . .

"But you certainly are not going to put up at a bed-and-breakfast in town." Laddy surfaced with a start to realize that Helen was speaking. "You must stay with us while you're here. Much more comfortable for you, and anyway—" she looked round "—it would cause comment if Laddy were suddenly to go looking for a bed-and-breakfast in Trefelin."

"I needn't be that close," Laddy said. "I could put up at a hotel in Fishguard." But Helen quashed that with a firm, "Nonsense. You can have one of our cottages," and none of the men seemed inclined to disagree with her. So it was settled that Laddy would come back to Tymawr House as soon as time and Harry Waller allowed.

The atmosphere relaxed considerably after this, and Laddy saw that everyone was grateful to her for having discovered the way out of an almost impossible dilemma. She realized with some surprise that the attitude of Richard, Helen and Ned Bear toward her yesterday had not been the hostile suspicion she had imagined, but horrified understanding that Mischa Busnetsky's attitude, however justified it might be in view of his past, had succeeded in creating a corner and pushing Laddy into it. If she had not reacted like a paranoid idiot last night, she might well have enjoyed the benefit of a joint discussion of the possibilities with these three, instead of battling things out alone in the small hours.

Helen confirmed this as the two women took a quiet walk along the Coastal Path after lunch, a few minutes before Laddy and Ned Bear were to set out for London.

"How long will it be before you can get back, do you think?" Helen asked as they tramped single file along a particularly narrow stretch of the track.

"At least a week, I imagine," Laddy said. "My holidays don't start for two weeks, and I doubt very much if Harry will give me more than another week at the beginning and perhaps a few days at the end. I hope that's going to be long enough."

"So do I, for your sake. I shouldn't imagine that what you're doing is easy to manage, and I must say I think you're bending over backward. I don't think he quite understood what he was asking."

Laddy thought Mischa had understood exactly what he was asking. But she did not understand why, and she did not contradict Helen.

"Will you have to cancel other holiday plans?" Helen asked. "It's very pleasant here in late spring, but—"

But sitting around a country village, trying to protect her interest in an exclusive story, however pleasant the village might be, would not make up for missing out on an exciting vacation, Laddy silently finished for her. With a certain degree of relief she realized that Helen had no suspicion that there was anything between herself and Mischa beyond Laddy's loyalty, perhaps, to her father.

"No, I really hadn't made any..." she began aloud, and stopped dead, remembering. John. John had asked her to go to Greece with him. And she had wanted to go—or rather, she had wanted to *want* to go, until Mischa Busnetsky came.

"Oh, damn!" she said violently. She had thought seeing Mischa Busnetsky again would settle things for her, and instead her life was being turned upside down; she was more uncertain than ever. Laddy sat down uncaring on a dirty stile and gazed hollowly at Helen. "How could anybody get their life into such a *mess*!" she demanded savagely. And she saw Helen looking at her in dismay and knew that Helen did not guess what was going on in her mind. Well, how could she? How could anyone know when she herself did not know? She was utterly and completely confused—she didn't know what she wanted, what was right, who she loved, for two minutes together.

Laddy sighed and looked out over the sea. The decision she had made out here last night meant that she was going to lose John Bentinck, she knew it.

Part of her loved Mischa Busnetsky, and part of her hated him.

CHAPTER SEVEN

ON THURSDAY the news came out that two major publishers—English and American—planned the simultaneous publication of two works of Mikhail Busnetsky, and thanks to Richard, the story broke in the *Evening Herald* under Laddy's by-line.

It was going to be a very noisy affair. The publication of two very different books by a newly released Soviet dissident was going to make literary headlines. And where had the manuscripts come from? Had Mischa Busnetsky managed to bring them out of Russia with him? People were tearing their hair out trying to find Mischa Busnetsky, but Mischa Busnetsky remained very successfully in hiding. They had to be satisfied with Mr. Busnetsky's agent, Richard Digby.

"What we're telling them," Richard said to Laddy over the phone the day after she had broken the first news, "is merely that the manuscripts had previously been brought out of the Soviet Union and were awaiting him here. We're deliberately leaving it rather mysterious. If you would like to let out the real story on that, we rather hoped—the publisher and I, not Mischa—that you might do that a little later on, Laddy."

Mischa Busnetsky might hate publicity, she observed wryly, but Richard did not—and he was going to do everything he could to assure good coverage while stopping short of actually countermanding Mischa's wishes.

"Did you tell the publishers the truth?" she asked.

"No. I merely mentioned that there might be an interesting story attached to that," he said. "We thought it might be better broken closer to the publication date."

Quite a story indeed, Laddy thought wryly, thinking of the flurry that would be kicked up if she were to suggest that her father's last act had been to obtain the manuscripts and that he had then died under mysterious circumstances. She sighed. Thank God that information resided in only one brain— her own.

And in that of whoever had run down her father in the street, of course. But she thought that the secret was safe between them.

"Aren't you afraid they're going to find him through you?" she asked Richard.

"We hope not," he replied. "I'm afraid I'm stuck here in town for the next few weeks until he feels strong enough to speak to the press, however. It wouldn't do to have me followed down there. But the house has always been in Helen's name. The town flat is listed as my residence."

"Still, I'm surprised he agreed to this."

"I'm afraid once we'd chosen our publishers there was no alternative," Richard said. "They have paid a very large advance, you know, and the news wasn't likely to be kept quiet. Possibly nothing will be kept quiet for very long," he added. "One never knows. When are you going to get down again, Laddy?"

To sit on her story, he meant, in case somebody enterprising found Mischa Busnetsky.

"Not before Tuesday, I'm afraid," she said, grimacing across the newsroom toward where Harry Waller sat and remembering the difficulty she had had getting even those few extra days.

"Will you be going down for the weekend, then?" he asked. Today was Friday. She could leave tonight and drive through the night again, but. . . but she was tired—exhausted—and suddenly she didn't care if this weekend, Mischa Busnetsky exposed the entire Soviet spy network operating in the Western world. She was sick of the dispassionate words she had been writing about him, sick of seeing Mischa Busnetsky as "good copy." She wished he had been a factory laborer in Murmansk who had never looked at a piece of anti-Soviet propaganda in his life. *Let* the story break this weekend. Let Harry pack her off to the astrology column.

"No," she said. "I've got to spend the weekend packing and arranging. I expect I'll go down on Tuesday night or Wednesday morning."

"Well, then, I'll talk to you again before you go," Richard said. "Will you give me your home number—just in case?"

She gave it to him, realizing there was a small

conspiracy between him and Helen. If an enterprising reporter located Mischa Busnetsky this weekend, Laddy would know within five minutes. She wondered why they were taking such care of her. For her father's sake?

She wrote the follow-up story Richard had given her on Mischa, then talked to a stringer in Jerusalem about a recent border raid from Lebanon in which four Israeli children had been killed on the beach near a place called Rosh Ha Nikra. The story had been on the front page all day, and the stringer had nothing new to report other than a general conviction that there would be reprisals.

"Shalom," the man said as he hung up. The Israeli word for both hello and goodbye also meant "peace," and Laddy sighed. Everybody talked about it....

"The world is not as we would make it," she heard a quiet voice say in her head, and she sat upright with a jerk. *"Shut up!"* she told Mischa Busnetsky's insidious voice, to the amazement of the blameless reporter at the typewriter beside her. She smiled a weak apology at him, rolled paper into her typewriter and concentrated on the inevitability of reprisal for the lives of four children who had been shot down while playing on a beach on a sunny day.

"OH, LASS...why not?" John asked quietly, his northern accent thickened through emotion. He dropped the menu onto the table and looked at her.

He had arrived back in town Friday afternoon after three days of getting pictures of an oil-rig disaster in the North Sea, and they had come to Charlotte Street to their favorite Greek restaurant for dinner. And she had told John she could not go to Greece with him.

Laddy looked away from his blue gaze, feeling a confusing swirl of emotions in which guilt vied with anger for predominance. She supposed she would never know now whether John Bentinck could have made her forget Mischa Busnetsky, because after this he would not be trying.

She was being forced into a decision that might or might not have been the one she really wanted to make. She could not go to Greece with John, and she would never know whether she had wanted to.

"John, I can't tell you," she said desperately. "It's business. I'll be waiting for a story to break—"

He interrupted her. "You're giving up your holidays to wait for a story?" he demanded, amazed. "Must be some story— What is it, the capture of a mass murderer?" He was half-serious.

"No, no, nothing that big," she said hastily. "But I've given my word to someone not to file a story until they—"

He interrupted again. "Well, hell, love," he said. "You don't have to hang around waiting, do you? Write the story up and get them to cable you or Harry when it can go! You know that."

She did know that, and as soon as he'd said it, he realized there had to be something more.

"Well?" he queried softly.

"John, they won't do that. They won't give me an exclusive.... I have to be right there when they decide to—"

"Now, just let me get this straight." He sounded as though he were battling to keep incredulity out of his voice. "You've got a story, and you've agreed not to file till someone gives the okay, but you haven't got the promise of an exclusive?" He spoke each word separately, small measured pauses between, as though he thought one of them might have trouble understanding.

Laddy nodded. He was right; it sounded absolutely incredible. She should never have embarked on this explanation.

The waiter appeared at his side, and John glanced up as though he had come out of a time machine.

"I'm not hungry, Laddy," he said. "Could we get out of here?" And almost before she agreed, he stood up, apologizing briefly to the waiter and passing him a couple of pound notes. He pulled her coat from the chair and flung it over his own arm, shepherded her rapidly past the tables and then outside.

They walked in silence to where her car was parked behind his at the curb. He opened the passenger door of his own car and she got in. "Damn!" he exclaimed suddenly. "I can't even drive you anywhere!" He slammed the door and walked around to climb in behind the wheel. He turned to face her, his arm along the seat back in the gloom of dusk. "You're not being honest with me, Laddy," he said roughly. "I want you to be honest with me. Tell me anything, lass, as long as it's the truth!"

But what was the truth, she wondered hopelessly. "Everything I've told you is the truth, John—so far as it goes. I can't tell you any more because—because I don't understand it myself, yet."

"It's a man," he said flatly, and raised a hand against her gasp. "Don't deny it—I know. Somewhere between last Thursday night and tonight you met a man, and he's—he's turned you upside down, Laddy. *Dammit!*" He hit the steering wheel with his hand. "How could it happen so quickly? How? We had something going, Laddy, I—"

"It wasn't quick at all." She could not stop herself from saying it or keep the pain and bitterness from her voice. "I knew him years ago, he. . . ."

"He's come back?" John hissed softly, a light of anger, danger in his eyes.

Startled, she gasped, "Who?"

"I always knew there'd been someone," he said. "But I thought he was gone, out of the picture. I always knew there'd been someone who'd hurt you."

She said, "He couldn't help it, John, but I. . . ."

"But you think you still love him," he said flatly.

"I don't know."

"But while I go off on my holiday alone, he gets a chance to prove that you do, is that it?" he demanded.

"No..." she faltered. "There's a story—"

Abruptly he pressed the starter and the engine leaped to life with an angry roar, then he held the wheel and looked straight ahead out the windshield.

"I hope I never learn the bastard's name," he said angrily. "I hope I never do. If you change your mind, call me."

She got out of the car and stood on the pavement and watched as he roared off down the street.

LADDY SPENT most of the weekend with Margaret and Ben Smiley in the garden, unaccountably wishing that she had gone down to Trefelin after all. She did not hear from John over the weekend, and she didn't see him at work on Monday. She wondered whether it was by accident or design.

Monday night at six o'clock a wealthy gold dealer was shot down in London in the street outside his home, and Harry phoned her late that night to ask her to cover it first thing Tuesday morning.

She was somehow quite certain that John would be at the scene the next morning, and she wondered with a sinking heart what they could say to each other. But he was not there. Laddy had been so convinced John would be covering the story, that for a moment she did not recognize the man who was, an old *Herald* hand named Bill Hazzard.

She and Bill spent most of the day between the "scene" and the hospital waiting for news. And during the long pointless wait it occurred to her that

John might have asked Richard Snapes not to send him on the same assignment as herself.

But that was paranoid and ridiculous. John was a professional photographer and he put that before everything; there had been many occasions in the past two months when they had not worked together for days at a stretch.

She knew she was not functioning well, and she was glad there were no intricate Middle-Eastern developments today to follow and report.

Laddy set out for Wales on Wednesday in greater confusion than when she had left it ten days before.

MISCHA BUSNETSKY had set up a study for himself in one of the cottages on the property. Both of what Laddy had thought were outbuildings were in fact self-contained cottages that Helen and Richard had had modernized—though not as extensively as the house—to serve as guest quarters. The house itself was not large enough to accommodate guests comfortably over a long period.

"For one thing we've only one bathroom," Helen explained. "But Mischa still sleeps and eats in the house—I'd be worried if he was sleeping in the cottage with no one within easy distance in case of accident.

"I've put you in the other cottage. The two are quite close together, but I don't think you'll get in each other's hair—I hope not."

The cottages were at right angles to each other, and at their nearest walls, the remains of an old construction that might once have been their common animal shelter ran between them. The walls were white stucco and the roofs and shutters were black. Large worn flagstones angled across the courtyard between the two front doors.

"They're charming," Laddy said delightedly. "I don't remember them at all from when dad and I were here."

"They were pretty broken down—you were probably expected to keep away from them. We had them done seven or eight years ago."

She showed Laddy into the cottage that lay farthest from the house, at a right angle to the cliff face. The door opened directly into a pretty little kitchen that had been repaired, painted and supplied with running water and electricity but still retained much of the flavor of the original.

"We had to have the floors entirely redone—" Helen pointed out the brick-red ceramic-tiled flooring "—but I didn't want the cottages turned into chrome-and-glass monstrosities."

To the left of the kitchen lay a completely outfitted bathroom, which Helen said had once been a pantry-storage room. To the right was the sitting room and through it the bedroom. The fireplace in the kitchen had been removed, Helen told her, but the one in the sitting room was working. At the far end of the cottage, the bedroom overlooked the sea.

It was like something she had dreamed of, a place she had always known. "I don't suppose you'd consider selling it?" Laddy asked. "I'd retire here and write a book." She had always planned to write a book someday—she might do some thinking about that during the next two weeks.

"Isn't it odd you should say that," said Helen. "Richard and I agreed only the other day to sell the other one to Mischa."

"Oh," said Laddy.

Although Helen said Laddy was welcome to take all her meals at the house and particularly hoped to see her every night for dinner, Laddy thought she would prefer to make her own breakfast and lunch, and when she had moved her luggage into the cottage, she drove down to the village store for supplies.

It was a beautiful warm spring afternoon, and Mischa Busnetsky was standing in the open doorway of his own cottage when she returned with her shopping, as though he had been waiting for her.

"So—now I have the press on my doorstep?" he asked quietly, and moved across to take one of her bags and open the door for her.

He was wearing black trousers and a black-and-white-check shirt rolled up at the elbows; there was appreciably more flesh covering his frame than ten days ago. His short black hair now had the look of soft fur, and it crossed her mind that it might be rather pleasant to touch it.

He wasn't serious; she laughed. "In fact, I was even thinking of putting in an offer on this little place, till I learned you were buying the one next door!"

"And why did that change your mind?" he asked lazily, his eyes smiling, and it was as though the hostile suspicion of last week, when he had accused her of wanting only a story, had never existed.

"I rather thought *you* might complain," she said nervously, setting her bag on the table, and when she turned he was close behind her with the other, and he was very tall and broad.

"About what?" he asked. "The distraction?" He moved to put the bag down, and then he was very close indeed. He put his hands on her shoulders and her body jerked as though electricity had passed through her between his two hands.

"You did not publish the story of my whereabouts," he said. "Why?"

Laddy blinked at him. "Did you think I *would*?" she gasped, amazed.

"No," he said. "I was not sure. Why did you not?"

His eyes were so deep, she could have drowned in them. She thought wildly that if she let herself fall into those eyes she need never come up for air again. She swallowed.

"Helen told me that this could mean great trouble for you, that you might lose your job for it," he said when she did not answer. "Is this so?"

"I would lose credibility with my editor if he found out," she said. "But there's no reason why he should." A week ago she had been hating him for putting her in this position, and now here she was telling him it didn't matter. She must be mad.

"This word 'credibility'—it derives from the Latin *credere*, to believe?" he asked, and this was a jump she could not fathom. She nodded dumbly.

"Your editor will stop believing in you because of me, therefore?" he concluded, and she gazed in admiration at an intellect that could translate from English to Latin to Russian and so add another word to his vocabulary.

"But this is no small thing," he said. "I was wrong to make this demand of you when it is so easy for me to promise you an exclusive story." She had stopped looking into his eyes; she was staring at a small white button on his shirt front. "I will promise you an exclusive story," he said quietly, "but I will make a condition." He put his hand under her chin and raised it, and she looked into his eyes. "On this condition," he said, and he was half smiling, but his eyes were dark. "That you tell me *why* you did not publish my whereabouts last week."

To her amazement she felt herself blush fiery red. She gazed up at him, unable to speak, unable to tear her eyes away from his. He was not smiling anymore. He was staring at her and his breathing had altered, and she watched his gaze slide to her mouth and her lips parted in a faint gasp.

The hand under her chin shifted, and she felt his thumb gently tracing her mouth. With a clarity so vivid it shocked her, she saw his hand touching the lips of the woman in the painting, and his touch was a burning brand on her mouth, and eight years melted away to nothing.

"Mischa..." she begged. He bent his head, and at last, at long last, his mouth touched her own.

It was the kiss they would have exchanged in that Moscow apartment if he had kissed her then, and in some extraordinary way, the girl who lifted her arms passionately, trustingly, around his neck and clung to him was a seventeen-year-old girl who had only just learned the secret of why she had been born a woman.

He took his mouth away from hers, and she moaned her loss as his lips followed the line of her neck down to the hollow of her throat, and she pressed his head with her two hands and trembled. He lifted his head and looked into her eyes, then pulled her tightly to his chest and held her.

"How I have dreamed to see you tremble for me," he whispered, and she could have wept at the perfection of it. He looked down into her face, her head cupped firmly in one large hand. "And you have no husband, no lover?" he asked.

"No husband, no lover," she whispered.

"Not for a long time, too, I think," he said quietly.

She dropped her eyes and said, "Not for a very long time. Not for eight years."

She counted the seconds till he understood, and he went completely still. Then his hand was in her hair, pulling her head back, and his eyes raked her face, harsh, almost angry, his own face all planes and angles in the shadowy room.

"You will learn about love from me?" his voice

rasped in his throat, and it was half question, half command.

When she could speak, she breathed, "Yes."

His broad hands encircled her face, her head; they trembled against her hair as though if he let go his control he might crush her, and she shook as his emotion enveloped her. "Why?" he demanded hoarsely, and she knew it now, she could say it now, it was so clear.

She said, "I love you."

His eyes darkened as though she had struck him, then he drew her body against the length of his, and the passion in his eyes blazed down at her. His thumb touched her lips, parting them, and he bent his head and his mouth covered hers; she went up like dry underbrush and heard the flames roaring in her ears.

He lifted his mouth from hers and buried his face in her hair. "Lady, Lady," he repeated hoarsely, over and over, as though the sound was being torn from him.

"I love you," she said, wrapping her arms tightly around him. "I love you so much." And she tasted the first heady joy of surrender to love without restriction, without fear. With a groan Mischa buried his face in her neck, and his body, pressed so tightly to hers, was burning, flaming with his need of her. His face pushed away the collar of her shirt as his warm seeking mouth ran over the hollows of her neck and shoulders, then her throat and finally found her mouth again. His broad hands touched her body as though they would remold her at breast, waist and hip. . . .

His hand left her hip then and reached up to wrap itself in her hair, stilling her for a moment as he gazed into her eyes.

"Never?" he asked, and his eyes were slitted with pleasure, with triumph, knowing the answer.

"Never," she whispered hoarsely, and his body leaped against hers so that she closed her eyes against the confusion of desire in her.

"Open your eyes," he commanded huskily, the hand in her hair shaking her head a little. "I have waited a long time to see this in your eyes. I thought I would wait forever. Open your eyes and let me see."

She opened her eyes with effort, and his eyes were gazing down at her, his mouth half smiling.

"What do you want to see?" she breathed, indescribably moved by the hungry possessiveness of that smile.

"I want to see what I have dreamed of seeing," he said softly, the silver thread of need glittering through his tone. "I want to see the first surprise of passion; I want to watch your innocence taste desire."

On the last word his voice roughened, and his hands dropped to clasp her denimed thighs. With a drunken, reeling sensation she felt the length of her torso slide up against his until her hips were above his belt, and aware of him in every pore, she looked down at his dark head and watched his involuntary tremor as he pressed his face to the hollow between her breasts.

He buried his face inside the confining folds of her shirt, his mouth moving moistly against the creamy fullness of her breasts, leaving a trail of fire and a high aching longing that she scarcely understood. Her hands pressed against his head, against the sensuous panther pelt of his hair, forcing his mouth against her skin; she felt his mouth as it kissed her breast.

"Yes," he said huskily, pushing his head back against the pressure of her palms, the mat of his hair fanning sensually against her incredibly sensitized fingers and his passionate, triumphant eyes glittering up into hers. "You see how your body makes its demands...my mouth against your breast now, but it shall want more than this before we are through...."

He kissed her mouth again. She was drugged with passion, with wanting him. When he straightened, holding her, and turned, she scarcely knew what was happening until the world reeled and she felt the hard table top under her back. She opened her eyes to see him standing between her thighs, his hands on her prominent hip bones warm through the thick denim of her jeans and his eyes burning into hers. Her eyelids fluttered as she drew a sudden breath through her teeth. Then he dropped forward over her, a hand falling on each side of her head, and smiled down at her.

"Lady," he whispered, his mouth tantalizingly

near her own. "Lady, Lady, Lady." He repeated her name in a passionate whisper, sending a frenzy of sensation down her spine into her arms, her stomach, her legs.

"Love me," Laddy pleaded, almost beside herself, feeling as though she had moved into some new dimension of consciousness, of existence. "Please love me."

"I do," Mischa said, and it was a promise. "I will."

Some barrier around her heart that she had never known existed began to crack then, and she understood that she had been a prisoner behind that barrier, that the barrier was her own self and that soon she would be free.

"I love you," she cried again, and the words were the distillation of a truth so profound she thought the world should shatter in its presence; and she heard the rasping intake of his breath in answer.

Her body was long since operating on a primitive instinct. Her hands moved over him, his back, his head, his thighs, wherever she could reach. His chest lifted away from hers and she arched up in search of the contact again. He held her head tightly, firmly, so that she could not move, and his hand on her jaw held her mouth open. The teasing kiss stopped and he deliberately lowered his mouth over hers in a thrusting, urgent, powerful kiss that told her more plainly than words exactly what he wanted of her. In answer to that same primitive instinct, she wrapped her arms convulsively around his back.

The kiss was destroying her, turning her bones to water, her flesh to fire, blotting out reason so surely that she felt she would never need to think again. She felt him tremble at the response of her body and his kiss deepened in fever and intensity. His hands ran along the length of her arms, and his fingers threaded between hers and clenched, holding her immobile; the knowledge that she was completely in his power burned white hot in her, and with every cell of her being, every iota of body, brain and soul, she wanted him to take her then, there; she cursed the thick rough denim that kept his body from her, kept him from making her a part of him forever.

As though that final yearning ache was transmitted to him, he lifted his mouth from hers and let go of her hands to stroke her hair. His jaw clenched tightly and then his mouth moved in a smile.

"I will," he promised roughly, "but not yet." And when she understood what he meant she felt dismay rip through her like a scream.

"Why?" she gasped, as though truth, beauty and life were all being torn from her at once, and she reached to hold his head as he moved to straighten up.

Mischa became still when her hand touched him, as though in spite of himself he was a slave to her touch. "Because I am going to court you," he said, his voice low and caressing. "Because I am going to teach you slowly about love—so slowly that you will hate me, so slowly that we will both be mad before you have learned. I will teach you that you are seventeen and a woman, as I would have taught you then. And each one of our eight lost years we will reclaim with love.''

She closed her eyes and felt tears on the lids, and immediately his mouth was tender on her lashes.

''Lady,'' he said. ''My Lady.'' And through the ache of loving that suffused her she could hear that this decision was hard for him; he was in her power as much as she was in his, could not stop now unless *she* allowed it—and suddenly she wanted him more desperately, more profoundly than ever.

''No!'' she cried, reaching for him.

He caught her hands determinedly and his voice ground out, ''Yes.''

But he had to fight both of them—her desire as well as his own. She had for opponent only his determination, and she wanted him with every cell of her being. ''Mischa!'' she moaned, as she had done in that Moscow apartment eight years ago.

And as though she had called down the canyon of time, she heard the echo, ''Mischa...Mischa!'' in a high young voice. Only when he let go her hands and moved to disentangle her legs from his did she understand that it was not her own voice she had heard, but that of a young boy. A boy who was knocking on the door of the other cottage and would doubtless soon turn toward Laddy's cottage and the door that still stood open to the setting sun.

CHAPTER EIGHT

"MISCHA," the young voice called, and Laddy raised
herself first to her elbows and then to sit on the edge
of the table. She gazed at Mischa as he pulled away
from her and took a long shuddering breath. She felt
as though she had been suddenly jerked into another
world, and she shivered as though that world was
achingly lonely and colder than the one she had been
inhabiting; as her passion left her, an anger born of
her sudden loneliness took its place.

"Friend of yours?" she demanded sarcastically
as the knocking on that other door continued.

Mischa nodded, holding her gaze with an expression in his eyes that said he delighted in her anger,
and she snapped, "His timing's excellent. I don't
suppose you bribed him?"

Mischa laughed outright, and his hand touched
her cheek caressingly. "Yes, this is good," he said,
the laughter dying out of his eyes. "Find anger, and
hatred, too—for we will take every emotion imagin-
able to our love bed."

She gasped against the sudden twist of emotion
that churned in her, and he bent and kissed her with
a sudden and swiftly curtailed passion.

"And every emotion will be destroyed," he said, "save love and the innocence in your eyes."

Running footsteps sounded on the flagstones, and he moved away from her toward the open door. Laddy dropped her head forward onto her heaving chest and tried to calm her breathing.

"Hello, Rhodri," she heard him say.

The young Welsh voice, full of admiration and hero worship, burst out, "There you are, then! You've moved into this cottage, have you?"

"Not I," Mischa explained. "My friend from London is staying here."

With heightened sensitivity she heard jealousy in the tone that repeated, "Your friend?"

In response to the answering jealous pang that scratched through her, she jumped off the table and moved over to stand beside Mischa in the doorway and smiled down at the thin, dark young boy whose gaze, when it transferred to her, held a worried frown.

"Lady, this is my friend Rhodri. Rhodri, my friend Lady."

Rhodri smiled up at her in sudden relief, and Laddy knew that he was responding to the warmth of Mischa's voice and the double use of the word "friend."

"Hello, Rhodri," she said.

"Hello, Lady."

She heard her changed name on his wide lips with a little shock, for somehow when Mischa said her name, she had never really heard it as anything other than "Laddy" in an accent that charmed her. She opened her mouth to correct the boy, and instead she was saying, "I was just going to make a cup of tea. Will you have some with us?"

"Oh, yes, please," he said. "If it isn't too much trouble.... I could go and take tea with Brigit, you see," he added in some anxiety, as though to dispel any suspicion that he might have come in search of a meal.

"No trouble at all," Laddy said, moving back into the kitchen and over to the table. One bag of groceries—not the one with the eggs, she devoutly hoped—was on the floor, the other on the table squashed up against the wall. It was a compelling reminder of what had just transpired, and as she stood up from the floor holding the bag, Laddy's eyes met Mischa's; to her annoyance, she blushed.

Mischa checked a sudden, involuntary move toward her, and suddenly all her anger was destroyed, wiped out by the knowledge that he could never have been proof against her if she had held him and begged him to make love to her. She stared into his eyes over Rhodri's head, the smile broadening involuntarily on her lips still swollen from his kisses, her eyes telling him she knew he loved and wanted her as much as she loved and wanted him.

"More," he said quietly. "But you will learn."

Laddy turned abruptly away from him to set the groceries on the counter.

"You know Brigit, then?" she said to Rhodri. "Brigit up at the big house?"

"Oh, yes, I know her, she is my sister, you know!" Rhodri laughed.

"Is she!" Laddy exclaimed, unloading the bag. It did hold the eggs, and four were broken. "And are you, by any chance, twelve years old?" She put the eight whole eggs into the straw basket on the counter and carefully poured the meat of the broken ones from the cardboard carton into a bowl. At the price of eggs in Trefelin, she would use them to make an omelet.

"I'll soon be thirteen," Rhodri said, with the air of a scientist setting the facts straight for a layman.

"Well, then, you must be the family genius. Brigit talked about you last time I was here." Laddy filled the kettle and put it on the stove, then went back to where Mischa and Rhodri sat by the table to get the other bag of groceries.

In Rhodri's young eyes she saw a reflection of the dark intensity of Mischa's, and the two could almost have been father and son. Husband and son, her heart amended, and with an intensity that swamped her, she suddenly wanted to have Mischa Busnetsky's child, she wanted to create someone who would be a part of them both, a child who would sit across the table from its father as this one did and smile at her from dark, intelligent eyes....

The feeling washed through her and left her in the space of a moment, but Rhodri had seen the look in her eyes, and Mischa had seen it, and the young boy smiled at her in a responsive kinship. The three of them were suddenly inside a bubble of sunlight, united by the bond of intelligence and dedication—and, incredibly, by the ties of love.

Laddy smiled at Rhodri as though he were the son she had had eight years ago when she had first met Mischa Busnetsky, and a warm sense of belonging settled on the room.

"Well?" she prodded, the sunlight bubbling into laughter inside her. "Are you a genius?"

His smile was remarkably broad. "Oh, yes," Rhodri laughed. "And you are, too, I think, and for certain *he* is!" He flashed his engaging grin up at Mischa.

"But of course," Laddy said, moving to the stove as the kettle began to whistle. "So then what would two geniuses like for tea?"

"That depends," Mischa interjected, "on what the third genius has to offer." And he stood up with the other bag in his hands and walked over to the counter.

She loved every pebble in creation from the dawn of time, every blade of grass, every living creature. Surrounded by a warm glow, the three of them laid the table and made toast with cheese and chutney and talked over the meal as though they had been friends for a hundred years.

Rhodri Lewis's passion was archaeology, in particular the prehistoric archaeology of Wales. It was his burning conviction that cave painters had lived in Wales, and his great ambition was to find an example of cave art. And he believed he would find it near Trefelin.

"You see, here we are beyond the line of the

furthest extent of the ice during the Würm glaciation," he said excitedly to Laddy, when she had asked him why. "From above Fishguard down through to Land's End, you see, was beyond the glaciation." He began to trace a map on the table with his knife. "But in Cornwall and Devon, the west coast faces the ocean. Here on the peninsula we face Ireland, you see. And the water level, then, it would have been lower. Perhaps St. George's Channel would have been only a river. The caves along out here—" he waved an arm toward the cliff edge "—would have looked down a valley to a river. You see, it was cold during the Würm glaciation, and you would not wish to face straight out to the ocean in arctic weather, would you?"

"I see the logic of it," agreed Laddy, who had been dredging up the very few and long-ago learned facts she could remember about the earth's history. "Better to be in a river valley even if it were a little farther north, than facing out over an arctic ocean."

"So," Rhodri said, taking a hasty sip of tea and throwing an approving smile at her, "they would have chosen to live between Fishguard and St. David's Head, and on the Bristol Channel and the English Channel."

"And why right here at Trefelin?" Laddy asked. "There must be a lot of caves between Fishguard and St. David's Head."

"I need a map," Rhodri said, as Laddy, realizing that the sun had set and they were sitting in near darkness, got up and put on the light. "Because we are on Pen Mawr here, and when the water level was lower, from the caves here you would have been able to see the whole length of the river valley.''

''Will you show it to me on a map sometime?'' Laddy asked, as Mischa, who had crossed over to his own cottage a few moments before, returned with a pipe and a tobacco pouch and began to press some strongly scented tobacco into the bowl.

''Perhaps you will come with us one morning when we explore the caves?'' Mischa said, raising a questioning eyebrow first at Laddy and then at Rhodri. ''Rhodri explores the caves nearly every morning, and sometimes I go with him.''

''Saturdays, too, when my work is done,'' Rhodri said, clearly delighted at the prospect of having them both exploring for proof of his theory.

''Well, I'd love to come,'' Laddy said, rather taken not only by his theory but by Rhodri himself.

''It's wet,'' Rhodri said, as though he had better tell her the worst of the matter before she got to it. ''Cold, too. And dark. But you will dress for it, won't you?''

The three of them were engrossed in their conversation and with one another, and the pool of soft light seemed to encase them in its protective glow, so that when the knock came on the door they all jumped, as though surprised that there was anyone else in their world. Laddy jumped up and opened the door to Brigit.

''Helen asked me to tell you that dinner's in an hour,'' she said to Laddy, then looked over Laddy's shoulder into the lighted kitchen.

"Are you here, then, Rhodri!" she exclaimed. "I wondered where you had got to. If you're not home soon, Mairi will be sending out the searchers. Good evening, Mischa."

"Good evening, Brigit," he said, a cloud of smoke encircling his head.

"Dinner in an hour," she repeated for his benefit. "Your special drink is in the refrigerator if you want to have it now. I'm going home now, Rhodri. Do you want to walk with me?"

Mischa and Laddy stood in the doorway as the two walked off across the field in the dusk, and silence fell between them. Mischa removed the pipe from his teeth and knocked it against the stone wall, and they watched the glowing embers drop to the grass.

"I have smoked shag for too long," he said, smiling ruefully. "Nothing else is strong enough."

"Shag?" she repeated, her voice, like his, subdued in the darkening dusk.

"Shag is a very strong, coarse tobacco," he said. "All we could get in prison. After a while one gets accustomed to it."

The darkness was increasing perceptibly, and the warm glow of the kitchen light spilled out between them as they leaned against opposite doorjambs, staring across the fields toward the slowly appearing lights of Trefelin.

"God damn them!" she said suddenly, fiercely, the cry coming out against her will.

He turned his head and she felt his gaze rest on

her. "You will have to say it," he said with weary acceptance. "Say it all."

"I couldn't say it all in a million years!" she burst out. "I hate them, I hate all of them, and I'll hate them forever!" Her body was rigid against the doorpost, and she kept her gaze fixed in the direction of Trefelin, but she was not seeing a small, peaceful village at night. Her brain burned with what she saw. "I looked at that boy tonight," she said, "but do you know what I saw? I saw you!" Her voice was cracking with emotion that was almost impossible to control. "I saw back twenty years to what you must have been—a brilliant, intense child, so full of life, so...so...." A sob caught her unawares, and she swallowed, choking on it. "And what did they do to you? What did they do? They took away your books; they threw you in those horrible places and they took away your books and your paper and pens. They tried to take away your mind, too—and they're sorry they didn't succeed! I hate them for that and I'll always hate them! They took away eight years of your life! That's what they did to reward you for your brilliant mind—they put you in a place where you got *accustomed* to things—where you got accustomed to smoking shag and eating a starvation diet and torture and things I have to grit my teeth before I can even read about them!"

Laddy was shaking now and breathing in jerking gasps, but still she did not look at him. His eyes were on her, unflinching, and she knew what look of quiet resignation she would see in his eyes if she turned her head; she did not want to see it. "And I hate them, and that's all I can do—hate. I want to kill them all—I want to scream at them the truth of what they really are, I want to rip the lies away and show them the truth, and then I want to tell them I hate them and wipe them off the face of the earth! And I can't—I can't! I'm powerless, helpless, impotent; I had to stand by and let them do that to you, and all I can do is hate them!"

The tears were pouring down her cheeks; she could no longer stop them, nor could she speak. But she held her head up, refusing to submit, and finally turned to meet his gaze.

It was not resignation but fierce pain that burned in his eyes as he watched her, and she stared at him in shocked immobility, as though a knife had stabbed her abdomen.

"Oh, God," she moaned, but he continued to watch her as though the pain was of no account.

"Lady, say it all," he commanded quietly, and then what she felt ripped its way through her. She sobbed uncontrollably and gasped out the burning anguish and pain of having loved him, knowing that each word, each sob was like a knife stabbing him, but unable to stop, incapable of holding it back any longer. . . knowing that her greatest sin lay not in the fact that she was hurting him, but that she was forcing Mischa to be strong enough for both of them; Mischa, who had had to be unremittingly strong for so many years and who had a right now to rest.

When it was finished she turned away from his

gaze, wiping her face childishly on her sleeve, and said hoarsely, "Oh, I'm sorry. I'm sorry, Mischa. It was unforgivable."

Her sleeve was soaking and she stared down at the black smears of mascara across the blue and white of the plaid and wished that she had died before doing what she had just done.

"It was not as difficult as you think," Mischa said quietly. But she had seen what was in his eyes and she knew he lied. Two gentle hands touched her cheeks and tilted her face up for his tender kiss. "But it will not happen again," he said. "You must not hate them anymore."

"I love you so much," she said quietly.

"Lady, I love you," Mischa said, his deep voice gentle, like a night breeze. Then he pulled her to his chest, his arms encircling her, his hand enfolding her head.

He held her while the breeze turned cold and the first stars appeared in the black sky, her hands curled close against his chest, protected and enclosed by him. She was safer than she had ever been and she knew she was safe forever.

LADDY DRESSED slowly, lovingly, relaxed and mellowed by her warm bath and the glass of wine she had sipped as she lay in the scented water. The silk of the burgundy caftan slid sensuously over her shoulders and hips, and her skin responded tremulously, as though, like a snake, she had lost the hard outer layer of skin and what was left was highly sensitized.

The caftan had a stiff high neck around a narrow front opening that plunged to the hollow between her full breasts, and she piled her hair loosely on her head with the help of combs and put on gold loop earrings. She looked like some pagan high priestess; the knowledge sparkled in her eyes, and she caught her lower lip suddenly between her teeth. If she had any power over Mischa Busnetsky, she had it tonight or not at all.

She took the flashlight from the kitchen and made her way across the field in the cool spring darkness. Halfway to the house she paused, shutting off the flash to stand in the light of the early stars and the subdued murmur of the sea against the cliff face.

Mischa, coming from the big house to fetch her, found her there, motionless in the starlight, and he took the flashlight from her nerveless fingers almost harshly.

"What are you doing?" he asked, his voice deep. "Calling up an ancient god?"

With his thin broad figure encased in black turtle-neck, black jacket and black trousers, his dark eyes frowning down at her, Laddy could almost imagine that that was what she had done. "I think so," she said. "I think it worked." And she felt as though she had drunk an entire bottle of champagne.

"What worked?" Mischa asked.

She smiled up at him. "The spell," she said, surprised to hear how seductive her own laughter could sound. "I cast a spell to call up an ancient god, and I got you."

His movement toward her was involuntary, and she looked into his eyes and felt his hand on her throat, firm against her chin. "Yes?" he said. His voice was subtly threatening, as though he dared her to go on.

"Yes," she said, licking her lips against the tension that was building up inside her. "Only I'm not the high priestess, you know. I'm just dressed up like one." She smiled slowly at him. "Actually, I'm the sacrificial virgin. The one who was locked up in the temple for the sole enjoyment of the god. And if she wasn't pleasing to the god he never came to her little room, and she just pined away, because she loved the god desperately, more and more as the years passed...."

In silent fury his mouth covered hers, stopping her words in her throat. He pulled her against him, her hands flat on his chest. His hands ran along her shoulders, her arms, then he clasped her wrists tightly and held her away from him, but not before she had felt his body's stirring response. The knowledge of her power left her shaken.

"What do you want?" he ground out. "To be taken without ceremony on the wet spring grass?"

She whispered, "Yes."

But he only bent to pick up the flashlight, flicked it on and, gripping her fingers, led her through the night to the big house for dinner.

Afterward she could never remember what or if she ate. She remembered the color of red wine against a white cloth, and she remembered Mischa

Busnetsky's hands in the soft light, and his eyes, and his mouth and music. But whether the music was real or imagined she did not know. And in the end it was drowned out in the electric tension that hummed in her ears, deafening her even to the sounds her own mouth was making. And then finally the evening was over, and with his arm around her, Mischa guided her back across the field to the cottage with a light in the window.

He opened the door for her, pulled her to him and kissed her. "You are so very beautiful," he said, "but tonight is not yet time."

She came to with a sudden cheated cry, moaning his name, and his arms tightened convulsively around her. His hands began to search through her hair for the combs that held it up. He took them out one by one and buried his face in the thick hair as it fell. The sudden weight of it slithering over her shoulders charged her senses and she clung to him, moaning her loss when he stood away from her. But he only gazed down at her, shaking his head.

"Why?" she cried.

"Because hunger, too, is a pleasure. And we will learn that pleasure first."

And, not wanting to, he left her.

CHAPTER NINE

"WHAT are you working on?" Laddy asked the dark head bent intently over the papers spread out on the table. She was standing at the open door of the other cottage, the morning sun warming her back through her cotton T-shirt.

Mischa Busnetsky raised his head and smiled at her, his eyes warm, approving, and she felt as though the sun had unaccountably shifted direction and now warmed her face.

"I am transcribing a book from my head to paper," he told her. "And what are you doing?"

"Just...watching you," Laddy said, with the sudden conviction that that activity might be enough to occupy her for the rest of her life. She straightened away from the doorpost and moved into the kitchen that, except in the color of the fittings, was almost the twin of her own. "Transcribing from your head?" she repeated. "Do you mean you have an entire book in your head?"

"There was a shortage of paper in the prisons," he said. "And a necessity to keep sane. During my last sojourn, I wrote a book in my head and memorized it. Now I write it down." He gestured to the paper-strewn table top. "But I am not sure enough of my English."

It took a moment for that to sink in, and then she gasped, "You wrote a book in your head in *English*?"

Mischa stretched a hand out to the pipe in an ashtray near him and began the process of cleaning and filling it. "It was a method of keeping sane," he said.

"I must say I think that writing a book in a foreign language in your head and memorizing it is a project that would drive most people mad," Laddy exclaimed, and she gazed at him, absorbing the fact of his truly awesome intellect with a respect approaching fear.

"Not you, however," he said matter-of-factly, as though she were protesting too much. He reached for a pile of handwritten pages. "If you have a few minutes, might you read two or three pages at random and see if my English requires a great deal of work?"

Laddy hungrily eyed the pages that he held. They were covered in thick black writing. "I'll read them all," she offered, dropping into a chair opposite him.

He looked at her in surprise. "Do you not have your own work?" he asked.

"I'm on holiday. And my work if any, is you."

In the act of gathering up the manuscript, Mischa paused, his eyes holding hers while his slow smile warmed her. "Your pleasure, too, I hope, will be me," he said softly.

Her heart leaped violently in response. In that moment Laddy knew exactly how Mischa intended to court and torment her. She realized suddenly that it was a delight she had never experienced before, that he meant to tear perfection out of the jaws of eight years of horror and emptiness for both of them. As the *frisson* of love and desire that trembled along her breath reached her throat, she laughed.

"That will depend," she said huskily, "on whether your pleasure is me."

His eyes narrowed at her in glinting admiration, as though a fencing opponent had pinked him, and she felt the heady excitement of embarking on a battle where losing would be a victory.

The week that followed was drenched in joy. It seemed to Laddy that the world was changed: colors were richer, scents were thicker, sweeter; the sun shone more brightly than she had ever seen it. Sometimes she stared at the new spring leaves that were opening everywhere around her and wondered how she had never before understood about the miracle of growth, creation, life.

In that week Laddy came to learn the joy of waiting, came to delight in the knowledge that her body was entirely sensitized to his, as though she were swimming in a cold fresh lake or climbing up a steep mountain into rarified air. She was electrifyingly clearheaded and alive in every pore. And the power that she and Mischa had over each other was a constant torment, a constant delight.

She was with Mischa almost constantly. They ate breakfast and lunch together and dined at the big house with Helen in the evenings. They went walking almost every morning, sometimes with Rhodri to explore his caves, and sometimes the three of them drove to archaeological sites nearby—to standing stones or tombs or Roman ruins, while Rhodri told their history. In the afternoons, Laddy made notes for the series of articles about Mischa she had begun to envision, while Mischa transcribed his novel at the kitchen table in his cottage. Laddy also worked with him to put it into more flowing English without destroying his powerful personal style. It was hard work, but after a few days she began to cultivate a sixth sense, an instinct that told her what he wanted to express.

Every moment of her day, every cell of her being, was steeped in happiness. She would lie beside Mischa Busnetsky's length on a grassy ledge overlooking the sea, listening to his voice or his quiet breathing in the sunshine, and feel herself on the highest possible peak of happiness; then later, watching his dark, intent head as he worked at the table, she would feel a jolt of emotion so profound it was like being kicked over the heart, and she understood she had scaled some new peak whose existence she had never known before.

When he held her and kissed her, her heart was molten gold. Mischa taught her about love slowly, as he had promised—as slowly as he could. At the end of a week he was still teaching her the hunger, and they were taking an immense delight in tormenting each other, with words, with looks, with unexpected caresses. Laddy was catching up on what she had missed at fifteen and sixteen, when instead of dating she had traveled with her father, and at seventeen, leaving Mischa Busnetsky in that Moscow apartment as she had to. And it was slowly borne in on her that Mischa was for her the single embodiment of every lover a woman has in her life: he was her first young love, her mature love, her true love... her only love. There were times when, giggling, she would have chalked "L.P. loves M.B." in a heart all over the pavements of Trefelin, and times, when he held her, that she could have sobbed out all the pain of a lifetime against his chest.

Laddy began to imagine that love was the last stage in the evolution of man, that one day she might wake up and discover herself part of a new species. The need to have him love her became an ache.

One morning more than a week after her arrival, Laddy's sleep was disturbed by a tapping at her bedroom window. In her dream she opened the door of the small cottage, and when the knocking continued she saw that there were many doors to open, and she flew through the cottage in her dream, opening door after door onto huge, richly furnished rooms that were filled with light.

"This is a palace!" Laddy exclaimed aloud, and awoke. The tapping was at the window over her bed, and exuberantly she knelt on her pillows, pulled back the curtains and opened the casement windows wide to a beautiful sunny morning and the figure of Mischa Busnetsky.

"Good morning!" she said in delight, the bubble of joy within her breaking down into a thousand little bubbles that spilled into her blood and sang along her veins.

"Good morning," Mischa agreed, coming close enough to lean over her through the window. She was wearing a plain masculine pair of red-and-white striped pajamas, but he looked at her as though he found the sight pleasing. "You are very beautiful," he said huskily, "and I should have known that I ought to wait until you were dressed and your eyes and hair had lost the memory of your bed." His hands on the windowsill, he bent down and put his face into the tangled cloud of her hair and left a kiss on her throat that burned against her like fire.

She gasped, and his mouth moved over her neck and down under her collar to her shoulder. Suddenly she was aware that his hand was at the top button of her pajama jacket; as though he became aware of the fact in the same moment, he drew back. He looked at her.

"In the question of breakfast," he said, taking a deep calming breath, "will you walk with me along the Coastal Path, and we will take our breakfast as a picnic?"

She laughed. When he stood back from her, her body swayed involuntarily toward him; she had no more control than if he were a magnet and she a stray piece of iron. He was asking her if she would go with him as though there were some possibility of her saying no, and he did it deliberately. He made her choose to be with him, always.

"I would love to." She smiled at him, then said meaningfully, "Shall I bother to get dressed?"

He took a ragged breath and laughed in the admission that she had scored a point.

"Yes," he said, "get dressed. When the time comes, it will not pain me to remove your clothes."

Game, set, match. All the butterflies in her stomach rose in a fluttering swoosh. She dropped her eyes and busily began disentangling herself from the sheets and got off the bed. "Give me twenty minutes," she said with forced calm, as though he might not have seen what effect he had had on her, and fled from his laughing face.

When she had showered and dressed, they walked up to the house and, finding Brigit in the kitchen, begged picnic supplies from her. Chatting to them about the routes they might take, Brigit found an old haversack with a tartan rug strapped to the bottom and helped them stow breakfast inside.

"You won't be wanting to carry along your special drink," she said to Mischa. "Why don't you drink it now before you go—I've got it ready, waiting." As she and Laddy added cutlery and napkins to the haversack and closed it, Mischa leaned against the counter and drank the creamy liquid.

"There now," Brigit said. "All set." Mischa

slung the strap over one broad thin shoulder and set his glass in the sink. "If you should happen to see Rhodri this morning, would you tell him he's got twenty-two minutes to get himself to school?" Brigit smiled.

As it happened, they did meet Rhodri, walking up the Mill Path as they walked down it, carrying his knapsack and flashlight.

"Hello!" he called up to them delightedly, scrambling into a run by the ruins of an old mill that had closed in 1839, shattering the town's economy. "Were you wanting to come out with me today?" He was full of excitement, coming toward them in uncontrolled little bounds, like a young mountain goat in spring.

"We'd be too late for that," smiled Laddy. Two morning adventures had taught her that Rhodri liked to get started with the sun. "Brigit asked us to remind you not to be late for school."

His dark eyes were brimming with news and he gazed up at them, almost transported. "Oh— school!" he said dismissingly.

Mischa hefted the knapsack more comfortably on his shoulder and said, "What have you found?"

The broad young grin swept from ear to ear as Rhodri gazed up at Mischa, then disappeared quickly, and his eyes became serious. "A rockfall," he said. "A cave I have been in before, too, and never noticed it. It was shallow, you see, and most cave paintings are deep in dark caves."

"What's a rockfall?" Laddy asked.

"The back of the cave is not bedrock," he said. "The ceiling or walls have collapsed, you know, and perhaps there is a much deeper cave behind. And then, you see, perhaps this happened so long ago that no one has been inside since prehistoric times, and if something had been in the cave, perhaps it would be preserved."

Rhodri turned away from them to look back along the beach that ran southwest of the Mill Path, then glanced at his wristwatch. "I wish I could take you now and show you," he said impatiently. "There is a groove on the wall, you see, right by the rockfall...."

He had their unwavering attention now. "A groove?" said Mischa. "A carved groove?"

Rhodri nodded. "It could be."

"I think, Rhodri, you need to take an archaeologist to the cave."

But Rhodri shook his head vigorously. "Not till I've found something," he said flatly. "I would like to show you now, but they say if I am late for school one more time—"

"Show us tomorrow then," Laddy suggested. "If it's lasted fifteen thousand years or so, it'll last another day."

Rhodri laughed, looking up at them warmly but saying impatiently, "School! They teach me nothing except the Wars of the Roses!" He ran by them up the Mill Path and turned and called to them, his knapsack banging against his leg, "Tomorrow morning, early? It is a promise?"

"Promise!" they called back, and watched him disappear over the rise before moving down to the stony beach. It was very warm for spring, and the air was fresh, clear, intoxicating. Laddy wanted to fling her arms out and spin like a dervish; she wanted to leap into the water and swim down and down to the strange realms under the sea. . . .

"He is so certain," Mischa said beside her. "One begins to think he has a special knowledge." He spoke musingly, as though to himself, but Laddy knew that he was talking to her. It was part of their extraordinary closeness that at times they seemed to think with the same mind.

"Perhaps he does," she said. "Perhaps he knows there are cave paintings here because fifteen thousand years ago he painted them himself." And she could almost believe that. Nothing seemed completely impossible to her anymore.

They walked at a leisurely pace along the shore that led past the foot of the cliffs back in the direction of Tymawr House. They passed the mouths of black wet caves, some of which they had explored with Rhodri, and then there was no more shore. A rather difficult ascent led up what might have been a dry waterfall bed to the cliff top.

They were then back on the Coastal Path and Tymawr House was behind them, white in the morning sun against the fresh spring green that enclosed it.

They passed farms and clambered over stiles from field to field, even their unhurried progress causing the sheep that ranged the cliff top to run off in baaing clusters when they suddenly took it into their woolly heads that Laddy and Mischa represented danger.

The sun climbed the clear sky and warmed them in their exertions until, with unerring instinct, Mischa turned off the path and moved down to the cliff edge and jumped over onto a grassy patch that had sunk a few feet down the face of the cliff, creating a sunny protected platform that was one of Rhodri's discoveries.

Mischa had dropped the knapsack and was unstrapping the rug, and Laddy moved to help him spread it over the thick rough grass. This sheltered place, protected by an outcropping of rock on both sides, caught the sun most of the day. She slid her denim jacket off and stood, in her blue plaid cotton shirt and blue jeans, in its rays.

It was not as warm as she thought, and she shivered a little and dropped onto the blanket. Laddy watched with pleasure as Mischa's two large hands pulled their food from the knapsack and laid it on the blanket between them.

"I'm starving," she said suddenly, rather surprised that after years of having an appetite for nothing but coffee in the mornings she was actually looking forward to breakfast.

"Good," he said, smiling over at her and tossing her an orange. "I, too."

She peeled the orange and ripped it apart, watching the juice droplets spray up and sparkle in the sun, her heart thudding hollowly. She wondered how it could be that she was so constantly aware of him, physically, emotionally, mentally—as though she were near a power source surrounded by a heavy electronic field.

Mischa sank into the grass-supported blanket as he finished off his own orange, and she saw how his body enjoyed the sensuality of the rough blanket, the softness underneath and the sun. He smiled at her.

"After a certain amount of time in prison," he said quietly, as though this were part of a conversation they had begun long ago, "your mattress gets very uncomfortable. Your sleep is broken, you wake up at intervals to get up and shake the lumps out of this thing they call your mattress, but no matter how you shake or beat it, the lumps are still there." She moved closer to him, and he drew her head down onto his warm shoulder and stroked her hair. "And then you realize that it is not the mattress at all, but your body. You are so thin that the lumps that stop you from sleeping are your own bones."

She accepted it wordlessly because she had to, because he had lived it, and she could only share it with listening. They lay in silence for a long time. "I sent you letters," she said at last. "My father always found out what prison you were in, and I wrote you."

"We were allowed only a certain number of letters each month," he said, his hand stopping its stroking motion to hold her head gently as though in comfort. "Often only one, or two. Sometimes I knew when you wrote, but I could not receive your letters. There were letters I had to have, from people on the outside, in Moscow, people who were fighting for me, who were sending me important information." He moved, and she felt his kiss on her brow. "But I knew when you wrote, and when the letters stopped I knew...."

When the letters stopped he knew she had found a lover, he meant, and she wrapped her arm around his chest and held him tightly.

"No," she said.

He kissed her brow again, his lips light against her skin. "No," he repeated quietly. After a moment he moved up onto one elbow, his face above hers, his eyes watching her, full of tenderness. Laddy's heart leaped in a response so deep it was almost pain. She brought a hand up to his cheek, and he caught it with his own hand and turned his face to press a kiss in her palm.

"Mischa..." she began quietly, and he placed her palm against his chest and dropped his hand to thread his fingers in her hair.

"Lady?" he answered.

"What was the worst—" she faltered "—what was the worst thing of all, the hardest to bear?" She spoke softly, quietly, but her voice was threaded with tension, with pain, with her need to share his anguish and horror. He gazed down at her, understanding, his fingers gently stroking her hair.

"In the end," he said, after a long pause, "the pains of the spirit hurt much worse than the physical tortures, the deprivations. When you cannot trust anyone, inside or out, the number of your friends grows smaller and smaller. Then you lose these friends to death or to the West. . . or because they have recanted, have betrayed you and everyone who is fighting. That is worse than if they had died, worse than looking at your own sure death."

For some reason it shook her to her foundations. That betrayal should be worse to him than starvation, cold, deprivation, injustice, imprisonment—the whole catalog of torture that through her father she had become so familiar with. Betrayal—in conditions where betrayal must surely have been the order of the day.

This was something she knew, something she could understand. If he had said the tortures, the cold, the isolation, how could she have hoped to understand, to share? She had never experienced even the smallest brush with real physical deprivation. But betrayal she knew and understood—and she had known it was the worst pain possible in the world from that moment when, at the age of six, she had sat in a classroom and heard her best friend tell the teacher, and thereby the whole class, her deepest secret. She could not remember now what the secret was, but she had never forgotten the pain of being betrayed.

Betrayal was the one unforgivable sin, and from that day to this, anyone whose loyalty had failed the test ceased to be her friend as irrevocably as if he or she had died. And she was looking into the eyes of a man who understood that and who would never betray her.

"I love you," she said, and it seemed as though no human language could encompass this truth.

"I love you," said Mischa Busnetsky, and drew her body against his and held her as though he would never let her go.

IN THE AFTERNOON, Helen left to spend a few days in town with Richard, and Laddy spent the early evening in her kitchen preparing a perfect dinner for Mischa and herself—the first they would eat alone together since her arrival. And she thought that tonight it would not be so easy for Mischa to leave her at the end of the meal.

When it was nearly ready she showered and slipped on the wine-colored caftan. She brushed her long hair over her shoulders, humming to herself as anticipation began to build slowly in her stomach. Her face was fresh and faintly colored by her days in the spring sun, and she used only a touch of mascara and a hint of perfume before she cast a last glance at the table and set out, barefoot, to tap on the door of Mischa's cottage. He should have come over before this.

Mischa had moved his belongings from the big house into his cottage shortly after Laddy's arrival more than a week before, but there was no answer to her tapping, and after a moment she opened the door and slipped into a dark kitchen.

"Mischa?" she called softly, a sudden irrational fear beginning to tinge the heady anticipation that bubbled in her blood. She groped her way to the sitting-room door in the near blackness of the cottage and saw with relief that there was a faint glow coming from a lamp in the bedroom. Mischa still tired easily, and Laddy was used to his dropping down for a sudden catnap whenever fatigue overtook him.

The sound of a tortured groan suddenly wiped the smile from her face and sent her headlong to the door of the bedroom, breathless and afraid.

Fatigue had overtaken him after his shower, for he wore his black toweling bathrobe, and the pillow slip was damp under his dark head. He lay half on his side, half on his back, one arm above his head, the hand on the blue pillow clenched into a fist, the other lying across the mat of dark hair where the robe fell open over his bare chest.

The golden glow of the lamp beside the bed fell softly over the bed and over his sleeping shape, revealing in its mellow light Mischa Busnetsky's tortured face. He was in the grip of a nightmare.

He moaned again and called out hopelessly in Russian something she did not understand, and Laddy flew to him and knelt on the bed beside him, softly calling his name.

His forehead burned as she gently stroked it, whispering his name over and over; his jaw clenched and relaxed, and suddenly his eyes were open, burning into her own. The torment left him as he recognized her, and then, so suddenly and devastatingly that it blinded her, she saw a naked, unprotected need of her that had its roots in the depths of his soul.

"Lady," he whispered, as though it were a prayer. "My God, Lady, Lady!" Suddenly she was in his arms, breathless with being pressed tightly against him, her face against the pulse beating powerfully in his throat and his buried in the softly perfumed cloud of her hair.

"Lady, I need you—" The words seemed torn from him, his voice was cracked with emotion; then his mouth found hers and clung with a need so fierce that her own need of him burst the careful barriers she had set up against it, swamping her, carrying away fear, reason, self.

"*Ya lyublyu tibya,*" he said against her lips, her cheeks, her eyes, his mouth urgent against her. And then, in English, "I love you, Lady. Do you hear it?" His mouth found her throat and the deep hollow between her breasts, which were unconfined under the burgundy silk.

She cried, "I love you, I love you so much!" and heard her own voice break on a sob. Every barrier was down; she was reduced to her essential being. It was a tearing, aching joy, like birth or death. And she knew there could be no drawing back for either of them now.

He took her not in passion but in love, from the

deep well of their need. His body found hers with a deep, thrusting urgency, as though the union of their bodies would make them one being for all time; she accepted the sudden tearing pain from the same deep need, remote from pain as she floated formlessly and drowned in the dark, dark eyes that accepted everything she ever was or would be.

He held her head in his two hands at the last and kissed her and cried out against her lips in passionate release. She knew she had made him tremble as he had said she would so many years ago; her senses staggered with the knowledge, and she thought there was no greater joy the world could bring her. She clung to him, knowing that at last she was perfect, at last she was complete.

Mischa was stroking her face, her hair. "Lady, you are so beautiful," he whispered, touching her long body, golden in the lamp glow. She reached her arm around his neck and gazed into his loving eyes.

"You, too," she said achingly. "So beautiful—"

He wrapped both arms convulsively around her while his eyes devoured her face. "I am afraid I will lose control," he whispered hoarsely, "that one day I will break your body against mine.... When you wake me from such a nightmare I am lucky you are still whole...." His arms tightened on her again and his eyes were dark.

She gasped, "What is the nightmare?"

"You," he said quietly. "You, walking down those stairs away from me, and I maddened with the need to stop you, to keep you with me. But I cannot cry out, and when I try to run after you they are holding me back—KGB men, Party members, sometimes my friends—and every time I tear one off my back another clings to me. And you do not know, you do not look back...."

Passion leaped in his eyes and he bent and pressed his lips to her throat, her breast. "Stay with me tonight," he whispered, desperate need in his voice, his mouth, his roughly caressing hand. "Lady, Lady, I can never hold you enough!" A wordless cry was torn from her, and Laddy arched her hungering body desperately against his, and they clung together as though they had both been starved of love since birth.

"Laddy? Mischa?" A woman's voice, high with emotion, pierced the night, and then came the sound of an urgent, desperate knocking on the door of Laddy's cottage.

"Rhodri? Laddy? Mischa?" the voice begged, and they both recognized Brigit's voice, unnaturally high and strained.

"Something's happened!" Laddy exclaimed, their bodies reluctantly parting as the world burst in on them. She found her silk caftan on the floor and pulled it over her head while Mischa slipped quickly into his robe and knotted the belt as he moved to the bedroom door.

Laddy was beside him as he pulled open the front door of the cottage onto the courtyard, lighted by the rays from Laddy's kitchen lights. The startled face of Brigit Lewis turned from the other door to gape at them in surprise and, after a moment, dismay.

"Brigit! What's the matter?" Laddy called, running barefoot over the cool flat stones to the other woman.

"Rhodri," Brigit said. "It's Rhodri—oh, we were so sure he would be with you, I rushed right over the moment we thought of it. . . . He's missing, Laddy. When it got late we checked with his friends, and he wasn't in school today—"

"Not in school!" Laddy and Mischa exclaimed in unison.

Mischa said quietly, his deep, quiet voice somehow calming Brigit: "We passed him this morning on the Mill Path, and he was on his way to school then."

"He never got there," Brigit said wretchedly, her eyes growing large in fear. "Oh God, do you think he was picked up by someone?"

Laddy and Mischa exchanged a swift glance, and Laddy's voice was filled with calm certainty as she said, "No. I think he went back to his cave."

CHAPTER TEN

THEY FOUND HIM when dawn's first long tendrils were snaking over the horizon to illuminate the cold mist that hovered above the sea and the cliffs. They had searched and called through numberless black caverns throughout the night, stumbling and sliding over smooth damp rocks, somehow fighting aching fatigue and near exhaustion, and going on.

When the light from Mischa's flashlight and the graying mist fell on the jagged back wall of a much shallower cave than any they had previously searched, it caught at Laddy's memory, and she gasped in sudden hope. "Mischa!" she said. "Didn't he say it was a shallow cave?"

The flesh of Mischa's face in the faint light was drawn tight with fatigue and self-discipline, and she knew that he was too ill to be taking part in such a prolonged search, but his stamina seemed somehow to come under the control of his enormous will-power.

"Yes, you are right," he said. He led the way into the cave, the light of his torch moving systematical-ly over the walls and the sloping floor.

"Rhodri!" Laddy called, and at the same moment

Mischa's light, moving along the jagged, sloping back wall of the cave, caught in its glare a spreading pile of angular rocks that lay on the floor of the cave and ran partially up the slope of the back wall.

Their two figures were gripped in sudden immobility, and then the light moved swiftly up the wall almost to the ceiling and found a narrow jagged hole of empty blackness.

"Rhodri!" Laddy called again, scrabbling up the loose pile of rock toward that sinister hollow darkness, and they both gasped to hear the faint response.

"I'm inside!"

"Thank God!" Laddy's voice cracked with relief and fatigue. "Rhodri, are you all right? Are you hurt?"

"Just my leg," Rhodri answered, his voice tired but bright. "And I'm awfully thirsty."

Clinging with one arm through the tunnel he had made, Laddy tried to see into it, but the light of her torch seemed frail against the darkness. Mischa climbed swiftly up beside her with his more powerful light, but even its glare seemed to be swallowed by the blackness.

"How could he have dug such a deep tunnel?" Laddy asked in faint horror, imagining him caught in its suffocating narrowness deep inside.

"All right, we have water, Rhodri," Mischa said in his deep calm voice. "Can you see the light?" He held the light steady with his left hand and slipped the knapsack of supplies they had carried all night off his right shoulder and dropped it at his feet.

"Yes, I'm nearly underneath it," the little voice said.

"Underneath it!" Laddy exclaimed, suddenly gripped with the irrational fear of the unknown. "How can he be underneath—has he fallen into a hole?" In the back of her mind was the fear that Rhodri was so ill he was delirious, but she did not say it aloud.

"More likely into a cave behind this wall," Mischa said.

In the steady light, they examined the jagged walls of the tunnel that soon disappeared in blackness. It was flat and narrow—too narrow for Mischa, it was obvious after a moment.

"I can get through," Laddy said, and Mischa glanced down at her as he bent to set down the lamp. He slid out of his dark-blue quilted jacket.

"I will fit," he said matter-of-factly. "I am used to squeezing through small spaces. We used to go under the fences every night to get some shag to the men in the box." He smiled at her wryly. "I am, in fact, ideally suited to this rescue."

Leaving her the smaller torch he took the more powerful one, lifted his arms and the lamp and eased into the opening, his shoulders filling the space so that it seemed he would become wedged.

"Mischa!" Laddy said, watching his legs as they scrabbled up the wall. "It's too narrow! The ceiling—"

She broke off with a short harsh scream as his

legs disappeared into the tunnel with a scraping sound. In the light of her torch there was nothing but blackness.

"Mischa!" she called hoarsely.

Then his white face was in the light of her torch only a few feet away, and Mischa smiled into the glare. "A large cavern," he said calmly. "I am going to look at Rhodri. Get the water canteen out of the knapsack and call me when you are ready to pass it through." Suddenly his face was gone.

"Lady, you come, too!" Rhodri's voice called through to her. "I want you to see!" The excitement in his voice was unmistakable, and stopping only to take the water canteen from the knapsack, Laddy put her arms and head through the hole and began to work her way into the opening as Mischa had done.

The tunnel, which had seemed to go on forever, was only three feet long, Laddy discovered, and within a few moments her head was projecting into a black cavern on the other side of the wall. The floor was higher on this side of the cave than on the other, as was the ceiling, and a few feet below her in the lamplight she saw Mischa's tall figure bending over the thin form of Rhodri, who sat on the cave floor, his back resting against the wall. In the light of the torch on the ground beside them, the faces of both Mischa and Rhodri were thrown into harsh relief, white plane and black shadow, and some essential kinship of character between them was revealed, as though in this eerie darkness Mischa had met his childhood self, or Rhodri the adult Rhodri.

Laddy let the canteen slide out of her fingers to the ground and, finding purchase on the sloping uneven wall beneath her, lowered herself almost noiselessly to the floor of the cavern beside them.

Suddenly the harsh glare of the lamp was in her eyes and Mischa cursed once in Russian. "What the hell are you doing?" he said, his strongly accented voice coming angrily out of the blackness behind the torch's blinding glare. "Did not you hear me say you must stay on the other side?"

"No," said Laddy, shielding her eyes from the light as she sat up, and abruptly the torch's glare was on the wall above her.

"That is a rockfall!" Mischa said harshly. "If the roof comes down again while the three of us are behind it, no one knowing where we are, what then?"

He was right. A thrill of fear pulsed through her in a split-second response to his words. Then she got to her feet, breathed deeply and smiled at him in the darkness.

"Well, we might all die together," she said, "but somehow I think you'd dig us out by sheer force of will."

"If you were on the other side of the wall I might," he said, his voice in the blackness glittering with an emotion she could not decipher. "When you are with me what could tempt me to want out of this cave?"

The light on the wall flickered as his arm found her in the near blackness, and she was pulled against his body and kissed passionately, ruthlessly, angrily, his body bending hers back with the force of his need of her.

Every nerve of her body stirred with the memory of what had occurred between them in the early hours of the night that was only now turning to day, and she clutched at him, but already he was forcing her away.

"Go back," he said. "It is foolhardy for all of us to be in such a place. And I must look at Rhodri's leg."

"Not yet," Rhodri said suddenly, the hoarse weakness of his voice startling Laddy so that she instinctively bent to the ground to grope for the water canteen she had dropped. "Don't go yet—I want you both to see it."

"I brought the water in," she said.

But Rhodri interrupted passionately, "Never mind the water, look at the *wall*!" And they understood in that electrifying moment that Rhodri did not care if his leg was mashed to a pulp and he died of thirst; it was more important to him that they look at what he had discovered. Without another word, Mischa directed the torchlight against the wall beside them.

The massive chest and shoulders of the great deer leaping bloodred in the torch beam startled Laddy so much that she leaped backward. So intent had they been on finding the boy and so exhausted had they become, that in the past few hours she had scarcely spared a thought as to why he was here.

"*Rhodri!*" she cried, her voice an amazed incredulous squeak. Mischa's light had wavered in that first moment of discovery, but now the beam was steady as he explored the maddened eyes and great tossing antlers of the animal and its huge, black-outlined body. They stared in silence for a long moment.

"Well done, Rhodri," said Mischa quietly, commendation woven through his voice like a laurel. "What period is this?"

"I think it must be Magdalenian," said the boy. Pride and a scientist's excitement burst through his tone, as at last he had a chance to say what had been whirling around in his head throughout the night, to the audience he preferred above any other. "The use of perspective, of the natural shape of the rocks, the color—there's a whole scene running right down that wall...."

While he spoke, Laddy and Mischa gazed at that dark-red, maddened animal, obviously stabbed through with spears, and at the scene of leaping animals that continued down the wall to a point beyond which the light of the torch could not penetrate. The colors and shapes were almost alive under the steady beam, and there was no doubt as to the talent and intelligence of the artist.

A deep sense of kinship grew between the three in the cavern as they silently drank in the proof of the ancient intelligence of their own species.

"How old is it, Rhodri?" Laddy asked softly.

"If it really is Magdalenian, it must date from ten to fifteen thousand B.C.," he said, and she absorbed that in a kind of reverent silence.

"And no one has seen it since then—until now?" she asked.

"That will be hard to say; it will depend on when the rockfall occurred. And perhaps there will be other artifacts." He paused. "I must phone the museum," he said quietly, his voice just reaching them as Laddy and Mischa slowly followed the ancient artist's progress down the cave. "They will send someone to look, and then everyone will want to come." His voice was filled with satisfaction.

"How far does it continue?" asked Mischa, when it was obvious they still had not come to the end of the artwork. On this side of the rockfall the cavern was enormous, high and deep.

"I don't know," Rhodri said. "I tripped and hurt my leg and couldn't stand up, so I crawled back here to be sure of getting air. I examined what I could till my torch batteries went dead."

That brought his rapt audience back to reality and the remembrance of his needs. When Mischa's searching light pinpointed the green water canteen lying halfway up the rocky slope under the passage, Laddy ran to pick it up and take it to Rhodri. He gulped thirstily while Mischa again ran strong fingers over his hurt leg.

"Nothing broken, I think," Mischa said. "A badly twisted knee, but we've got to get you through that hole. I think we should splint it if possible."

There was a crowbar lying on the ground beside Rhodri's tattered knapsack, and Laddy picked it up. "Can you bind this to his leg?" she suggested.

In another second she had stripped off her shirt and handed it to Mischa.

"What the devil are you doing?" Mischa demanded. "You'll freeze!"

"I can wear your sweater, but you can't wear my shirt," Laddy pointed out. "If we use your sweater you'll get cut to ribbons on the rocks when you crawl out, and what good is that?"

She bent over his kneeling figure in the torchlight, her long black hair curtaining down, falling on his shoulder like a perfumed shadow. For a moment, as he reached to take the shirt from her hand, he turned his face deliberately into her hair's softness, his forehead brushing her cheek.

"Beware," he said hoarsely. "You are in a cave where primitive passions have been locked up for ten thousand years." Laddy straightened suddenly to combat a sudden hollow feeling and in a few economical movements Mischa bound the crowbar to Rhodri's leg with her shirt. Then, putting his arms around Rhodri, Mischa climbed up the short sloping wall to a point a few feet under the jagged hole, now showing a gray silhouette against the blackness all around them.

"Can you hold on here for a few minutes?" he asked as Laddy climbed up beside them to help hold the stiff-kneed boy. They both nodded at Mischa, and in a moment his body had stopped up the faint gray light of dawn that was showing on the other side of the tunnel. In the torchlight Laddy and Rhodri smiled at each other. His face seemed lighted by its own extraordinary inner glow.

"How do you feel?" she asked him, smiling.

He grinned. "Like a million pounds."

"What are you going to do now?" she asked, aware of a change in him, a new maturity that gave him an adult confidence for all his gamin grin.

But at that moment Mischa called from the other cave and she bent to fix the lamp on a rock so that it would shine on the wall in front of them. When she stood up to give him a hand, Rhodri paused for a moment and smiled at her.

"I'm glad you came," he said. "I was waiting for daylight to try and get out, you know, but sometimes in the night I was sure I would never get out. I thought I would die here. I knew that if it weren't you and Mischa, you know, no one would find me."

Her breath caught at this bald revelation of what it was that had changed him into an adult overnight, and she was filled with admiration for him. He had faced death alone, in the dark, for endless hours, and when the ordeal was over he had demanded that his rescuers examine his great discovery even before giving him water! Her arm around Rhodri tightened for a moment.

"We had to find you," she said softly. "There was no way we would have let you die in here alone."

Gingerly, painstakingly, he was eased through the tunnel, and Laddy was alone with the painted figures and the torch in the dark cave. For the first time she shivered in the chill dank air. At that moment Mischa's black sweater reached her through the hole. The warmth of his body enveloping her and the masculine smell of him reaching her nostrils as she pulled the sweater over her head reminded Laddy sharply that she had lain in his arms so recently, and the hollow excitement that churned within her made her feel faint. He was her lover! He had escaped whole from every form of horror and torment, and after eight years they had found each other again. His mark was on her now and she could never belong to any other man if she lived for a thousand years.

In the dank, dark cave Laddy gazed at the evidence of an ancient, unknown ritual of her distant ancestors and felt a deep-rooted kinship with their primitive passion. She had discovered a deep well of unexplored emotions in her nature, of which she knew almost nothing. But she had a strong conviction that her artist-ancestor could have told her all about them.

"GOOD LORD, Laddy, is this true?" Harry's voice crackled incredulously over the wire, and stifling a yawn, Laddy assured him that it was. It was ten in the morning and she still had not been to bed.

"When was the discovery made?"

"Rhodri—that's the boy who found it—dug his way through to it late yesterday," she said. "We found him in the cave early this morning."

"We?" Harry pressed.

"A friend and I," she said, her heart skipping a beat for who the friend was and what Harry would say if he knew. "There were about a dozen searchers out all night."

"And when you found him he was sitting beside the only known example of cave art in the British Isles," Harry said wryly. "Any professional opinion as to their authenticity yet?"

"The national museum has been notified and someone will be arriving for a look probably before noon," Laddy said. "But I'm sure they haven't been faked, Harry. It's no hoax."

"What about photos?"

"If you send someone down here tonight, you can have exclusives by morning. Only three of us know where the cave is," Laddy told him.

"All right," Harry said. "We'll get a photographer down there. I suppose you want to cover it yourself in spite of the fact of your being on holiday?"

"Yes, thank you," she said, sighing. She could stop another *Herald* reporter from arriving on the scene, but there would be no stopping the other members of the press and public who would very likely descend on Trefelin as a result of this story. And on Mischa Busnetsky. The peace of Trefelin was going to be disrupted for a few days at least, and every time Mischa walked abroad he was going to run the risk of being recognized.

But there was nothing she could do about it. This discovery could not possibly be kept quiet; this exclusive she would certainly lose within twenty-four hours if she did not file it.

Harry was congratulating her on what was really a very exciting story, and she said, "Does this put me on the credit side of the ledger, do you think?"

Harry sighed. "What favor do you want now, dear girl?"

"Isn't it a touchy editor today, then?" Laddy responded lightly. "No favor at all, Harry. I was merely thinking that if I happened to be going after something in an unconventional way one day, and it happened to blow up in my face, and you happened to be upset by it. . . well, it might help to have such an exciting exclusive to remind you of. Don't you think?"

Harry exhaled noisily, and the sound conjured up his face for her, his large thumb propping up his chin, a fat cigarette between two upraised fingers, his mouth pursed in exhalation and one eye pensively narrowed as he tried to see through the keyhole of her soul.

"It might," said Harry. "That would depend on the story and just how unconventional your methods were. How unconventional are you being?"

"This is all hypothetical, Harry," Laddy responded with a grin. "I'm on holiday, remember?"

"Umm-hmm," grunted Harry, and she knew he was unconvinced.

When he asked her where she could be reached, she read him the number of the phone she was using in Richard and Helen's sitting room, then told him how the *Herald* photographer could reach her when he arrived.

Laddy was dropping with fatigue when at last she locked the door of the big house and headed toward the cottages. But the morning was crisp and fresh, and small field flowers were blooming underfoot in the green. She breathed in the fresh, damp-earth smell and looked about her at sun and sea and sky. Some distance away along the cliff a neighboring farmer's white horse wheeled and snorted in the breeze.

She breathed deeply and willed herself to relax, but her mind could not stop churning over her central problem: how to tell Mischa Busnetsky that by tomorrow afternoon Trefelin would likely be housing a number of her colleagues, so that he must either curtail his activities or run the risk of being recognized, and more—how to tell him that it was her fault.

A FEW MINUTES past six o'clock that evening, there was a knock on the door of her little cottage. Laddy had just showered and dressed after a sleep of several hours, and she felt refreshed and alive and glowing with love. With a secret little smile she raised the perfume bottle to give her hair one final spray, and then, with her long skirt rustling around her legs, she ran to the door to let Mischa in.

The sight of the good-looking blond man on her doorstep startled her so much that she gaped at him for a moment in the blankest amazement. He was smiling warmly but quizzically at her, as though almost but not quite sure of his welcome.

"Hello, Laddy," he said, and the tones of his northern voice jolted her into the realization that this was no stranger. It was John Bentinck! Yet for a moment it had seemed to her that she had never seen his face before.

"John!" she gasped.

"Are you so surprised to see me, Laddy?" he asked wryly, smiling.

"Well, I...but aren't you supposed to be on holiday?" she asked lamely.

John shrugged apologetically. "Oh, well, there wasn't much point in going. And it was better for Richard if I didn't go just now. How are you, Laddy? Your story broke all right, I see."

He was standing on the flagstones outside her door—the one man from the *Herald* who could not possibly fail to recognize Mischa Busnetsky if he happened to come out of the door opposite. With an awkwardness born of utter dismay Laddy stood back and invited him in.

"This looks very comfortable," John remarked, glancing around as she closed the door after him. "I'm in a rather dark bed-and-breakfast near the pub. I shudder for the blokes coming tomorrow, they'll get nothing at all."

"There are at least two good bed-and-breakfasts in Trefelin," said Laddy, "even assuming that Mairi Davies won't be taking in—"

"All full," John said succinctly.

She gasped in horror, "With whom?" But with a sickening lurch she knew before he said it.

"Well, ITV, the BBC and CBC are here already, to my certain knowledge, and there seem to be quite a few local...."

"Oh, Lord, so soon?" she whispered in dismay, her brain churning in misery. She should have told Mischa this morning; she shouldn't have waited. But coward that she was, she had decided to tell him over dinner....

John was staring at her in surprise. "I take it you haven't seen your story yet," he said. "I suppose you didn't realize that there's been no other news at all this week—not even a strike threat." And he reached into the ever-present camera bag over his shoulder and threw the noon edition of the *Herald* onto the kitchen table.

The folded paper hit the table with a little slap, and the glaring black headline leaped at her: "BOY DISCOVERS CAVE ART, from Lucy Laedelia Penreith, Trefelin, Wales."

With an amazed little laugh Laddy sank into a chair, unfolded the paper and began to read.

"The only known example of prehistoric cave art in the British Isles may have been uncovered today in a cave on the south coast of Wales. Twelve-year-old amateur archaeologist, Rhodri Lewis, who made the discovery early this morning after months of searching...."

"Good grief!" Laddy exclaimed in half-laughing dismay. "He's going to be a hero!"

"Of course he is," John said. "Isn't that what you intended?"

"Among the archaeological community, yes, I did intend it. But this...." Suddenly she saw an image of Rhodri holding court in front of the television teams of two countries tonight, and delight overruled her dismay. She began to laugh in earnest. "Oh, he's going to love this!" she exclaimed. "No school for a week at least! And he's the perfect little hero, you know—intelligent and engaging. They'll love him. I wish we'd had a picture with this, but...."

"I must say I was surprised you didn't," John said. She looked at him in perplexity.

"Well, I do have my camera here, but we only found him this morning, you know."

"Yes? But then how—" John began, then changed his mind and looked out the window. "The light's fading," he said. "Can we get those pictures in the cave now, do you think?"

Laddy refolded the paper and stood up. "Yes, we'd better get going," she said. "Give me a moment to change my clothes."

She carried the paper into the bedroom with her, and when she had changed her skirt for jeans she located a felt pen and wrote above the headline: "Mischa— Lots of press people in the village tonight. Be careful. Love, L."

"What's that for?" John asked a few minutes

later as she ran across the flagstones to prop the *Herald* against the door of Mischa's cottage.

"My neighbor is a writer," Laddy explained rapidly, scrabbling through her thoughts for an innocuous explanation. "When they called out searchers he came along—he and I found Rhodri, and I thought he'd be interested in seeing the story."

None of which was exactly a lie, Laddy thought as she led John along the Coastal Path by the house. Interested Mischa would certainly be—and he would understand how this fame would go to Rhodri's head—but at the same time he might wonder why Laddy had given him no warning of the fact that the town was filled with the people to whom, at the moment, he least wished to talk.

"Is there anyone guarding the place?" John asked as Laddy led him along the Coastal Path toward the beach, moving west into the brightly setting sun.

"A man from the national museum came to look at it around noon," Laddy replied. "He left, but he was coming back. If he's camped out there already, we may not get any pictures."

"We'll get the pictures," said John firmly, "even if an army of archaeologists is camped out there. This is Crown land and accessible to the public until they get a permit to close it off. They won't have that yet." He was thinking these might be exclusive pictures, Laddy could see.

"Well, there won't be an army," she said mildly. "Just Roger Smith."

But there was no evidence of the young archaeologist as they approached the cave, and Laddy wrinkled her brow in dismay. She had expected—from what he had said to Rhodri and to her this afternoon after examining the inner cave and congratulating Rhodri on his find with an air of awed excitement that thrilled Rhodri more than his actual words—to find that Roger Smith had returned hotfoot to the site to set up his tent. It would be too bad if the paintings were discovered by sightseers in his absence.

Laddy and John, having made sure that no one was in sight on the cliff above or on the beach, climbed the last few feet of sharply sloping shingle to the mouth of the cave. Inside the duskily lighted outer cave, John glanced around.

"This is the right cave?" he asked.

"Yes," Laddy said. "To get to the paintings you have to crawl through there."

John Bentinck eyed the narrow passage with some disfavor.

"Not unless we make that hole larger," he said dispassionately, and there was some justice in that. He was not as tall as Mischa, but he had a good deal more flesh on his frame.

And he was not used to squeezing under the barbed-wire fences of a Siberian labor camp to get shag to the men in the box, she thought wryly.

"Well, we can't do that," she said firmly. The larger the hole, the more likelihood there was of sightseers finding the paintings before archaeologists could protect the site. "Set up the camera for me, and I'll get the pictures. I've been in there before.''

John was a photographer before anything else. He did not demur but immediately began asking her questions about the size and position of the paintings.

When he had adjusted the lens and instructed her on the use of the camera, Laddy held the torch in front of her and inched as before into the ancient artist's breathtaking gallery.

The magnificent red-brown-and-black reindeer postured in death as before, though she had almost expected it to have moved. Laddy stood on the rocky slope for a quiet moment, staring at the painted figures, and shivered suddenly. She flashed the torch toward the back of the cavern, but the light could not pierce the black depths or show her where the cavern ended. Laddy gazed blindly into the empty darkness for a chill moment. Then with a shake of her head she turned away from the unknown depths and called to John in a matter-of-fact tone, ''Ready!'' She aimed the light through the hole and reached to take the camera he held out to her.

He had set it properly; all she had to do was focus as well as she could in the weak light and shoot. She chose the best bit first: fixing on the huge, powerful, black-outlined animal, she took several shots, the flash attachment blinding her after the first one so that thereafter she closed her eyes each time she pressed the button.

She moved down the cavern over the uneven floor, shivering now under the combined effects of the chill air and nervousness, until she had taken nearly twenty shots in all. Then, picking up the flashlight from the floor she stumbled back up to the passage and passed the camera through.

"Good girl!" John exclaimed. Now she had only the painful job of inching through the jagged tunnel again.

As she crawled along the narrow tunnel, her head almost into the front cave, her feet still in the black cavern behind, she was seized by a sudden irrational fear of the unknown that lay behind her in that endless cavern, a fear so near to panic that she wanted to scream to John to grab her and drag her through. But she soundlessly fought the fear and slowly made her way back to reason and the outer cave.

John shot pictures of the narrow tunnel, of the pile of rocks on the sloping floor of the outer cave, and then declared himself satisfied.

"Am I going to get a shot of the child prodigy?" he queried, carefully consigning the film to his camera bag and rolling a new one into the back of the camera.

"Rhodri!" she exclaimed. "We'd better hurry if we're going to catch him before he goes to bed!"

John laughed. "If the lad goes to bed before midnight tonight, I'll be surprised. He's tomorrow's news, remember? And no doubt enjoying it hugely."

Rhodri was indeed loving his sudden fame. In the small warm house where Mairi Davies and her husband made a home for her younger sister and brother, Rhodri was suddenly king.

He sat on a chair in the center of the sitting room while two television teams and several journalists and photographers surrounded him, asking questions, taking notes and listening to his excited young voice with a flattering deference. His family sat on the fringes of the room, Mairi and her husband Alun, Brigit and her fiancé Bran; several neighbors also were there watching. It was his moment, and Rhodri's flushed cheeks and bright eyes told Laddy as she and John entered the room that he was taking full advantage of it.

"I didn't *happen* on the paintings," he was explaining clearly and patiently to a man holding a microphone whom Rhodri plainly thought rather slow. "I was *looking* for cave art—I was hoping to find it." He fixed the man with a look. "I was not out looking for a lost sheep, you know. Please do not tell them that I was," he said sternly, and everyone in the room laughed.

"No chance," drawled the man in a transatlantic accent, laughing, too.

Beside Laddy, John was attaching a lens to his camera. "Bright kid," he said briefly. Before she could reply he was moving away to find a clear angle for photos. Laddy followed him.

"Take some pictures of him with the newsmen, John," she whispered. "The family might like to have them." Intent on his subject, John nodded, and Laddy went to sit on the settee beside Brigit.

"Proud?" Laddy whispered. Brigit reached out and squeezed her hand.

"We're very grateful to you and Mischa, Laddy," Brigit said quietly. "If it hadn't been for you, we might never have found him. I keep thinking how differently we'd have been feeling tonight if...."

"My two friends found me," Rhodri's clear, carrying voice was saying suddenly, and Laddy tensed in sudden horror, her eyes fixed on his glowing face. She had not warned Rhodri to say nothing of Mischa in this affair! If he mentioned that name in this gathering!

Brigit bent forward. "I warned him not to say Mischa's name," she whispered. "Don't worry." Brigit had guessed who Mischa was from the first day, but she had said nothing about it to anyone— even Mairi. Laddy looked at her now in surprised gratitude. That in all the excitement of this day she had found time to remember and protect Mischa Busnetsky's privacy....

Rhodri was saying, "They knew I was looking in the caves, and when I didn't come home, they came and found me."

"Are they school friends of yours?" called the reporter of a local paper, who was thinking that three children would make an even better story than one.

"Oh no," Rhodri said with a broad smile. "They are quite grown up, you know. I think...I think they are going to get married."

THE CAR SCREECHED to a halt in front of the white gate, with inches to spare, and Laddy was climbing out the passenger door before John could reach to turn off the ignition.

"Don't get out, John," she said flatly. "I don't want to talk about it anymore."

When she was halfway through the gate, the car door slammed and she knew John was coming after her. Resolutely Laddy kept her face forward and began walking over the meadow toward the warm light that beckoned her from Mischa Busnetsky's cottage.

"I want to have this out, Laddy," John's voice said behind her in the night air. Realizing that he would follow her right across the meadow to the cottages and knowing that she must keep him from catching sight of Mischa, Laddy turned.

"John, there's nothing to have out," she said. "I've told you that Rhodri was being fanciful. What else is there to say?"

She had lied to John, telling him she scarcely knew her neighbor in the other cottage, saying anything that would keep him from trying to get a look at Mischa.

"You can say you're coming back to London with me, if that's true," John returned.

"Well, I am not going back to London with you, John," Laddy said, her anger beginning to show. "I am waiting for a story to break and I'm not leaving Trefelin till it does, if I can help it. Besides that, Rhodri—"

She was interrupted by a harsh incredulous laugh. "Come off it, Laddy!" John said loudly. "You're forgetting yourself—your story broke this morning, remember? That's why I'm here."

There was a little silence between them as she realized that John thought she had had advance notice of the cave paintings. Perhaps it would have been better if she had let him go on thinking that— but it was too late now.

"No, *that* just happened," Laddy said. "There's another—"

"Laddy," he said, and his voice was pleading now, "don't lie to me. I love you, Laddy. I've tried not to tell you because I didn't want to scare you, but I love you. Now tell me the truth."

Starlight bathed his golden head, but she could not see his face in the darkness. She swallowed suddenly.

"I can't tell you all the truth, John," she began in a low voice, wishing now that she had been more honest with him in the beginning.

He responded harshly, "Then just tell me this: do you love me?"

Not even the sound of the ocean was there to break the silence. "I'm not in love with you, John," she said quietly, after a moment. "I—"

Suddenly he pulled her against him so roughly that the camera slung over his shoulder struck her ribs. "You would have been! You would have been, if it weren't for him!" he said in a hoarse whisper. "Damn him!" And as she pushed to get out of his arms he bent and kissed her, a hot, tormented, possessive kiss. She did not struggle. She stood rigid and unmoved under the searching attack, and when he let her go his face was bitter.

"After that, don't try to tell me it's work that's suddenly come between us," he said angrily. "If it is, you sacrifice one hell of a lot for a story. You just sacrificed us!" He turned on his heel in the moonlight and strode toward his car.

Weary and shaken, she turned to cross the meadow. A few minutes later her heart leaped as she saw the door to Mischa's cottage open, the warm inviting light inside framing his lean, tall figure as he waited for her. On a half-sob of desperate need, Laddy began to run toward him through the cool scented moonlight like a wanderer who has seen home. She ran straight into his arms and clung to him.

"Hold me," she said. "Hold me."

And Mischa Busnetsky's arms closed warmly and securely around her body at her plea, but over her head his voice was saying, coldly, incredibly, "But of course. A woman who has sacrificed so much is entitled to a little comfort."

CHAPTER ELEVEN

"WHAT do you mean?" Laddy drew back in be-wilderment, and immediately his arms released her. Never in her life had she been so bereft. His eyes were remote, condemning, and with the sudden conviction that he was going to close the door in her face, she stepped quickly past him into the warm, softly lighted kitchen. "What is it? What do you mean?" she asked again.

Closing the door, he said, "You should not have forgotten my habit of taking a nocturnal walk, nor how the sound of voices carries at night."

"What are you saying?" she asked, bewildered. "That you overheard my conversation with John? But why has that—" She broke off as she saw a movement out of the corner of her eye, and she turned her head suddenly toward the window. "What was that?" Laddy said. "There's some-one—"

But Mischa's dry voice halted her. "I don't think so," he said ironically, and perhaps he was right. Not in thinking it an attempt to distract his atten-tion, but that perhaps her nerves were making her jumpy.

"Let's go into the other room," she said, nonetheless. "The curtains are drawn there."

"By all means," Mischa said blandly, following her into the cozy sitting room. "But don't you think you did enough acting last night?"

"Mischa," she begged, her heart beginning to pound, her stomach hollow with fear. "What's the matter? Don't look at me like that."

She reached for him. If she could touch him all this would disappear; it was a nightmare, his looking at her like that, so cold, so angry....

"I would advise you not to touch me again," Mischa said. "Unless you are willing to repeat the sacrifice you made here last night."

She gasped at that, her wide dark eyes filled with the consciousness of what he meant, her stomach suddenly burning at what she saw in his eyes.

She crossed to him and wrapped her arms around his neck. "I don't know what you think you heard out there," she said, willing him to touch her, to hold her. "But whatever it was, you're wrong. I love you."

A flame burned behind his dark, dilated pupils as he looked down at her, and then his broad hands gripped her waist.

"Or perhaps you feel you were shortchanged last night," he said as though she hadn't spoken. "I was so desperate for you, was I not? You did not achieve the kind of pleasure you have a right to expect. You must forgive me. But tonight I shall not be so desperate."

She tried to step away from him then, away from the anger in his eyes, but the hands around her waist were suddenly steel.

"Mischa," she begged, and he bent his head. While her lips were parted, his tongue came between them and his mouth branded hers.

She felt the kiss in every nerve, and in spite of herself her fingers gripped his shoulders, convulsively, and her lips begged him silently not to take his mouth away. In answer he pulled her body roughly to his, and she gasped for the breath she suddenly needed.

The response of his mouth was to pillage deeper, and he bent her backward to increase her body's passionate awareness of his, igniting sudden fires in her bloodstream that chased down her veins as though her blood were gunpowder. She was lost then, and she clung to him, her mouth stretching wider under his, her hands clinging desperately around his neck.

Suddenly the long muscles of his shoulders tensed, and she felt herself lifted off the ground, his hands warm now on her denimed thighs, and against her body she felt the slow rhythmic glide of his hips as he carried her through the darkened doorway of the bedroom.

He lay down with her in the darkness on the soft bed. Then his long arm reached out over her, and a moment later the soft glow of the bedside lamp was in her eyes. She gazed hungrily up at him, feeling as though she had forgotten her own name.

His hooded eyes staring into hers hid from her everything except his passion. His hand unbuttoned the cream silk shirt she had put on for him so many hours ago, and his rough palm pushed the cloth aside. The white roundness of her breast was immediately exposed in the golden lamplight, and as his hand closed on its female softness, his eyes flickered up to hers and she caught the flash of the hard anger she had seen before.

"Mischa," she asked pleadingly, because she saw no love in his eyes, "do you love me?"

Mischa smiled grimly. "I love you," he said roughly. "But do not be troubled in your conscience. They say every man loves a cheating woman once in his life. This will not kill me."

Laddy gasped aloud. "Cheating?" she repeated in stupid amazement. "Mischa, I love—"

"Shut up," he said quietly, brutally, and his mouth came down on hers. "I can take only so much."

His hand cupped her breast and his rough-skinned thumb brushed back and forth over her sensitive nipple, and when he lifted his mouth from hers to run kisses down over her neck and throat to her breast she was shaking so that she could only moan.

The thin cloth of her shirt was sensuous torment on her flesh as he slowly slid it from her body, his mouth and tongue finding each square inch of her sensitized skin as the sliding silk bared it to his eyes. He removed her blue jeans, and she lay trembling under the onslaught of his mouth and hands.

"I love you," she cried, her head arching back into the pillow as the fire set by his mouth and hands blazed in her body. He stopped to throw off his own clothes, and then his skin was against the length of hers, and this was the touch she had yearned for.

"I love you," she said, looking into his eyes, and she saw pain suddenly reflected there, as though she had struck him.

"Be quiet," he commanded, kissing her. In defiance she cried it again under his lips as they moved over hers, unable to believe that her love could cause the pain she had seen.

"I love you," she whispered against his kisses, feeling the shuddering response of his body to her words, "I love you. I—"

"Be quiet!" he repeated in a strange, harsh cry, and the ecstatic pain shooting suddenly through her body cut off her words like a knife, as she gasped on a moan that she hardly recognized as her own.

She had not understood, she had had no idea what it could be. Even last night had not prepared her for this. Pleasure suffused her trembling body, and when he looked into her eyes they were drugged with an innocent, sensuous surprise.

The hooded expression left Mischa's eyes then and they blazed at her, desire and love nakedly triumphant as he watched passion make its first mark on her face.

"Lady," he whispered hoarsely, "Lady, my Lady." And he shook when her body arched in answer to his.

When the long crescendo began, her hands stopped their exploration of his body and gripped his shoulders tightly. She no longer knew herself. She moaned and cried his name aloud and strained against him. "Please," she gasped, "please, please Mischa," not understanding what she was saying, knowing only that this was pleasure beyond endurance. In the moment when her endurance reached its limit he cried her name aloud, and a torrent of sensation coursed through her body like molten gold, flowing into every cell, engulfing her. She cried his name on a high, keening moan until his mouth covered hers again in triumph and possession.

When it was over, they did not let each other go, but clung together, their bodies entangled, for minutes that seemed like eternity.

At length Mischa's long fingers began to stroke the damp hair from her forehead, and he bent to kiss each eyelid. His eyes were still dark with emotion. "After eight years," he said, "one begins to live." And she knew that for him, too, the world had changed in these past days, that love had transformed him as much as it had her.

"I love you," she said. "I couldn't live without you. I haven't been alive for twenty-five years, but I'm alive now, and I don't know how I got through life without you." Her voice trembled, and she broke off to stroke his cheek and hair. Mischa caught her hand in his and kissed her palm as he had done eight years ago on a dark, hopeless stairwell.

"The memory of you kept me alive during those eight years," he said. "Even though I did not believe I would ever see you again, I had to stay alive while you were in the world."

She reached up to kiss him, and his arms encircled her tightly as his mouth took hers, and nothing could ever come between them.

"Why were you angry with me?" she said gently when he lifted his lips to kiss her forehead.

He said simply, "Your friend told you he loved you and then kissed you and said you were sacrificing your love for your work." He dropped another kiss in her palm. "I thought you had lied to me for the sake of a story."

"No," she said.

"No," he repeated. "I saw the truth later, in your eyes. Forgive me."

"John is a photographer on the *Herald*," she said. "We used to date, but then you came...."

He caught something unconscious in her voice. "So close?" he said. "After eight years, I came so close to losing you?" And he wrapped his arms tightly around her as though her body was his barrier against unbearable pain, and to let her go would kill him.

LATE IN THE MORNING they were awakened by a knock on the door, and still half asleep, Laddy felt Mischa slide out of bed beside her.

"Roger Smith," she guessed drowsily on a smile. "Rhodri's archaeologist. Wanting breakfast, I'll bet."

"I will tell him we are out of supplies," Mischa said, tying his robe as he bent to kiss her. "Don't go away."

"Uhm-hmm!" she agreed, without opening her eyes, drifting drowsily.

The sound of voices went on a long time, and eventually Laddy realized she was straining to discern who the second voice belonged to. But she did not recognize it; with a sudden feeling of alarm she swung to a sitting position and reached for her clothes.

She dressed quickly and was doing up the buttons on her shirt when Mischa came back to the bedroom. She looked up with a smile, but at the sight of him her smile died.

Mischa was standing in the doorway, his face white, his eyes dark, and he was looking at her as though he had never seen her before in his life.

"Mischa!" she screamed. "What's happened? Who was it?" She started to run toward him, but she came up before the brick wall of his eyes, and she stopped, staring at him in horror. "Who was it?" she repeated.

He said tiredly, coldly, without emotion: "It was Duncan Foster of the *Times*. It seems you are a better actress than I thought." And at the look in his eyes she quailed.

"*What?*" she gasped.

"If I had known you would go to these lengths I'd have given you a story two weeks ago and saved us both the trouble."

She said, slowly and calmly because she thought she must be losing her mind, "What are you talking about? I hardly know Duncan Foster. And I certainly...."

"Perhaps you don't," Mischa said. "But Mr. Foster knows you. And he knows there were pictures and a story about Mikhail Busnetsky in the first edition of the *London Evening Herald* this morning."

She stared at him in wordless dismay. "In the *Herald*?" she repeated incredulously. "*You?*"

Mischa smiled at her without warmth, saying nothing.

"It can't be true," she said. "It's barely ten o'clock. The *Herald*'s hardly in the streets." Fifteen minutes, she thought. And fifteen minutes was enough time for Duncan Foster's editor to phone him and, since he was already in Trefelin, for Duncan Foster to get here.... And there was only one way the story could have got into the *Herald*.

"John," Laddy said with quiet conviction. "He guessed or he got it out of Rhodri somehow.... But you said pictures?" She looked up to find Mischa's gaze on her as before, cold and withdrawn, and stopped speaking.

He said, "I told Mr. Foster that I would hold a press conference at two o'clock. Perhaps you will come to it." And he stepped aside politely as though to let her through the doorway, but Laddy did not move.

"I did not give John that story," she said passionately. "You've got to stop suspecting me every time something goes wrong! You've got to trust me—or don't you understand what that word means anymore?" And she remembered his voice saying, "Betrayal is worse than looking at your own death," and she wondered how many times in those dark prisons he had heard betrayal on someone's lips.

"I understand the word," he said with ironic emphasis, and she closed her eyes for a moment against pain.

"Then if you love me, you must trust me, Mischa, otherwise it isn't love."

There was a look in his eyes then that filled her with terror, because she could imagine that he had looked at a cell mate in just such a way after learning that he was a KGB plant. Before she could stop herself she cried, *"Don't!"*

He raised his eyebrows inquiringly at her, still without saying a word, and suddenly she felt sick, bruised, as if he had beaten her; she could no longer look at him. Turning her head away, she asked dully, "Do you love me, Mischa?"

"No," he said quietly, but she had heard the answer long before he said it, a thousand years ago she had heard it, and its echo reached her now only distantly.

"Why did you lie to me?" she asked.

And he replied, "I did not lie. You are the first woman I have known in many years. It would have been hard for me not to believe I loved you."

"But easy for you to realize your mistake?" she asked.

There was no answer.

"I love you," she said quietly. "I love you more than my life. I never loved anyone till I loved you, and now I love the whole world. How could I sell out your peace of mind for a story that might sell a few thousand more copies of a newspaper? How can you believe it?"

A knock on the front door made her jump, but Mischa calmly turned his back on her and walked to answer it. By the time he had closed the door on another journalist she had joined him in the kitchen.

"Hold me," she begged. "If you hold me you'll know the truth, you'll—"

He laughed without humor. "If I touch you I have no doubt that you can convince me of anything. I might believe I could breathe underwater if you told me so while I had you in my arms."

"You love me," she said, but he stared at her, unmoved, and there was no getting through the barrier behind his eyes.

"You *want* to believe it," she accused him suddenly, and felt the hot tears begin to slide down her cheeks. "You don't want to know the truth, you prefer to believe a lie. Why? Why, Mischa?"

He said dryly, "Self-preservation."

"Self-preservation?" she repeated, and looked at him as though he had struck her. "Against me?"

"Against you," he confirmed, and at the look in his eyes she could easily believe she was the deadliest enemy he had in the world. Her heart began to beat painfully, like the wings of a dying bird.

"How can you want to preserve yourself against love?" Laddy asked, her voice an unbelieving whisper. This was beyond her comprehension; she felt suddenly as though she had spent her whole life searching for love. She said, "I love you. What is more important than that?"

But he had gone into a region where she could not reach him. When he looked at her she could almost believe he didn't know who she was. How could the love of a stranger matter to him?

"Mischa," she said earnestly. "I didn't tell him. I didn't file the story. John must have—" She broke off, remembering. "Last night, when I thought I saw something—that must have been John, taking a picture! He would have recognized you, he was at the airport—"

Distantly, cynically, Mischa Busnetsky was smiling at her.

"Last night," she repeated. "Don't you remember?"

"I remember. A woman would have to be a fool not to cover her tracks. And you are no fool."

Yes, she was; she had been a fool ever to think herself safe in his arms. She should have known that nothing was safe in this world.

"I am, though, you know," she contradicted him quietly. "My father always said that the first sign of a foolish woman is that she falls in love with a—" Laddy broke off. "Bastard" was the word her father had used, but she could not say it to him, she could not apply the word to Mischa Busnetsky. Suddenly she laughed, a long peal of self-deprecating laughter as the truth dawned. "And the second sign," she said, her tone harshly cynical in spite of the sound of her laughter, "is that she refuses to admit it."

Mischa reached for the door. Knowing he meant to open it and make her leave, Laddy flung herself in front of it, pressing her back against the panels with an urgency that bruised her shoulder blades.

"Don't send me away!" she begged him passionately, her hand reaching out to clasp his arm; feeling the hot tears on her cheeks, she understood that her laughter had turned to weeping. "I'll die if you send me away. Mischa, I can't live without you." She had never believed it possible that she would say that to anyone, but she heard herself say it without surprise, learning only as she heard it that it was true.

For a moment, fire flickered in his eyes and she thought she had won, but as quickly as she thought it, the fire died. He touched her without passion, moving her away from the door and opening it.

"You are a fighter," he said with a calm indifference, as though sizing up her qualifications for a resumé. "You will survive."

And there was nothing to do but walk out the door he held open for her.

CHAPTER TWELVE

"HARRY," Laddy said breathlessly into the phone, "are you running an article about Mischa Busnetsky this morning?"

"Dear girl, of course I am," Harry replied. "And a very nice piece of work it is, too. I perceive it has *not* blown up in your face."

What on earth was this? He was sounding as though *she* had filed a story. Slowly, she said, "What exactly did you run, Harry?"

She heard the sound of deep inhalation and could almost see his compressed, frowning eyebrows.

"Just a teaser about the exclusive and one of John's photos."

Laddy stopped breathing; even her heart seemed to stop for a suffocating moment. "The exclusive?" she repeated.

"Dear girl, this world-weary editor is trying to wrap up the city edition of a newspaper just now," Harry said, friendly but impatient. "We are running the first part of your excellent interview with Busnetsky starting tomorrow. You could hardly have hoped for greater celerity. What else would you like to know?"

She could not believe her ears. She actually took the receiver away from her ear and looked at it as though it had a life of its own.

"Harry!" she said stupidly after a moment. "Harry, where did you get the interview copy?"

"Dear girl," he said, "were you afraid John would funk it? He handed your package to me as neatly as you could have wished—this morning early. If that's all—"

If her heart had forgotten to beat before, it was working double time now to make up. Laddy hung up the phone and gazed sightlessly around the blue sitting room of Tymawr House, her brain whirling. John had not only taken a picture of Busnetsky, he had also given to Harry copy purporting to come from her. And there was only one way he could have come by that. . . .

Slamming and locking the door behind her, Laddy ran breathlessly across the meadow in the spring sunshine and burst through the door—unlocked as always—of her little cottage. She did not stop running until she got to the small desk that held her portable typewriter by the sitting-room window.

The neat file that held the draft of her articles on Mischa Busnetsky was gone.

RICHARD AND HELEN DIGBY arrived by plane at one o'clock that afternoon and let it be known that the press conference would be held in the big house. When Laddy arrived there just before two o'clock, extra chairs had been brought into the sitting room, and they and the blue-flowered settees were all turned to face two straight-backed armchairs behind a small table. Except for the microphones bunched together on the table top and the TV cameras, it looked like a room set up for a lecture.

There were many more media people waiting for Mischa Busnetsky this afternoon than had met Rhodri Lewis last night, Laddy saw as she took an empty seat in a corner of the room as far away from the small table as possible. And though, no doubt, most of those here had originally arrived in Trefelin to talk to Rhodri Lewis, she saw a few faces of people who could only be here because of Mischa and who had therefore flown down to be here for the press conference.

Not the least of those whose object could only be Mischa Busnetsky was the correspondent from the Russian news agency Novosti.

Pavel Nikolaivich Snegov was in comfortable conversation with the man next to him when Laddy entered the room, but immediately after she sat down in her corner with her back to the broad window, he was there, nodding and smiling at her, and interrupting the reporter in the chair in front of her who had turned around to speak to her.

Laddy neither liked nor trusted Pavel Nikolaivich Snegov. She was quite certain that he knew all about her and her father, and as she looked into his smiling, cool eyes she wondered fleetingly whether Pavel Snegov had come down to Trefelin last night because of the story of the archaeological discovery or because that story gave him a good excuse to be in Trefelin to watch Mischa Busnetsky. It was easier to fool the press than the Russian spy system, she had no doubt.

"And so you have outwitted us all not once, but twice!" Pavel Nikolaivich Snegov said grandly, one reporter to another, as he sank into the empty chair beside her, and however much she feared and disliked him, Laddy could hardly ask him to go away.

"Outwitted?" she repeated with a raised eyebrow. "You could hardly call it that, surely?"

"My dear Miss Penreith," he said cozily, smiling at her in excellent imitation of a Dutch uncle, "to have tracked down this taciturn man when all the press of England are unable to find him *and* to be given an interview? If this is not outwitting us, what deserves the term?" He looked as though he wanted to pat her hand to complete the confiding image, but did not dare. "Hmm?" he pressed.

Laddy regarded him thoughtfully, wondering what his game was. "Well, certainly I seem to have been ahead of the rest of the media," she said quietly, "but are you telling me he had managed to keep his whereabouts a secret from *you*?"

She managed to inject amused disbelief into her tone, but her heart sank. Suppose it was true; suppose Mischa had managed to escape the vigilance of the Soviet spy network. Then it was not merely the press he had been so desperate to avoid till he was stronger, not merely the press that this morning's article had brought down on his head...?

Amid the chaos of her thoughts, she became aware that the buzz of conversation in the room had died, and in the silence Richard's voice greeted the ladies and gentlemen of the press.

"Mr. Busnetsky is still unwell and tires very easily," Richard said. "He will answer questions for one half hour and no more. After that I will be available for further questioning if you wish."

The noise of a footfall sounded in the expectant hush, and feeling as though her eyes were being dragged up by a force more powerful than her own will, Laddy met Mischa Busnetsky's gaze across the room.

His eyes rested on her for only a moment, moved away to the man on her left and stopped abruptly. He stared at Pavel Snegov for a long, long moment and then flicked his gaze, cool and dismissing, back to Laddy. His lips tightened, and he turned to the table and hung his jacket on the chair back before seating himself behind the mikes.

He wore a white shirt without a tie, open at the neck and rolled up at the cuffs, and a navy vest and well-fitting navy trousers that emphasized his tall leanness, his flat waist.

"With one or two exceptions," Mischa Busnetsky said in a deep, tired voice, "I do not know you—" his glance flickered imperceptibly to the corner where Laddy sat beside Pavel Snegov "—so you must forgive my not acknowledging you by name. Mr. Foster, I know your name, however, and I am sure you will initiate me into this Western rite gently." He nodded smilingly at Duncan Foster of the *Times*, and everybody laughed, liking him; those who had expected Mischa Busnetsky to be withdrawn and laconic were relaxing under this evidence that they would be met halfway.

Their questions ranged wide, from the conditions existing in his old homeland to his plans in his new one. Mischa answered them openly, matter-of-factly, with a dry wit that kept their laughter always on call. But the humor did not prevent him from making points, from showing his anger.

"Mr. Busnetsky, how many political prisoners would you estimate there are in the Soviet Union?" a dark-haired woman in the front row asked when the half hour was coming to a close.

He responded quietly, "I do not need to estimate, I can tell you exactly. The answer is two hundred and sixty millions."

There was a short pause then, and beside Laddy, Pavel Snegov raised a negligent hand.

"The gentleman beside Miss Penreith," Mischa's deep voice said without the least hesitation over her name, though he had never spoken it before. Pavel Snegov stood up.

"Snegov, Novosti," he introduced himself. "When do—"

Mischa raised his hand, cutting the question off. "I am sorry," he said, and there was a glitter in his eyes that was not quite a smile. "The Russian State has asked me all the questions she is going to ask me. I do not answer any more." There was a flurry of indrawn breaths, but Mischa's gaze calmly moved on. "The gentleman in the second row?" Pavel Snegov, calm, and smiling with his mouth only, sat down again.

"Gerald Harding, Reuters," said a blond young man who reminded Laddy of John. "How long will you be staying here in Wales and where do you plan to go when you leave?"

"I shall be traveling to the United States within a week," Mischa said, and Laddy sat up with a gasp. She had heard nothing of this. "First I go to a clinic for health treatment, and later I am asked to do a lecture tour which, if I am well enough, I shall do." He leaned back in his chair then, and Laddy knew he was exhausted, more exhausted than he had been after a night searching for Rhodri. "At the moment this does not seem to me very likely," he smiled self-deprecatingly, "but the doctor tells me it is quite possible." He moved to stand up, weariness etched on his face for all to see.

In the moment before the applause started, a woman's high voice called out, "One last question, Mr. Busnetsky?" When she saw him nodding at her, Laddy realized that the high, strained voice was her own. "One of your compatriots, another dissident, has said that while he was in prison, in order to keep himself alive it was necessary to have a dream. What was the dream that kept you alive, if you had one?"

"You," he had told her once. "I told myself that if I stayed alive I would see you again...."

Forgive me, she prayed silently now, her eyes on his face pleadingly. *Forgive me, but I have to remind you now that this is me, that you love me....*

His face was suddenly drawn under the bright lights the television crews had set up. "I had a dream," he said in a voice suddenly harsh. "But the lady whose memory kept me alive is dead now."

"Dead?" she gasped unbelievingly.

"Dead to me," said Mischa Busnetsky shortly. He nodded to the room and crossed to the door while the journalists made friendly applause. Laddy could feel her own palms slapping each other at regular intervals, but the sound she heard was not applause. She was hearing Mischa's voice on a sunny morning against the rushing sea, Mischa's voice saying, "Their betrayal is worse than if they had died."

"How on earth did it happen?" Helen and Laddy sat across the table from each other in the large bright kitchen of Tymawr House. Laddy was gazing helplessly at the early edition of that day's *Herald*, where a picture of Mischa that had obviously been taken within the past few days lay over the small headline "Busnetsky Exclusive."

Soviet dissident Mikhail Busnetsky, recently released in exchange for a Russian spy, last week spoke to *Herald* reporter Lucy Laedelia Penreith about the dissident movement in Russia, about life in the camps, about his first impressions of the West, his plans for the future.

Starting tomorrow, watch for this series of exclusive interviews....

The headline story, over a photo of the painted deer, was "Cave Art Authentic." Under her by-line was the story she had filed last night after talking to Roger Smith, the young archaeologist from the museum.

Laddy looked at the paper helplessly.

"I don't know how it happened," she said to Helen. "But I can guess. I suppose this is the only time in my life when I'll get credit for two front-page stories at the same time." She laughed mirthlessly. "If anyone had ever told me that that would give me no joy at all...." She took a breath. "John must have broken into my cottage last night before he went back to town and taken the papers I'd been working on. There's simply no other explanation."

"Would your editor run the story without speaking to you about it first?" Helen asked. She had come to find Laddy as the press conference broke up, and Laddy had asked to see the copy of the *Herald* that she and Richard had brought down from London with them...that Mischa had read before the press conference this afternoon.

"It's hard to get me on the phone here," Laddy pointed out. "Besides, John gave him those articles with a message that I had sent them." She stood up disconsolately. "I've got to talk to Harry again, Helen. May I use the phone?"

"Harry," she said when, after ten minutes of listening to him argue with someone at his desk, she finally heard his voice in the receiver talking to her, "Harry, John stole those papers he gave you out of my house, out of my desk. He went in when he knew I wasn't home and searched my desk. You can't run the interviews, Harry. Not yet. I promised Busnetsky to let him read and approve them and he hasn't seen them yet. I also promised to hold the story till he was ready to talk to the press, but it's too late for that now."

There was a pause during which she heard the click of Harry Waller's cigarette lighter, then the long exhalation of his breath.

"John had pictures of Busnetsky—of you and Busnetsky," Harry said.

"Which he stole through the kitchen window," Laddy replied, unable to keep disgust and contempt from her tone and not trying anymore, "*after* I told him the story wasn't ready to break yet."

"I suppose you realize, dear girl," Harry said, "that if you'd told me what you were doing in the beginning, this wouldn't have happened. But never mind that now. Have you got carbon copies of this stuff John gave me?"

"Yes," she said dryly. "He did actually leave me those."

"Check it out now, Laddy," Harry said. "You've

got it there; have Busnetsky go over it today as soon as you can to approve it.''

Laddy breathed deeply. ''He is extremely angry, Harry. He may just say we can't run it at all.''

''He won't do that, dear girl,'' Harry said, meaning Harry would ignore it if he did. ''He did give you the interview in the first place. Tell him to be sensible and recognize the fact that these things happen. Through nobody's fault. Get back to me as soon as you can with any changes.''

By rights, the articles belonged to Laddy. She could refuse to let them run at all, if she were willing to fight hard enough, if she were willing to make Harry angry, make the *Herald* look foolish, shatter her own reputation....

But Mischa's hiding place was already discovered; the whole world knew where he was. What purpose could be served now by not publishing the interviews? The damage was done.

''I have to talk to you,'' she told the steely-eyed stranger sitting at the kitchen table in his cottage.

Mischa replied shortly, ''I don't think so.''

''Helen told me you saw this morning's *Herald*.'' Laddy held up a sheaf of carbon copies of typewritten sheets. ''These are the articles Harry wants to start running tomorrow. I told him you would want to approve them—read them and delete what you don't want printed—but you have to do it now, Mischa.''

He regarded her steadily for a moment. ''Since I have no doubt that there is nothing there I would like to see printed, I shall not waste my time," he said, and turned back to his work.

Laddy said desperately, "You had promised me an exclusive, Mischa. I drafted these articles— I was going to show them to you, see if you liked them! I'd no intention of giving them to Harry! *Mischa!*" she cried as, ignoring her, he continued to write. He looked up at her slowly. "John stole them from my desk last night, and now there's nothing I can do about it. The damage is done. But please, read these and make sure there's nothing in them that shouldn't be published."

Her voice was pleading as she dropped the sheets on the table in front of him, but he didn't touch them, didn't look at them.

"I told you once before," he said unmoved, "that I do not make bargains with my freedom. I told you you must make up your mind to steal it. Apparently you have done so. You will publish what you wish to publish. Do not engage me in the farce of seeking my approval."

"Mischa," she begged, feeling somehow forced to pick up the papers again, "I can stop them. It will cost me, but I can stop them. But you haven't read them, you don't know what's there. Don't make me fight this for nothing, Mischa. If after reading them you feel that no part of what I've written should be published, I'll stop them. But please don't ask me to pay so highly when I don't know why I'm paying. Please read the articles."

His face when he looked at her was without emotion. "And what words would I have to use to convince you of my right to privacy?" he asked. "You think that I should read those papers and find justification for what I do not wish the world to see— that perhaps this sentence endangers such and such a cause or that paragraph puts a life in danger. But I have given you no such information at any time. There is only one person's freedom I have placed in your hands—my own. And I tell you that I do not bargain for that. Nor do I plead. We all pay for our own actions, and now I pay for mine. Publish your stories. You worked hard and well to get them."

"I love you, Mischa. Don't you believe that?" she said desperately.

"No doubt to the extent of your limited ability you do love me," he said dispassionately. "But perhaps you will understand that I have had enough of people's limited ability for loyalty."

"There's no limit to my love for you," she said quietly, knowing it was hopeless. "I'd die for you, Mischa. I love you more than my life."

"I don't think so," he said, in the calm tones of a judge.

Laddy drew herself straight in front of the table. "You're talking to me as though I were no more than a reporter you scarcely know," she said, her voice choked and hoarse. "You're asking for everything and giving nothing. Tell me—as the man I love, as the man who. . .who loves me—tell me not to publish these articles, and I'll stop them."

She paused, while Mischa looked at her, saying nothing. "Mischa," she begged, "can't you see? You want me to give in the name of love what you are not prepared to ask in the name of love. You want me to do it all myself. But I can't. I can't give up all the respect, the reputation I've earned at the *Herald* over three years to walk in a void where you don't even speak to me...." She stopped, choking back tears, waiting.

His eyes were dark, full of messages she could not read. He smiled faintly at her.

"Goodbye, Laddy," he said.

He picked up his pencil and turned back to his work, and after a moment Laddy turned helplessly toward the door. "Unless you are leaving," his voice arrested her, "we shall be neighbors for several more days. This cottage is my property. I do not wish to see you on my property again."

It chilled her to the marrow. Her hand on the open door, she turned her head to meet his eyes, and for the first time since she had met him, the person who looked at him was Lucy Laedelia Penreith, journalist.

"You couldn't have said *that* in Russia, could you?" she remarked coolly. "You're admirably quick at adapting to the West. Try to remember, in future, that one of the great differences between dictatorship and democracy lies in the freedom of the press!"

THURSDAY MORNING, after a sleepless night, Laddy got up to find a cold and rainy day. It was the first day without sun since she had arrived in Wales, and the Coastal Path was transformed.

She walked for an hour on the Path, high along the cliffs over the sea, the fine mist wet on her face and hair, the wind blowing away the cobwebs in her mind. She walked till she stood overlooking Aberdraig, a small town nestling in a cove below her, protected by the high cliffs and by a thick seawall.

She sat on the white gold wood of a farmer's stile and gazed across to the cliff on the other side of the cove, where what looked like an ancient standing stone was silhouetted high on the headland. She wondered if it was one, and if so, why Rhodri had never brought Mischa and herself to see it.

Perhaps he had wanted to show them more important sites first, not knowing how much time they had, knowing the three of them could only be together for a short time. She herself had never thought of that, Laddy realized now. Somewhere deep inside her she had accepted that she and Mischa would always be together, and she had never stopped to wonder where. Laddy laughed a little and was surprised to hear the sound of her own voice against the murmur of wind and sea. She might, she reflected, have awakened one morning in the cottage in Trefelin to find that five years had passed, wondering what had become of her house in London, her friends, her job, so besotted had she been. . . .

She had drafted those articles as an exercise in love, as an exploration of who Mischa Busnetsky was, to try and understand what he had gone through. She had not thought of their being read by anyone except herself, though perhaps the time might have come when she would have asked Mischa to approve them for publication. But while she wrote them—from notes, memory and tapes she had twice made of their conversations, piecing together his observations and experience into exploratory questions and answers—it had been a labor of love. "A Discovery of Mischa Busnetsky," she might have called it, showing it to him. A discovery of her love.

The man who would continue to be her love, no matter what he said to her. He had said he did not love her, but first he had told her, much more strongly, that he did. And he had not been lying then, she knew he had not. He loved her, but he believed she had betrayed him, and so she had become "dead" to him. That was his method of self-preservation. He had had years of practice of steeling himself against the betrayal of people who were close and dear to him, fellow warriors in the freedom battle who had sold out. He must know so well how to close himself off to such things that it was second nature to him, an automatic response that he no longer consciously controlled.

But she had *not* betrayed him. Her only sin was her stupidity in not locking her door against a man who said he loved her and whom she had thought of as a friend. *Had thought,* she repeated to herself with a grim laugh, and noticed how the same unconscious mechanism that operated in Mischa had operated in herself. John Bentinck had betrayed her, but she did not even feel the pain of it, because already he had ceased to be her friend. If he had come to her then and told her he loved her, she would have stared at him as distantly as, yesterday, Mischa had gazed at her.

Laddy stood up with a bound of release and threw her head back to feel the light droplets of water that seemed to be materializing rather than falling on her skin, so soft were they. Joy and resolution filled her like light. She would *make* him listen, make him understand. She would refuse to leave him until he had heard her out—no matter whose property she was on, she thought with a laugh.

She clambered over the stile and set out at a slipping run along the muddy Coastal Path. Ahead of her the white horse galloped across a field, his tail high, his spirit as free as her own.

The proprietress of the small shop on the main road in Trefelin had had the foresight to order additional copies of the national morning papers from Fishguard, so when Laddy arrived, shortly after the bus that brought the papers had passed through, she was able to buy one of each. The *Herald* was a London paper, not a national one, so she would see no copy of it today—unless John Bentinck came down from town again to check on the rift he had caused between her and Mischa, Laddy thought sardonically.

She was very wet when she arrived back at the cottage, which now, in the rain, seemed cozier and more protective than ever. Dropping the papers and her bag of provisions on the kitchen table, Laddy headed to the bathroom for a warm shower. Then, wrapped in a robe, she set a fire in the sitting-room grate and settled down for a lazy morning with the papers while she waited for the sound of Mischa's footsteps to announce that he was home. Outside the sky was growing darker and the rain on the roof became gradually more insistent.

The photo of the dying reindeer, which had yesterday run in the *Herald*, had been picked up by the wire services and was running in all three of the morning papers. It was a good picture: she had not taken the time to examine it closely yesterday, but now she saw that even in the harsh glare of the flash, justice had been done to the powerful talent of the artist.

"Courtesy of AP/UP," read the acknowledgment under the photo in the *Telegraph* and the *Guardian*, but in the *Times* the tiny printing read "Photo by John Bentinck."

Laddy let the paper fall into her lap and gazed unseeingly into the bright crackling fire on the hearth.

So John had not been prepared to achieve his dream honorably. Having in his possession exclusive photos that were of enormous interest to the world, he had not been able to resist the temptation to claim them as his own. It was a breach of professional ethics that a week ago she simply would not have believed him capable of. But now she knew him better, and she knew that John Bentinck could not have let this opportunity slip by. He would have had to justify this to himself, perhaps telling himself that he set up the camera, that if the passage had been wider he would have pushed the button himself; telling himself, more importantly, that Laddy would not benefit from the picture credit and it would be foolish to waste such a chance—that it could make no difference to her, but all the difference in the world to him. . . . Laddy knew the arguments that a weak man would use in justification for what he wanted to do, as surely as she knew, looking at that credit caption, that the arguments had prevailed in John Bentinck's mind.

Because the only opposing argument was the simple question of ethical behavior. . . and she knew that the man who had stolen papers from her desk would think nothing of stealing a credit that was not rightfully his. Laddy shook her head in bewildered disbelief. And this was a man who three weeks ago she thought she knew well enough to love.

She was reading the papers' various reports of Mischa Busnetsky's press conference—only one of them giving any play at all to his refusal to hear a question from the correspondent from Novosti—when there was an urgent knocking on her front door. As though there could be no other human being in the world, she was immediately convinced that it was Mischa, and scattering the newspapers and tripping over the hem of her bright red toweling robe, Laddy rushed into the kitchen to let him in.

Rhodri Lewis and Roger Smith, looking like two rats caught in a rain barrel, grinned sheepishly at her in the pouring rain. Laddy burst out laughing and stood back, holding the door open.

"Goodness, what happened to you? Come in, come in, you look drowned."

"I'm afraid we'll dirty your floor," said Roger Smith warningly, as though she would not be able to see that for herself, but Rhodri took her instantly at her word and leaped through the doorway, shaking the water from his head like a dog.

"It's tile," Laddy assured Roger Smith, who had scarcely been out of Rhodri's sight since his arrival from the national museum Tuesday morning, and still hesitant, the young archaeologist stepped into the kitchen and allowed her to close the door.

"We were coming to ask you for elevenses," Rhodri announced with a wide grin that glinted in his eyes through rain-studded eyelashes. "We were coming up the dry waterfall bed, you know, which was very foolish on such a wet day. We could hardly move on those wet stones—we were caught halfway up and halfway down, and then it began to rain *very* hard."

Under his thin jacket Rhodri was wet through, and so, obviously, was Roger Smith.

"Well, what you need now is a hot shower—both of you," Laddy said, smiling down into Rhodri's irresistible grin. "Suppose you go first, while Roger stokes up the fire and I find you both something to wear."

Roger Smith was embarrassed, but it was obvious that he could not go back to the tent he had set up in the cave in his present condition, and he put a cheerful face on it, taking off his wet outer clothes and expertly adding more coal to the fire.

In the bedroom Laddy changed into a sweater and cord trousers and set out her blue jeans and a sweat shirt for Rhodri. They would be too big, of course, but he had to have something while his own clothes were drying. For Roger Smith, who was a slim young man, she pulled out her oldest and most comfortable blue jeans, the largest item she had in the minimal wardrobe she had brought with her to Wales.

Elevenses ran into an early lunch and the clothes hanging around the fire slowly dried, but the pouring rain did not let up.

They talked about Rhodri's cave, and Roger Smith proved to be so keen on the subject that finally Laddy pulled out her tape recorder to get down what he was saying.

"The odd thing is the reindeer," he told her. "Although Magdalenian man, as far as we know, painted animals often, the treatment of this reindeer intrigues me. The artist seems to have given him great prominence, you know.''

"Does that mean that Rhodri's cave might not be Magdalenian?" Laddy asked.

"Well, it might. But other points of comparison—superficial ones until we get the chemical people down here—show these drawings to be very similar to the ones in France. Except for the prominence of the deer.''

"Tell her what you think!" Rhodri demanded, bouncing on the sofa in his excitement, and Laddy's ears perked up. She smiled at Roger expectantly, saying nothing.

"Well—" he paused and ran his hand over the back of his head "—it's possible, if the cave is very extensive, if perhaps there's another rockfall deeper in the cave—and I haven't done a great deal of exploring on my own—it's possible that in fact the reindeer, which is, after all, in a relatively shallow part of the cave, is not as prominent as we now think him.''

Laddy's gaze rested on Roger Smith for a long moment, then for several seconds flicked back and forth between the two faces watching her.

"If that magnificent beast does not have the prominence we think, it can only be because elsewhere in the cave are far richer, far more prominent paintings," she said slowly at last.

Rhodri crowed: "I knew she'd get it!"

"Right!" said Roger Smith simultaneously.

"And that means," continued Laddy, "that it

228 CAPTIVE OF DESIRE

would be such a rich discovery that every archaeologist north of the equator would be clamoring to work on the site."

"Right again," said Smith. "Fortunately the year is only half gone, and the museum still has some of this year's funding to be starting with. There'll be a team coming down this evening or tomorrow to start the preliminary work."

Laddy's smile broke into incredulous laughter. "This is extraordinary!" she exclaimed. "You must be walking on air, Rhodri, aren't you?"

"Well, you know," he said, smiling broadly, "sitting in there with that reindeer all night—before you found me—I thought it was a little strange. Not like the ones in France."

"In fact," Laddy said, as the light dawned, "this is Rhodri's theory!"

Roger Smith was not entirely pleased with this, but he said, "He drew my attention to the extraordinary prominence of the reindeer, certainly."

"Is this for publication?" Laddy demanded, completely infected now by Rhodri's suppressed excitement. "Can I do a story in tomorrow's paper?"

"As long as you stress that it's theory only, based on very insufficient fact," Roger Smith said, while Rhodri hugged himself and beamed at her. "I don't see why not."

The downpour continued steadily into the afternoon, and Rhodri began to fret over not being able to see Mischa to tell him the news.

"Come and help me make tea," Laddy said,

"and then you can borrow my mac and run across and see if he's in."

"He's got a mac, hasn't he?" Rhodri demanded. "Why hasn't he come here? He always comes for lunch, doesn't he?"

Laddy filled the kettle without replying. She did not want to talk about Mischa's absence, and besides, she had something to say to Rhodri while Roger Smith was out of the room.

With her blue jeans belted tightly, rolled down at the waist and up at the ankles, and her sweat shirt hanging on his small frame, he might have been the well-scrubbed orphan in any one of a hundred sweetly revolting Hollywood movies, except for his thin dark face and the intense intelligence of his eyes.

If you didn't have Brigit and Mairi, Laddy thought suddenly, *I'd adopt you tomorrow.*

"Listen, Rhodri," she said softly, "they haven't named the site yet, have they?" He shook his head, frowning curiously. "In tomorrow's *Herald* I'm going to have a good stab at naming it for you," she said. "Once it's got a name, you know, it just might stick. So what shall I call it tomorrow? The Lewis Cave? Rhodri's Cave?"

Laughter leaped in his eyes. "Rhodri's Cave," he said unhesitatingly. "Can you really do it?"

"Well, we'll see, won't we?" she said, and they smiled at each other like conspirators.

She could not prevent him then from setting out to bring Mischa over for tea, but he came back in a moment, reporting the door locked and the cottage dark.

"I suppose he went up to Tymawr for breakfast and got caught there, same as we did," Rhodri said comfortably, digging into his scrambled eggs. It was early for such a heavy meal, but they had had an early lunch, too, and as Rhodri said, rain made one hungry. "But he'll be back soon now, because it's clearing," Rhodri finished. "You will have to sleep at our house tonight, Roger. Everything in the cave will be too wet."

By four-thirty the rain had stopped, and both Roger Smith and Rhodri insisted that their clothes were dry enough to put on. Laddy stood in the doorway as the slight blond figure and the slighter, shorter dark one set out across the meadow toward Trefelin, then closed the door and sat at the kitchen table with a cup of coffee, watching out the window for another, taller figure to appear.

But Mischa did not come.

SHE AWOKE in the pitch blackness, calling and weeping, and imagining that it had all been a dream. That waking dream enclosed her as she stumbled through the darkness of sitting room and kitchen, through the chill wet air of the night, through another kitchen and another sitting room to the bright darkness of Mischa Busnetsky's bed.

"Hold me," she begged, trembling in the endless warmth of his bed, of his body, and his hungry sleeping arms reached out for her, and she knew it had all been nightmare. "I had a dream," she whispered. "Love me, please love me."

His mouth searched for hers in the darkness, moving down from her temple across the corner of her eye, to her cheek, to her parted lips, hungry, urgent, demanding. His hand caressed her neck, his thumb forcing her head back over his arm under her, and then for a moment in the darkness there was a still waiting, before his mouth covered hers.

With a small keening noise of need she arched against him, reaching her arms around his body, and realizing with mingled shock and pleasure that he was not wearing anything at all.

Under the loose top of her pajamas his hand found her breast, pressing its fullness with passionate force as she cried out, then breaking off to brush the sensitive hollow of his palm over its soft tip. When he felt it swell into sensual awareness of him his lips left hers, and through the cotton of her pajamas she felt the heat and damp of his mouth on her breast with a pleasure that rippled through her entire body.

Lifting his mouth, he buried his face in the neckline of her pajamas, and she wanted his mouth on her skin, then, with almost desperate need.

His hand found the top button of her pajama jacket in the darkness and struggled for a fruitless moment to undo it. He laughed, above her, where she could scarcely see his shape, but she heard the rich thread of passion in his voice.

"I am the beggar at the gates," he said, in his

deep, thick voice. His other arm moved from under her, and for a moment the weight of his two large hands was between her breasts. "Am I not?" he said.

"No," she moaned, for if anyone would be reduced to begging she knew it would be herself.

"No," he said with sudden violence, and she heard a tearing as his hands parted and then his lips were against her naked breast.

With agonizing deliberation his mouth and hands began to move over her body, teasing, tantalizing, bringing her to an ever higher pitch of sensuous excitement. His hands stroked her head, his fingers pressing and caressing her scalp and her thick hair till she learned that her hair was composed of nerve ends. His mouth delicately traced the shape of her nipples till her breathing was a series of gasps through her open lips. He stroked her body, her long legs, with a suppressed passion that was almost savage, calling up in answer her own deep savagery.

In the end his mouth against her became a torment and she felt that if he did not take her now, she would go mad.

"Please," she begged, pulling at his arms, his back. "Please, Mischa, love me, love me now," she whispered, and was rewarded in the darkness with the sudden weight of his long body against hers.

"Yes," he said quietly into her ear, the added sensation of his warm breath against her overloading her system so suddenly that she thought she

would explode. "Oh yes, my Lady, I will love you.
But I want you to tell me something."

His voice was low and filled with promise, and
she responded to the tone, hardly conscious of the
words.

"Anything," she whispered smiling. "Anything
at all."

"What information did Comrade Snegov ask you
to get from me tonight?"

"What?" asked Laddy in distant perplexity.
What she had heard was gibberish to her.

Mischa repeated the question slowly, word for
word, and the first thin trickle of fear slid down her
back like a shard of ice. She remembered then that
not all of her nightmare had been a dream. Some of
it had been real. In spite of the heat of Mischa's
body against hers, she shivered.

She raised her hand and found his cheek in the
darkness.

"Mischa, what are you saying?" she whispered,
horrified.

"Tell me," he urged roughly. His thumb was on
her lips, and his mouth came down and kissed hers
with hungry anguish. "Tell me, and then we will
love each other one last time to remember." His
hand caressed her. "I will not judge you, Lady, not
tonight. Tomorrow, perhaps. But tonight we will
only love."

"You think I'm a spy—a Soviet spy?" she asked,
her voice high, her mind coldly clear now. "Why—
because Pavel Snegov sat next to me at your press

conference yesterday?'' Freezing suddenly and shaking, Laddy struggled out of his arms. For a moment it seemed he would keep her there, then he let her sit up while he reached to turn on the bedside lamp.

She blinked at him for a moment in the soft golden light. His eyes were burning steadily into hers as though he had been able to see her all along, as though he did not need the light to see.

After a moment, he said flatly, "So you do know that he is a spy."

All the buttons were missing from her pajama jacket. Shivering, she pulled the cloth over her breasts and held it tightly.

"The whole world knows it!" she exclaimed harshly. "But if everyone who has ever talked to Pavel Snegov is also a spy, don't forget that that includes you!"

"Everyone who drops casual information in a spy's ear is not necessarily a spy," Mischa said softly.

She shouted, "Have you forgotten who I am? Who my father was? From the time I was twelve years old I knew better than to drop information into the ear of anyone like Pavel Snegov!" She looked at him and saw the truth behind his eyes. "But you haven't forgotten, have you? You'd never forget a thing like that. You knew that if I were dropping information into Snegov's ear, it would have to be deliberate, done in cold blood. It would have to be." She dropped her eyes from his and turned her head away. "But you believed it," she said softly, shaking her head as she felt the tears begin. "You believed it, without evidence, without reason, without proof. You believed that everything I said to you was a lie—my love, my. . . ." She broke off, turning to look at him. He was resting on his elbow, beside her on the bed, unmoving, his mouth drawn tight, his eyes watching her. The wrinkled blue sheet lay lightly over his hips, revealing rather than disguising his long lean frame under it.

In sudden anguish she turned and kicked her own legs out from under the thin sheet and sat on the edge of the bed, her back to him, her face in her hands. On the floor at her feet were her pajama bottoms, their red-and-white stripes twisted and angled. Bending, Laddy picked them up and pushed her legs into them, then stood and pulled the elastic up around her waist with a snap.

Tears were streaming unchecked down her face, but she stood straight in the lamplight as she turned to face him.

"Well, here's something you don't know!" she said bitterly. "And I'll give you this information free: your country, your compatriots killed my father three years ago, and they killed him because of you! They killed him because he'd obtained your manuscripts, and because if he'd stayed alive he would have published them. They searched the house after he was killed. I knew they'd searched it, but I didn't know what they wanted. They wanted the file on you," she said bitterly, staring down at his dark, unwavering eyes. "Yes, they took that, but they didn't get the manuscripts. My father had hidden them too well. So well that it was three years before they were found. Four months ago I found them, your precious manuscripts, and that's when I knew what had killed my father—your countrymen and your manuscripts. I sat there looking at a lot of paper covered with words—*your* words—and I had to accept that in my father's judgment they had been worth his life.

"Well, I did accept it," she said, her voice thick with sobs. "I did accept it, and when you were released I only thanked God that you had come back to me safe. The memory of my father never stopped my loving you. But it will now. It will now. Because you aren't the man he thought you were. His death was nothing but a joke.

"You think Pavel Snegov was getting information from me yesterday? Let me tell you something about your own countrymen, since you seem to underestimate them so badly: Pavel Snegov doesn't need to ask me a damn thing! He probably knows everything about me right down to the shade and brand of my toenail polish! *He* has not forgotten, if you have, who my father was!"

Mischa lay motionless, his eyes dark with what she had told him, the muscles of his face tight, his skin pale in the lamp shadows.

"I didn't know," he said gently.

But she interrupted, not wanting to hear: "No,

you didn't know, and you didn't have any faith either, did you? I loved you," she said. "I loved you more than anything that moved on this earth. I would have taken anything from you and still have kept coming back for more. I sat waiting for you for hours tonight with my little explanation of how innocent I was, and I was going to *make* you understand that I hadn't betrayed you. I never judged you for believing what you did, I couldn't judge you, but I was going to make you see the truth. I thought if I did that, that you would know that you still loved me." She sobbed once, running an impatient hand over her wet cheeks, staring at him. "But I know now you were right. You never loved me, even if you believed that you did. Never. If you had, you could not have thought even for a moment that I would betray my father and myself by coming to your bed to betray you. I thought there was nothing I wouldn't take from you, but I was wrong. That's the one thing I can't take."

The sobs had stopped now, the tears were dry on her cheeks. Her heart ached as though there were a knife impaling it. Suddenly everything went out of her: life, love, spirit; only pain was left.

She gazed into the dark eyes she had loved so much and felt as though she had been ripped away from the being who gave her life.

"If your object was to get rid of me, you chose the only method in the world that could have worked," she said quietly. "I don't care now what you believe of me. You won't have to tell me again to keep off your property. I don't want to be any-where near you."

Laddy turned on her heel and walked toward the door.

"Lady," he said when she had reached the door-way, in the voice of a man waking from a dream. But the woman who would have turned and listened then was dead. Without a sign that she had heard, without the least break in her stride, Laddy walked out of Mischa's bedroom into outer darkness.

CHAPTER THIRTEEN

THE SUN WAS BEAMING down on London as if it had never done anything else in the whole course of its existence, though in fact it was the first warm weather the city had seen in ten days. Along Oxford Street, tourists and natives alike were smiling with the happy surprise of those who have just discovered the miracle of spring.

In the bustling Saturday morning throng of shoppers, Laddy wandered, unaware of the sun on her skin, the faint warm breeze or the sprinkle of summer green glimpsed down side streets along the busiest street of the city she loved most in the world. She felt like a ghost. Never before had the touch, the air of London failed to put the world right for her; never since her father had brought her here at the age of ten had she been in this city without the comfort of knowing that here was home.

She had left Trefelin on Friday, after lunch with Richard and Helen, without seeing Mischa again. She had driven to London almost nonstop, like a robot, and when at last she had pulled up in front of the dark and empty house in Highgate, she could not remember one mile of the trip.

Margaret and Ben Smiley had not been at home upstairs, and since they had not expected her home, there had been nothing welcoming in her flat, not even milk in the fridge for tea. Laddy had stripped off her clothes in the middle of her bedroom and had crawled shivering into her cold empty bed and had lain waiting for exhaustion to pull her into unconsciousness. As on the long drive, her mind had been a blank. She had not thought of anything, of anyone....

"Oh, excuse me, I very sorry," a voice said, disrupting her thoughts, and Laddy blinked into the politely perturbed face of a Japanese gentleman who carried a camera around his neck.

"Sorry," said Laddy, for if they had bumped into each other it had to be her fault. "I wasn't looking where I was going, I'm afraid."

"Please, okay," said the man, nodding his head and smiling, and his wife and two children at his side smiled, too. The camera around his neck was of German manufacture, she saw, and Laddy smiled as she moved past.

A Japanese man with a German camera taking pictures of England, she would have said to Mischa, and he would have laughed with her, as taken as she by the incongruity.

Suddenly the sunlight was hurting her eyes. Blinking, Laddy stepped into an Italian trattoria she was passing and made her way to a table against a wall that gave her a view of the Oxford Street crowds through the large tinted windows.

She did not often shop on Oxford Street, and certainly never on Saturday. But today she had come here deliberately, to be in the crowds, to be assaulted by the music from the boutiques, to breathe in the diesel exhaust of the black London cabs. . . as if the presence of so much life around her might make her feel alive. But nothing touched her. Even Oxford Street moved along the periphery of her senses, like a half-attended-to television program.

"Good morning, Miss Penreith," said a voice above her, and with her cup of coffee halfway to her lips, Laddy glanced up and then froze. The fat white face of Pavel Snegov smiled down at her.

"Good morning," she returned, sipping the coffee and placing the cup very methodically in the center of the perfect white saucer before looking at Pavel Snegov again.

"What a surprise to meet you in London— May I sit down? I had thought of you as being in Wales for several more days," said Snegov, dropping into the chair opposite without waiting for her nod, stolidly adjusting the knees of his gray suit, then leaving his hands on his knees, as though he had forgotten them.

Laddy's mouth curved in a wary half smile. "That's a coincidence," she said. "I thought *you* would be there for several more days."

Pavel Snegov ignored that. "I must congratulate you on your interview with Busnetsky. The segments that appeared on Thursday and Friday were most excellent," he said comfortably. "I am looking forward to seeing the rest. He is a most interesting man, is he not?"

Laddy gazed at him a moment, her face grave. It occurred to her that she was frightened of Pavel Snegov. And she did not think she had sufficient energy to spar with him.

"On Monday he talks about his time in prisons and labor camps," she said. "Are you familiar with prison conditions in Russia?"

Pavel Snegov spread his hands. "Prison conditions are regrettable the world over, I am sure," he said sadly.

"Yes, I think they are," Laddy agreed. "Not all nations, however, subject their best thinkers and artists to such conditions."

"Best thinkers and—" Snegov shook his head in disbelief. "My dear Miss Penreith, what would you? A disruptive element even in his early school life, thrown out of the university. . . ."

Laddy smiled in real amusement. "You know, I rather thought you might spare me that," she said, and he fell silent. Finishing the last of her coffee, she set down her cup and dropped an exorbitant fifty pence on the table beside it.

"Tourist prices already," she said, "and it's only the last day of May."

"Supply and demand, Miss Penreith," responded Snegov with a smile. "The essence of the capitalist system."

"And what is the essence of the communist system, Mr. Snegov?" she asked.

"Equality," he returned, so promptly that she laughed aloud.

"Not repression?" she said, opening her eyes at him, as she got to her feet.

"Certainly not," said Pavel Snegov lightly, but he was no longer smiling.

Laddy stopped smiling, too. "Now that *is* news," she said. "I only wish my father were alive to hear it."

With a brief nod she left him, and in a few moments had threaded her way through the tables to the street. After the restaurant's cool, dark interior, the sunlight hit her with blinding force, and Laddy realized she had a headache.

It was a long walk through nearly deserted side streets to her little red car, and Laddy thought about Pavel Snegov all the way. What did he want? To frighten her a little? To pick up any information she might inadvertently drop? Or, perhaps, to assess the possibility that hell had no fury like a woman scorned?

"I SAVED you the papers, in case you haven't seen them," Margaret Smiley said as she refilled their coffee cups and returned the pot to the stove.

"I haven't seen Thursday's or Friday's," Laddy said. "Thanks, Margaret, I'd like to have a look at them."

They were sitting in Margaret's kitchen, which was immediately above Laddy's, overlooking the blooming back garden. Before her father's death, the room had been first Laddy's playroom and later her study. With the remodeling of the house they had had stairs built onto the tiny exterior balcony to give the flat access to the back garden, where Ben Smiley spent most of his time. Laddy gazed down at him now, moving lovingly through the plants and flowers.

"Ben's made the garden a showpiece in these past three years," Laddy said. "Look at the lawn, Margaret. There isn't a square inch anywhere that isn't green."

Under Ben's tutelage, the garden was in flower from May till October, with everything from lilac to magnolia, pansy to anemone.

"It's therapy for him," Margaret said prosaically. "It takes his mind off his problems. Stops him brooding. And, of course, flowers don't bite the hand that nurtures them."

"No..." Laddy agreed slowly. The door to the balcony was open, and a soft perfumed breeze, warm with the sun, blew into the kitchen. "*I* need to get out in the garden," Laddy said suddenly. "Will he need any help tomorrow, do you think?"

"Oh, Ben can always find something," Margaret said, sorting through some papers on the top of the refrigerator. "There are Thursday's and yesterday's," she said, dropping two copies of the *Herald* on the table. "Really, Laddy, those are excellent interviews. I don't know when I've read anything so good."

Margaret Smiley was the features editor of the *Herald*; this was praise indeed.

"Margaret!" Laddy exclaimed, overwhelmed. Margaret had twenty-five years of newspaper experience behind her, and she was not often lavish in her compliments.

"Harry had the good sense to copyright the interviews, of course," Margaret said. "I should think the American syndicates will want them, especially as Busnetsky's going over there next week."

"Oh, my God," said Laddy, closing her eyes in dismay.

"My dear, what on earth is wrong with that?" demanded Margaret, astonishment rippling through her tones. "You surely are delighted?"

"The interviews weren't for publication at all, Margaret," Laddy said quietly. "John Bentinck stole them from my desk and brought them to Harry as being from me, and by the time I knew anything about it, it was too late."

"Good Lord!" exclaimed Margaret, utterly incredulous. "*Stole* them? John Bentinck? Why, for goodness' sake?"

"Oh, Margaret, don't ask. In a fit of pique, I suppose. He told me he loved me."

"Why weren't the interviews for publication?" Margaret asked, frowning. She had long ago learned to believe anything she heard in the realm of human behavior, and the real anomaly in this story was not John Bentinck's underhanded activities but that the interviews should exist, and not be for publication.

"Mischa Busnetsky was a friend of my father's," Laddy explained dully. "He talked to me as a friend, but he was giving no press interviews. I was going to show them to him later on, ask if I could use them." And that was as near the truth as she was going to get. "It's bad enough just having them appear in the *Herald*. If they're syndicated, he'll be so angry I expect I'll be blackballed by every dissident group in London."

"No, you won't, my dear," said Margaret, with brusque good humor. "If the last two articles are anything like the first two, you've done the dissident movement more good than they've seen in years. They'll love you. And so will Busnetsky, when he calms down. But I must say, John's behavior is very shocking. Does Harry know about it?"

"He does now," said Laddy dryly. She paused. "There's something else about John," she said hesitantly. "I've thought it over, and I'm going to keep quiet about it, but I'd like to tell you about it, Margaret, if you wouldn't mind."

"Of course," said Margaret.

She listened intently, stroking her lips with forefinger and thumb, shaking her head. "He doesn't look the type, does he?" she said, when Laddy had finished the story of the photo exclusive of the cave art.

"I never thought so," Laddy agreed. "Am I right to keep quiet about it, Margaret?"

"I think you can only follow your own instincts," said Margaret. "Have you talked to John since you discovered this?"

"No, and I simply don't want to," said Laddy. "I don't want to speak to him ever again. I wish he'd just disappear."

But John Bentinck was not about to disappear. As Laddy sat over her typewriter and telephone in the *Herald* newsroom Monday morning trying to get back in touch with her job, she became aware of a presence in front of her desk and knew without looking that it was John.

Laddy continued to read the copy she had just typed, her hand stretched across the typewriter to hold up the paper in the carriage.

"Congratulations, Laddy," John said, his northern voice warm but hesitant. "That stuff on Busnetsky was really good."

"Go away, John," she said quietly, her fingers dropping onto the typewriter keys as she resumed typing.

"Laddy, I want to talk to you," he said in an urgent undervoice. "Come to lunch with me today. Please."

"No," Laddy replied. She had so far not looked at him, but she did so now, her eyes cold, distant, accusing.

"Laddy, I've got an explanation!"

"No doubt you do," she said shortly. "So does everybody. I don't want to hear it. For the record—" she pulled the copy from her typewriter, ripped the carbons from it and separated the sheets into their various piles "—I don't want to listen to you, talk to you, be with you, dine with you, see you or hear from you."

"And when we have to work together?" John asked. Laddy stood up and pushed the chair under the desk.

"Get out of my life, John," she said tiredly. She turned and walked past the clippings library toward the coffee machine. She could feel herself shaking from head to foot, and there was a scream rising in her throat that would surely escape her if John Bentinck said another word to her.

Gratefully she reached for the plastic cup of coffee the machine produced in response to her ten pence and brought it shaking to her lips.

"I did it because I love you, Laddy," said his voice beside her, and in another second she was looking at a stunned John Bentinck shaking his head and gasping, and blinking hot coffee out of his eyes. For a timeless moment Laddy watched the stain spread over his dark shirt, then she turned on her heel and strode down the corridor toward the newsroom and her desk.

Harry was looking for her. "Your Busnetsky stuff has been taken by the syndicates, dear girl," he told her. "It'll be running all over the States and Canada next week. If he's running as scheduled, that gives him a full week after his arrival to generate interest, tell him."

Laddy laughed shakily. "That's. . .that's terrific,

Harry. Thank you." She knew Harry had worked hard to sell the interviews. "Aren't you afraid I'll get so bigheaded you'll lose me?"

Harry looked at her consideringly. "Frankly, dear girl, I am," he said. "But never mind. You keep onto Busnetsky while he's in America, will you? There's a lot more there than we've seen."

"Could you give it to somebody else, Harry?" she said, striving to keep her voice toneless. Harry gave her a long look from under raised brows. "He was really angry about those articles," she explained hastily. "He won't want to speak to me again."

Harry laughed. 'He'll soon get over that, if he's got any sense. Those articles are the best thing that could have happened to him. The Americans will love him before he's opened his mouth."

Shouting his name, somebody waved the phone receiver at Harry from the back bench, and he sidestepped Laddy to go to take it. "You stick with him, dear girl. He's all yours," Harry said as he moved away. Laddy sank into her chair and automatically reached out her hand as her own phone rang.

It was the Israeli stringer, calling her from The Good Fence on the Lebanese border. There had been a dogfight in the air over Israel and Lebanon, and three planes had gone down. The stringer had an exclusive on the identity of the downed Israeli pilot: he was the son of a famous general who had fought in the 1948, 1956, 1967 and 1973 wars and who had lost another son in the 1973 Yom Kippur war. No one knew whether the young pilot was dead or taken prisoner in Lebanon.

"Thank you," said Laddy, when she had got the story.

"Shalom," said Saul Ben-David.

"Shalom," agreed Laddy. "Do you think it's possible on this earth?" But Saul Ben-David had rung off.

"DON'T close the door, Laddy," John pleaded. "Please, I just want to talk to you, I just want to explain."

"There's no need to explain what's self-evident," Laddy said tightly, and moved to shut the door. The sight of John on her doorstep filled her with such anguished hatred she could hardly speak. Was that what Mischa had felt when he told her to stay off his property, she wondered? The thought tore at her, screamed through her body. If what Mischa felt for her was any shadow of this horrid, evil feeling, it would kill her.

"Please, Laddy," John was begging her in the summer dusk. She closed her eyes, felt her nails digging into her palms.

"All right, John," she said, and stepped back to let him in.

"I can't clear myself, Laddy," he said when they had moved to the sitting room. "I can't make it look any better. I just want you to know how it happened, that's all. Okay?"

He sat with his elbows on his knees, his hands clasped lightly between them, his blond head hanging forward as he looked down at the floor. Laddy took a breath.

"Okay," she said flatly, and waited for the explanation she did not want to hear.

After she had left him on the meadow that night, John said, he had followed her across the meadow at a distance. He had really thought only of speaking to her again. Then, he had noticed Mischa walking to the cottage from another direction, and by the time Mischa had opened the cottage door, John knew who he was. He had taken several pictures, some at the open doorway, two through the kitchen window.

Except for their first embrace at the open door, the meeting between Laddy and Mischa had not seemed very friendly, and John had gone into Laddy's cottage to wait for her. After an hour Mischa's cottage was dark, and John was insane with jealousy. He began to search through the papers on her desk for some evidence that she and Mischa were lovers, had known one another before. When he found the interview file, he had thought of nothing except that if the press knew Busnetsky's whereabouts, the idyll would be over and Laddy would return to her senses. He had driven back to London like a madman.

"You loved me, Laddy, you know you did," John said. "If he hadn't been released just when he was, damn him, you and I would have gone to

Greece together. Don't say we wouldn't,'' he said sharply, "because I know we would. Those bloody Russians! If they'd waited one lousy month, Laddy, it would have been all the other way around.... I kept thinking about that, all the way back to London. I drove straight to the *Herald* and got there just as Harry was getting in, at seven. I gave him the file. I said you'd asked me to give it to him, and then it was all out of my hands. I was sorry afterward: I'm sorry now. But Laddy, after all those years, if they'd only kept Busnetsky one more month!'' he said pleadingly.

Mischa had said the same thing, on the same night. "After eight years, I came so close to losing you?" he had whispered. But they were both wrong, and she knew it as surely as if she had lived her life twice: there was no way she would ever have been lost to Mischa Busnetsky, whether she had gone to Greece with John or not. She loved him, she had always loved him. No matter where she was, who she was with, if he had called, she would have run to him.

John saw it in her eyes, and squeezed shut his own and turned his head away.

"God," he said bitterly, and then, "Laddy, I'm sorry. I didn't know.... Laddy, say you forgive me for it!"

"I can forgive you for stealing my papers, John," she said tonelessly, "but not for the damage you caused by it. I can't ever forgive you for that. You made him think I betrayed him, and that made him betray me. Nothing can ever fix that, and I won't forgive you for it as long as I live.''

John was white to the lips. *''Laddy!''* he whispered hoarsely. ''Laddy, don't look at me like that. Laddy, listen to me—I was crazy, I was insane with jealousy! I've never done anything like that in my life before, I swear it!''

It was an impassioned plea, and his handsome blue eyes were imploringly apologetic. If she had known less, she might have been moved. But she was untouched.

''No?'' she said dispassionately, looking at him from what seemed a great distance. ''But you have since, haven't you? Or don't you consider taking an undeserved photo credit to be theft? No, please don't say anything. Just go. I don't want to listen to you anymore.''

When it was all over and she had seen John's car drive away, she phoned Harry at home.

''Harry,'' she said. ''You originally gave me most of this week off, remember? I came back today because it seemed stupid not to, but would you mind if I stayed off tomorrow and Wednesday after all?''

''And whose trail are you on now?'' Harry joked.

''My own,'' she said. ''I'm exhausted, Harry. Do you mind?''

''No, dear girl,'' he said. ''You looked like death warmed over today. Why don't you take the rest of the week off, since you can hardly be said to have had a holiday? And I'll see you next Monday looking more like the Laddy we all know and love, hmm?''

"Thanks, Harry," she said, and when she hung up she sat without moving for a long time.

BEN SMILEY had been a union man all his life. He had fought hard for the workers in the plant where he had worked for forty years. He had fought for the promotion of workers through the ranks into management and then refused such advancement himself in order to stay in the union. Ben Smiley had been a fighter, and he had won his battles.

One day a young man who, thanks to Ben's efforts, had been able to cross the line from worker to management had done what management had not previously been able to do: he had engineered Ben Smiley's dismissal. From that day, Ben Smiley was a broken man. He had refused to fight the dismissal and refused to look for another job, and he gave up on life.

Three years ago, forced to move by loss of Ben's income, the Smileys had moved into the converted upper story of Laddy's house, and shortly afterward Ben had begun to take an interest in the garden. He had been perfectly willing, when she asked him, to share his interest with Laddy.

Margaret had told her that the garden was Ben's therapy, but although Laddy had worked hard there the whole of yesterday, all she had achieved was enough fatigue and soreness to put her soundly to sleep the entire night. The peace that Ben seemed to find there she had not found.

Laddy sat back on her heels now and stretched the tired muscles of her back, then twisted round till she caught sight of Ben's gray-haired stocky figure by the rose trellis on the garden wall. He was wearing old gray trousers and a V-neck sleeveless pullover over a casual shirt left open at the neck. The column of his throat was thick and brown, and with a new awareness that love had given her, Laddy realized that Ben Smiley was a very virile man. His thick workman's hands moved among the delicate rosebuds with a gentle strength, an expertise that, for the first time, Laddy recognized as sensitive. She did not know Ben Smiley very well; he was a silent man, though he had been a vociferous fighter once, and she had always been a little afraid of pushing conversation on him.

Yet when she had asked him if he could use her help in the garden for a few days, saying that she needed some exercise, he had looked at her as though he understood that what she really needed was a measure of the peace he had found.

"Ben," she said now, wiping the back of her hand across her forehead. He turned to look at her, and suddenly everything was very simple.

"Ben, how do you learn to live with betrayal?" she asked quietly.

He was silent a long time, working among the rosebuds, and Laddy watched her trowel turn over fresh damp earth onto the gray surface soil.

"You become accustomed to being less of a person than you were," Ben's voice came at last, and she knew that it was the first time he had said it, even understood it in this way. "When someone betrays you, they kill a part of you, the part that knows, that feels the betrayal. Or perhaps you kill off that part because it knows too much. The worse the betrayal, the larger the part of you that knows it, that must die."

There was perfect silence around them suddenly, inside and outside the garden. No noise of traffic or of distant voices reached her ears, only the sound of wind in the flowers, of insects in the summer sun, framing the quiet deep-toned voice that came to her from across the garden.

"The first pain of betrayal, profound though it may be, you overcome almost automatically. And you're grateful; you think it wasn't so bad after all. But sooner or later you understand the price you paid to overcome it—you understand that part of you has died, that you are no longer a full human being. The most difficult thing to live with is not the betrayal but the awful bitterness you feel at not being a whole person. It's like learning to live with being crippled, I've often thought."

Laddy had turned to face him, her arms around her drawn-up knees. When the sob welled up inside her, she did not fight it, but dropped her head forward and wept openly, unashamedly, wildly, like a wounded animal.

Ben let her weep. He did not console her or touch

her or look distressed. He merely stood and let her weep.

"Thank you," she said wiping her face, when the storm had passed.

"Those are marigolds," Ben said, gesturing to a row of potted bits of green that were sitting on the grass. "You can plant them up against the wall there. Space them out to run the whole length between the shrubs."

After a few moments, Laddy laid the trowel down and began to dig with her bare hands. The sun burned on her back and head, and the earth was rich and moist under her fingers. Suddenly her nose caught the pungent odor of fresh, fertile earth and growing things. At least the plants were alive. It was comforting to know that something was fully alive in the world.... Laddy turned her head and glanced at Ben over her shoulder.

"They don't ask questions, do they?" she said softly.

"No, they just grow," agreed Ben.

ON FRIDAY MORNING Richard Digby called her.

"Are you ill, Laddy?" he asked in concern. "I tried you at the *Herald* and they said you'd been off all week."

"No, but I needed a rest after my hectic holiday," she meant to say it jokingly, but somehow it sounded bright with pain.

"Yes, I see," said Richard after a moment. "Are you interested in news about Mischa, then?"

Her heart began to hammer. "Of course," she said, feeling oddly stifled. "He's always good copy." She knew what was coming, and she squeezed her eyes shut, waiting for it.

"We came up from Trefelin last night—he's catching a British Airways flight at noon. He's flying to New York and then to Denver."

If Mischa Busnetsky had been on his way to the moon he couldn't be more distant from her than he was right now, yet Laddy knew by the sudden wrenching inside, that somewhere, somehow, a tiny seed of hope had been sprouting undetected in her heart. "He...he didn't ask you to give me this item, by any chance, did he?" she asked, her voice rising high and hoarse on the last word.

"Well, I..." Richard began hesitantly.

"No, never mind," said Laddy, managing a matter-of-fact tone. "Why is he going to Denver?"

"From there he'll be going to a health clinic for a month or two, mostly for rest, supervised diet and exercise," Richard said. "He's considering several lecture dates after that but hasn't agreed to anything yet."

"Any chance for pictures at the airport?" Laddy asked. "Or a few comments?"

"Well, in fact, we'd prefer to have you hold this till the noon edition so he can get away without any fuss," Richard said.

"No one else knows?" she asked, wrinkling her brow. "Are there no media people in Trefelin keeping an eye on Busnetsky?"

"If there are we managed to avoid them, we think."

"Someone's bound to be staking out the airport," Laddy said. "They must realize by now that you've left Trefelin."

"Perhaps," Richard said. "Brigit is a rather able conspirator, though, you know."

Laddy smiled. "I believe you," she said. "How did you leave them, Richard? How's Rhodri?"

"Well, the archaeological team is all set up, but I suppose you knew that."

"Yes," said Laddy. She had kept in regular touch with Roger Smith by phoning him at Trefelin's pub every night when he went in for dinner.

"Rhodri, if you want the truth," Richard said with a chuckle, "is playing the twelve-year-old Christ in the temple among the rabbis. And they are all enjoying themselves hugely."

Laddy laughed aloud for the first time since she had left Trefelin.

"I can just see him," she said, conjuring up the memory of his dark eyes, his wide grin.... They chatted for a while and then Richard said he must go.

"Will you be telling Mischa you called me?" she asked, driven by a need that superseded reason.

"Oh, yes, I think I must."

Her heart began to beat loudly, painfully, so that she felt it through her entire system. She could not let him go without a word, not while there was still a chance. She had to keep the possibility open, even if the pain were to destroy her. Pride didn't matter nor did pain—nor, in the end, did betrayal. All that mattered was that she loved him. Laddy swallowed.

"Tell him...tell him I hope to see him again sometime, would you?" she asked.

"My dear Laddy, of course you will. He'll be coming back, you know," Richard said heartily.

"I suppose so," said Laddy. "Will you tell him, though?"

CHAPTER FOURTEEN

IT WAS a clear, hot summer in London. Wimbledon was rained out nearly every day in a chilly two-week stretch of bad weather, but thereafter the sun scarcely set on the British Isles. Each day was hot and golden, and, it seemed, even more so on weekends. Every Londoner who owned so much as a four-foot-square plot of grass either gardened it or sunbathed on it, according to his inclinations, until by mid-August the entire population of the city appeared to have had a holiday on the Costa del Sol.

There was rain too but, astoundingly, only after sundown or in a brief afternoon shower that left everything refreshed and the sun shining brighter and warmer than before.

In a troubled economy, seeds, at least, were cheap, and almost overnight window boxes began to appear on office buildings and in front of shops and boutiques, so that throughout central London, one was constantly catching sight of fresh-growing flowers and odd spots of bright greenery.

The garden behind the house in Highgate flourished like a jungle under the constant attention of Ben and Laddy. By late July, the August plants were flowering already, and all the earlier plants were refusing to die. In August they stopped thinking about what should be blooming when: it seemed as though everything was going to bloom at once and forever. The climbing roses ran wildly along the high garden wall like a thick blanket of pink that expanded its territory every day and perfumed the air of the whole garden.

"There hasn't been a summer to equal it since before the war," Ben said.

"Do you suppose England's drifting downstream?" Margaret asked in a sudden brainstorm. "That by now we're off the coast of Spain, and no one's noticed?"

"It's a thought," said Laddy.

Laddy was losing weight. She had always been slim but rounded, and she was the sort of woman who would not become angular no matter how thin she was. But over the course of the summer the effects of long hours working in the garden and her almost unnoticed loss of interest in food combined to make her very slim indeed.

She was not sleeping well in the warm summer nights. She dreamed constantly of Mischa, and she awoke to find the bed empty beside her, with a sense of loss as deep and tortured as though he had left her yesterday.

You have slept alone for twenty-five years, she told herself sternly as she lay wakeful, as usual, at five o'clock one morning. *Only one morning in all those years did you wake up at the side of Mischa*

Busnetsky! A man doesn't become a habit after one night!

But that was her mind talking: her arms and her heart knew better.

That summer she began a series of interviews with a beautiful young woman named Beth who had become a prostitute to support her heroin habit. Laddy spent hours with the woman, who was bright, intelligent and articulate—as long as she had had her fix. Twice during the summer Laddy had watched Beth change from a confident, with-it lady into a sweating, anxious spitfire who had not got home on time. On one of these occasions a traffic jam had held them up for over an hour, and for the last ten minutes of that hour Laddy had piloted her little red car with an unrecognizable woman beside her blaming and cursing her in the repetitious but pithy vocabulary of the streets, which gained immediacy from the barely controlled violence behind it.

Laddy wrote of that experience from two points of view: her own and Beth's. "And Don't Be Late," she called the article.

"You're not going to the extreme of trying it yourself to get a story, are you, Laddy?" Harry asked when he read it. "This description of being late for a fix is almost too good. How do you know so much about it?"

Laddy smiled and shook her head. *I'm cold turkeying from Mischa Busnetsky, that's how, Harry,* she could have said. *And believe me, he was some habit.*

It was not the sort of series that the *Herald* generally printed. Normally such things were the province of the large Sunday newspapers. But Laddy's interview articles with Mischa Busnetsky had been a prestige item for the paper and had been picked up by syndicates all over the Commonwealth and the States. When Laddy had argued with Harry for the right to do this series, he had privately thought it was the sort of violent switch that was needed to counteract the gently falling standards of the *Herald*. He had gone to battle with the *Herald* editor for the series, and no one was more surprised than Harry when he had won.

"I can't let you use all your time on it, Laddy. I'm still going to have to see you around here," he had said. "I've been informed that the *Herald* 'can't afford the luxury of investigative journalists'—so you're going to have to earn your keep in the regular way."

They had laughed together and shaken their heads over it.

"There's foresight for you," said Laddy.

So a great deal of her own time was spent with Beth, whose identity she kept secret even from Harry. Laddy was glad of the involvement. The harder she worked and the more time she spent with people, the less time she had to herself to think. Thinking was the great enemy. She avoided it religiously, working hard and late till she was too exhausted to do anything except fall into bed and sleep.

By the end of August she was operating on five hours' sleep a night.

In mid-September she spent three days on a visit to Wales to get a follow-up story on Rhodri's Cave, as the media were now unanimously calling it. She spent the three days with Rhodri's family—Mairi and her husband Alun, and Brigit.

Rhodri Lewis had become a minor celebrity, Laddy discovered on her first evening, as she sat with the family around the table in the homey kitchen, looking through his collection of clippings. It soon became evident that his pride and joy was the coverage he had been given in the international edition of *Time* magazine: an article and a two-page color spread of the now-famous photos Laddy had taken so many months ago in the cavern. There was also a photo of Rhodri himself, standing in the cave mouth with an air of being lord of all he surveyed. Underneath this photo was the caption, "Not looking for a lost sheep."

Laddy threw back her head and laughed. "Rhodri," she said, "you are a journalist's dream! You're so newsworthy—I'm surprised you haven't been approached to do a talk show!"

Brigit clapped her hands and let out a yelp of joy. "He has!" she whooped, and Rhodri's face broadened in an ear-to-ear grin.

"An American show," he bubbled happily. "I am flying to New York in two weeks, and Brigit, too. She is coming to look after me. I am a little nervous, you know, but I will be very interested to see the Americans.''

Laddy hugged him, laughing, congratulating him. ''I guarantee you they'll return the interest,'' she said.

The cave art almost without doubt was felt to be Magdalenian, she found when she visited the team on the site. The pigments matched, the medium matched; there were many points of comparison.

There were odd differences, too, not least of which was the predominance of the now-famous reindeer. But the archaeological team was taking its time, and the real item gleaned from her visit to Wales was Rhodri's impending visit to New York.

''How is Mischa?'' the young boy asked her Sunday afternoon as she climbed into her car for the trip back to London, and she bit her lip at the look in his eyes.

''I don't know, Rhodri,'' she said. ''I haven't heard from him since he left for America. I suppose he's still in the clinic, getting well.''

''I wish we could see him,'' Rhodri said.

And Laddy replied softly, meaning it: ''So do I.''

It gave her the courage, when she got back to London, to ring up Dr. Edmund Bear, who was connected with the Colorado clinic, and to ask him for news of Mischa.

''Well, as far as I know, he's still in the clinic,'' Ned Bear said. ''I can't imagine them keeping him much longer, though, unless....''

''Unless?'' prompted Laddy.

"Unless he's a much sicker man than I thought," Ned Bear said.

There was a short, thick silence.

"Look," said Ned Bear. "I'll make inquiries if you like, and why don't you take the address of the clinic and write him? He would certainly tell you his plans. In fact, I thought—" Tactfully, he broke off. "Let me get the address," he said.

In the small hours of a sleepless night, Laddy got up to write Mischa Busnetsky a letter. "Rhodri and I were talking about you yesterday..." she wrote, sitting at her kitchen table in the circular glow cast by the hanging lamp. In the peaceful solitude of the kitchen at night, the memory of Mischa was suddenly strong, so strong that she felt that if she turned her head he must be there. She deliberately did not turn her head, reveling in that sense of his presence, not wanting it destroyed.

When she let it out of its tiny box, her love, her need to see him, expanded like a magic tent, and in seconds it attained uncontrollable proportions.

She would beg one more time, she told herself. She would beg for the third time for Mischa Busnetsky to love her—the third and last time. There was nothing to prevent her except pride, and Laddy cast that impatiently aside as though she had never had more than a nodding acquaintance with it. She *was* a beggar, anyway—starving and needy, and pride would provide no nourishment. So she forgot his betrayal, forgot his accusations, forgot everything except love, and very gently she begged Mischa Bus-netsky to love her.

That night autumn arrived, and the air was suddenly crisp and alive. In the morning the garden seemed thick with fall colors: bright red and gold and burnt orange. Going out the back door with the letter to Mischa in her hand, Laddy paused and breathed deeply in the bright autumn air. It was the season of the dying of the year, and yet for her it had always been a source of energy, excitement, new resolution.

And optimism. At the corner of the street she slid the letter into the mouth of the round red postbox and listened to it drop. *Third time lucky,* she told herself gaily. *If he doesn't answer this I'll make myself stop loving him. I'll never think of him again.* But in her heart she knew he would answer it.

On Wednesday afternoon, Salvatore, the copy-boy, paused by her desk with a pile of teletype newsprint in his hand.

"Are you still covering Busnetsky?" he asked, so unexpectedly that she snapped forward in her chair and spilled her coffee.

"Yes, yes I am," she said, her heart pounding. "What is it?"

"Here," he said, dropping a scrap of newsprint in front of her, and ignoring the stain spreading on the knee of her trousers, Laddy snatched it up and devoured it with her eyes. It was a bulletin from a wire service, short and to the point. Soviet dissident Mikhail Busnetsky was going on the lecture circuit in the United States, and to kick it off, he would be making his first appearance on a talk show the following week.

DURING THE FIRST WEEK of October, one of the prestigious national dailies approached Laddy with the suggestion of an offer of a job as reporter in the newsroom: her interview pieces with Mischa Busnetsky and Beth had not gone unnoticed. It took Laddy completely by surprise, but when she had absorbed the impact, she was thrilled. That such a paper should come to her was an enormous compliment. Holding her breath with excitement, Laddy agreed to meet with the paper's editor.

She was buoyant with an accumulation of excitement and expectation now, for on top of this staggering offer was the deep-seated realization that if Mischa were going to answer her letter at all, it would have to be very soon.

For three days she lived in a bubble of almost unbearable excitement. She met with the famous editor on Friday, and he told her quite frankly he was impressed. There would have to be another meeting on Monday, and he expected to be able to make her a firm offer by Monday afternoon. Suddenly Laddy knew it would happen. It had to: the time was right, the feeling was right, everything was perfect.

And it was only fitting that on Saturday she should walk out to the front hall to see a letter on the mat with an American stamp on it. From Mischa, she knew at once; it could only be from Mischa. She bent and picked up the letter, smiling, and inside she felt her heart opening like a flower. She perceived how cold she had been in past months by the sudden warmth that flowed through her. Mischa loved her; there was nothing else in the world that mattered.

The address was typed, the postmark was New York City. Ten days ago, she knew, he had been in New York for his talk-show appearance. Laddy moved down the hall to sit in the kitchen.

The letter was typed too—a single sheet.

Dear Ms Penreith,

Mr. Busnetsky is very busy now, as I am sure you will understand, with his travel and lectures taking up a great deal of his time and energy. He has read your letter, however, and has asked me to thank you for it. He appreciates your warmly expressed support and encouragement and hopes that you will understand why he cannot answer your letter personally.

Yours sincerely,
Marsha Miller, Personal Secretary

Laddy stood up, her breath coming through her open lips in uncontrolled gasps, her hands clasped over her mouth. Like a demented brutalized animal she ran, wildly, gasping, stumbling against the furniture and doors in her erratic path, until finally she reached the bathroom. There, feeling as though she had drunk in sickening poison through her eyes, she threw up.

Then, sweating, shaking and colder than she had ever been in her life, she bathed her face in warm water. Then she reached for a towel and patted her face dry. Now she was calm. She took a deep breath and stood straight. She felt different, strange, and it was a moment before she understood the difference: the pain was gone. The nagging ache she had lived with for the past four months had disappeared as though it had never been. Mischa Busnetsky had no power to hurt her; she was only surprised that she had ever thought he did. How could he hurt her? People could only hurt you if you loved them, and she had been mistaken in thinking she had ever loved Mischa Busnetsky.

She caught sight of herself in the mirror over the sink and gave her pale haggard reflection a cool smile. Of course she didn't love Mischa Busnetsky. How could you love someone you hated?

ON MONDAY MORNING one of the unions went out on strike against the national paper that Laddy had been thinking of as her new home, and the editor called her with his apologies.

"I'm afraid this is going to put off any hopes of your joining us for the duration," he said. "I'm really awfully sorry, Laddy. I hope that when this is over there's enough money left in the till to warrant our talking to you again."

"I hope so, too," she said, and discussed the details of the strike with him with interested concern. She knew she was disappointed, but the disappointment did not touch her. She felt as though she were hearing the news at a distance or reading an item in a ten-year-old paper: it was unfortunate, but it had happened so long ago. "Well," she muttered to herself as she hung up the phone by her typewriter—the editor had called her at the office as soon as he heard the news—"at least I didn't hand in my resignation." She sat for a moment wondering when she would get another chance like the one that had just passed by.

MISCHA BUSNETSKY was making waves on the lecture circuit. Not content with the traditional dissident fare of a discussion of Soviet methods of suppression and prison-camp conditions, he had begun to tell the Americans how Western capitalism was contributing to the maintenance of that system and what mistakes they were making in their perceptions of and dealings with the Soviets. His name began to come over the wire-services teletype now and then, more and more frequently attached to the epithet "outspoken."

Oddly enough, the Americans loved him. "This is not the traditional anti-Communist dogma," a prominent newspaper said in an editorial. "Mr. Busnetsky is not concerned with Reds in the woodshed but with the real attitudes underlying Soviet policy in Asia, Africa and the Middle East. He deserves a hearing...."

"He's being cheered by the college audiences," a stringer in Florida told Laddy over the phone late in October. "No one knows exactly why, but the magazines are starting to say that he's 'tapping the new mood in America.' "

"What new mood is that?" asked Laddy, dryly, smiling at this sample of journalese.

"You tell me," said the stringer.

"Have you talked to Busnetsky at all yourself?" she asked.

"Not so far," the stringer said, "but I cornered his secretary for five minutes in the hotel bar last night, and she—"

"His secretary?" Laddy interrupted, her voice growling oddly over a sudden frog in her throat.

"His personal secretary—his traveling companion, if you want my opinion. Marsha Miller—of a New York family that has enough money to guarantee that the beautiful Marsha is *not* performing this arduous duty to keep the wolf from the door," he said, with heavy double entendre.

"No?" Laddy asked, unable to open her mouth on another word.

"The salary, if she's getting one, might be keeping her in panty hose—no, strike that—I can't believe the beautiful Marsha wears anything as prosaic as panty hose. The salary keeps her in nylon stockings, if she's getting a salary."

"What does she look like, Gary?" Laddy couldn't stop herself from asking.

"Hair as black as midnight," the stringer answered with warm promptness, "and blue eyes that could turn a man to ice at twenty paces and a Southern-belle charm that she can turn off and on like a tap. I tell you, whatever Busnetsky has been through in the past ten years, she intends to be his compensation—and in my book she stands a very good chance of succeeding. She could compensate me for nearly anything."

The newsroom was drafty and cold, and Laddy shivered as a block of cold October air settled chillingly around her. When she had hung up on Gary Boyle in Florida, she rolled copy paper into the typewriter carriage and with awkward fingers made stiff with the cold, began to type.

"Soviet dissident Mikhail Busnetsky, who was expelled from Russia to the West six months ago, took his American hosts to task yet again yesterday in a hard-hitting speech that accused the American government...."

"Wasn't Busnetsky a friend of your father's?" Harry asked mildly, nudging her copy with a negligent hand when she crossed to the back bench later to ask him a question.

"Well—he was certainly one of my father's pet causes," Laddy said. "Why?"

"He must have thought you were his friend, too, when he gave you those interviews."

Laddy sighed. "What are you trying to say, Harry?"

"This sounds like a pretty hostile reading of the facts, Laddy," Harry said, exhaling smoke and looking at her with one considering eye squeezed nearly shut.

"I just spoke to a stringer in Florida, Harry. That's what's going on. Do you want me to lie about it for old times' sake?"

Harry did not answer that. "Do you know what it is, dear girl?" he said, after a moment. "You lose your objectivity where this man is concerned. And you've done so right from the beginning. Right from the first time you mentioned his name to me."

"Harry, that's simply not true," she blustered.

"Think it over," was all Harry said.

After that she toned down her accounts of Busnetsky, because if she did not, Harry would. Nevertheless, other people noticed her change of attitude, and not least of these was John Bentinck.

In the last week of October there was a major jewel robbery in central London. Harry got the tip almost the moment it happened and, his crime reporter being out of reach, asked Laddy to rush over to cover the story for the *Herald*'s final edition.

Shortly after she arrived on the scene—a large exclusive jeweler's shop patronized by the very wealthy—John Bentinck arrived, camera bag over his shoulder, having been routed out of a Fleet Street pub by Richard Snapes.

They had worked together several times since Laddy's return from Wales and had always kept conversation to a minimum, but today John kept up a friendly intermittent chatter as he tried to get a clear photo of the interior of the large glass-fronted store, where it was obvious that Scotland Yard was still questioning the patrons who had been in the shop when the armed but bloodless robbery had occurred. And when Laddy came out of the phone booth after calling in the story, John was waiting for her outside.

"Harry ask you to stick around?" he asked, and she nodded shortly.

"If you want my opinion, they'll be in there till it's time for us to go home," he said, with his old, easy smile. "If we grab the front table in that restaurant before anyone else we can keep an eye on the proceedings in comfort. Quick!" he whispered conspiratorially, taking her arm. "Here comes whatshisname from the *Mail* to grab it."

They began to run toward the restaurant in the crisp exhilarating fall air, Laddy nearly stumbling in her high heels and being saved by John's firm grip on her arm. By the time they had made their way to the booth in the window, they were laughing together like truant schoolchildren and were just in time to see "whatshisname from the *Mail*" hail a taxi and drive off.

"Now there's a sore loser," John said in exaggerated northern lugubriousness, and set them both laughing again. They ordered coffee, and it came strong and hot. Laddy comforted her chilly hands on the cup and sobered suddenly, looking at John.

"Oh, Laddy," he said ruefully, smiling. "It's so good to laugh with you again."

"John—" she began warningly.

But he interrupted her with, "Don't put me off saying it. Maybe I'll look a fool and you'll tell me you still hate me, but I don't care. It's been five months, Laddy—I know because I've counted every day. I don't want to go on like this. I want to be your friend again, on whatever terms you say."

She was silent, looking at him, her lower lip between her teeth.

"You don't love him anymore, Laddy. If you ever did. That stuff you're writing these days isn't bitter, it isn't hurt—it's just cold. You've got nothing for him.

"I know how badly he hurt you, lass, I know because I know you. And I know you think that it was my fault. But if he'd really loved you, Laddy, a few newspaper articles wouldn't have changed his mind. He might have been angry, he might have come and killed me—but he couldn't have put that look in your eye, not if he loved you, Laddy. Don't forget I saw that look. It ripped my guts out. If I'd made you look like that I'd have crossed the desert naked to put things right for you again." He paused and rubbed his hand across his face. "As God knows I tried."

"What do you mean, you tried?" Laddy asked, frowning with surprise.

He looked at her a long moment. "You mean he never told you?"

"Told me what?" she demanded.

"Laddy, I wrote Busnetsky and told him how those interviews got in the *Herald*," John said slowly. "Didn't he ever mention it?"

Laddy felt suddenly breathless.

"When?" she asked, her eyes big with attention, like a battered child waiting to see if it will be struck again. "When did you write him?"

John's mouth tightened and she saw in his eyes that he knew that what he said would hurt her. "Last June," he said gruffly. "Before he left Wales."

Long before she had written him herself. Long before he had let his beautiful secretary read and answer Laddy's own pleading letter. Laddy laughed shortly, a harsh bark of self-deprecation.

"What a bastard!" she exclaimed, shaking her head. "Why do we always fall for the bastards?"

John reached out his hand and covered hers. "You fell for me first, remember," he said softly. "And I'm no bastard. A fool, an idiot sometimes, but no bastard. Don't think of him anymore, Laddy."

She said calmly, with perfect truth, "I never think of him, except when I do a story. You were right—I don't feel anything for him—I can't remember now why I ever did."

His handsome face crinkled into a devastating smile that made the waitress coming up with their check inhale audibly and smile back with a hypnotized air.

She was a very pretty young girl who had erased most of the Cockney from her voice, and breathily she asked, "Are you an American?"

"Not likely, love," John said, emphasizing his northern accent, and she laughed delightedly.

"I thought you were a film star," she said. "You should be, really."

"No talent, love," he replied, rolling his eyes at Laddy, and reluctantly his admirer left them.

"I wouldn't go so far as to say *that*," Laddy said, smiling at him, and John laughed.

"Be fair, now. Did I encourage that?" he asked.

"No," replied Laddy. "You were encouraging me, and all she got was the spillover. That's what makes you so dangerous."

"Too dangerous for you to have dinner with me tonight?" he asked.

She dropped her eyes uncomfortably.

"John, I don't think...."

"Just dinner, Laddy, no strings attached. I'm not expecting anything. Come on, lass—say yes."

She had to start living again sometime.

"Yes, all right, John," she said.

"LADDY," Richard Digby said over the phone a few days later, "who's your source for these stories you've been doing on Mischa lately?"

"No one particular source, Richard," she said easily. "Why?"

"Because the stories are slanted. Mischa isn't insulting the Americans, and the Americans aren't feeling insulted. Helen and I have just come back from California where we heard him speak, and he is being extremely well received."

"Thanks for telling me," Laddy said. "He must be enjoying himself, then."

"Yes, perhaps," Richard said. "But he's not really a public man, you know. He's very much looking forward to coming back."

Laddy paused. "Coming back?" she repeated.

"He gives his last lecture on November tenth in Seattle, flies back to New York for the party the American publisher is giving on the twelfth and then straight back to London for another publication party on the fourteenth. A very big party, indeed; the media are invited as well as the reviewers. I hope we'll see you there?"

"Of course!" she said, successfully injecting enthusiasm into her tone. "The fourteenth—is that the publication date? For both of the books?"

"That's right," said Richard.

"They've worked fast, haven't they?"

"We had excellent translators, and the Americans were very definite about coming out in time for the Christmas market."

"Oh, of course," Laddy said. "I expect he'll get a good sale in the States, with his lecture tour just finishing."

"We think so," Richard agreed placidly. "I've had review copies sent to you, of course; if you haven't received them yet, you will soon."

The package arrived at the newsroom late that afternoon. Laddy tore open the end and was just pulling the books out of the wrapper when her phone rang. It was Margaret Smiley.

"My car's gone in for service again," she said. "Could you give me a lift home tonight? I'll be a bit late."

"Sure," Laddy said. "I'll wait for you in the pub."

"And I'll buy you a drink," a familiar voice said as she hung up, and she looked up to see John standing over her desk. She wrinkled her nose at him. "In that case I'll have something very exotic and very expensive," she said.

John sighed. "If only you wanted something homegrown—me, for instance. Come on, love, before the barbarian hordes move in and there's standing room only."

She sat at a corner table while John stood at the bar to be served, and her curiosity getting the better of her, she pulled off the wrapper to look at Mischa Busnetsky's new books.

To Make Kafka Live was a large volume of at least four hundred pages, its dust jacket navy with yellow gold lettering and trim. "Mikhail Busnetsky" took one-third of the front cover. There was a photo of him on the back, obviously taken recently. His dark hair was longer than the panther pelt she remembered, and his face looked fuller and healthier.

"My dear Miss Penreith, good evening," she heard, and before she could look up, someone sank into the chair opposite and the face of Pavel Snegov glided into her vision. "I see you are reading our friend's latest contributions to Western literature," he said with a raised eyebrow.

"Yes," she said noncommittally, unable to prevent the sudden tension that always gripped her in this man's presence. "Have you read them?"

"For what they are worth," he shrugged. "I am

afraid you will think that your father's trouble was scarcely worth it.''

A chill began creeping through the tension in her body.

"That would not be for me to judge," she said softly. "The choice and the judgment were my father's."

"And you ask no questions?" His faint accent thickened slightly with sarcasm.

"Not of my father," Laddy returned with emphasis, wishing John would come back with their drinks or Margaret would arrive.

"Of whom, then? Of Mr. Busnetsky, perhaps?" Snegov insinuated.

This was too much for Laddy. She fixed her eyes on him coldly for a long angry moment and then said icily, "I really shouldn't be surprised at your suggestion that I would blame Mr. Busnetsky for my father's death, should I? That's just the sort of unspeakable, irrational obscenity your government practices every day. Let me jog your possibly failing memory, Mr. Snegov: my father and Mischa Busnetsky were friends, and when my father was killed, Mr. Busnetsky was behind the barbed wire of prison camp number thirty-six in Perm province. He could hardly answer any questions about my father's death."

"Here's your exotic drink at last," John said, and Laddy had never been so grateful to hear his deep thick tones. "One glass of exotic, imported white wine."

CAPTIVE OF DESIRE 283

Pavel Snegov bowed and slipped out of his seat, which John immediately occupied.

"I was just having a word with Gerry," he said. "Did you know he's going to Canada?"

"Gerald Parkinson?" she asked, sipping her wine and trying to forget that Pavel Snegov had ever spoken to her. "That's a surprise. Where's he going?"

"Canada, I told you, love."

"Canada is a very big—"

"Toronto. He's going to one of the Toronto papers. I told him you were Canadian and could tell him all about it."

"John, do you know how many miles Toronto is from Vancouver? And I left there when I was ten," she said, laughing.

"Yes, I know that, but Gerald doesn't, you see," he said conspiratorially.

They were laughing together when Margaret found them, and there was a quizzical look in her eyes as she glanced from one to the other.

"I didn't know you were seeing John again," she commented to Laddy as they drove home in the wintry dusk.

"Mmm. Since a few days ago," Laddy said. "He told me he wrote to Mischa to explain that it was his fault about the interviews getting into the *Herald*. And we're just being friendly, not romantic."

Margaret absorbed that in silence.

"And how did he explain away taking the photo credit?" she asked at last.

"He said he never thought of it, he was so concerned about Mischa and the interviews. He said he handed the film over and the next thing he knew, he'd got credit for those pictures and they were all over the wire services."

"And you believe him?" asked Margaret.

"Don't you?" Laddy glanced over at Margaret in the erratic glare of the street lamps.

"I don't know. Yes, I suppose I do. And yet— once suspicion has been planted...it's not something I'd want to believe about anyone. When did he tell you this?"

"A couple of days ago," Laddy said. "By the way, have you heard about Mischa coming back to London?"

"For the publication party? Yes, we've had the invitation and the advance copies of those books. And you know, Laddy, I've been wanting to ask you— Do you remember last winter around about February, those manuscripts I found? Were they by any chance—"

"This is not for publication, Margaret: Yes, they were," Laddy answered quietly.

"I say!" exclaimed Margaret in happy awe.

Laddy carried the books into the kitchen and filled the kettle for tea. Then she settled down at the table and opened the larger volume, turning over the pages one by one.

To Make Kafka Live read the first title page, and she thought of how she had knelt in her bedroom— such a long time ago—and had seen that title in

Russian and the name beneath—M. Busnetsky—
and she could not suppress a little burst of excitement at the thought of the journey that manuscript
had made in order to arrive back in her hands at this
moment.

"Truly we were born to make Kafka live," she
read on the next page, a quote attributed to another
well-known dissident, whose name she knew.

The third page held the dedication. "To the
memory of Dr. Lewis Penreith—humanitarian,
scholar, martyr," she read.

CHAPTER FIFTEEN

MISCHA BUSNETSKY ARRIVED at Heathrow Airport on Friday morning, the fourteenth of November, and once again the media were out in force to greet him. This time, however, they awaited him in the airport VIP lounge, comfortably at their ease as they adjusted cameras, mikes and notebooks and waited for a man who would not, this time, be "uncooperative."

Laddy had a chair near the door and not too far from the cluster of microphones that marked where Busnetsky would stand to talk to them. She was wearing a black wool suit of a softly casual cut over a delicately feminine white blouse. With her black hair falling thickly around her shoulders and her pale face, the only relieving color came from her cherry-red lips and the matching red carnation on her black lapel. She leaned sideways in her chair, talking to her neighbor, her long legs smoothly crossed, her hair falling away from her ear to expose a hoop of thin gold.

She had not gained back the weight she had lost during the summer, and she had bought this suit to fit and emphasize her extreme slimness. She looked very chic, very smart, very dramatic. As she had chosen to look. And she stood out against the casually dressed, motley group of her fellow journalists like a full-color fashion model against a sepia background.

When at length they heard footsteps in the corridor outside, the members of the media focused their attention and turned expectantly to face the door, and the loud murmur that had filled the room died away. Only Laddy did not move from her elegant, negligent attitude, except to reach for a long yellow pencil from the little table beside her and allow her slim, well-manicured hands to toy carelessly with it.

The door to the lounge opened, and a man in a casual, well-fitting suit without a tie first appeared, then turned to talk to someone still outside the door. Laddy watched him curiously, for this was no airport official, yet she had not heard from the New York stringer that Busnetsky was being accompanied by either the British or American Secret Service or that he had hired a bodyguard.

Bodyguard this man certainly was, however, whatever else he called himself. Very tall, with broad muscular shoulders, a flat waist, lean hips and strong thighs and the physical air of a man who feared no one, he was the sort to set old ladies pleasurably atwitter and scare off potential trouble-makers with a glance. He had thick dark hair that curled attractively over the collar of his open-necked white shirt, and his skin was deeply tanned.

He was intensely masculine, entirely physical and somehow dangerous, and with a sudden lightheadedness, Laddy discovered what a pleasure it was to watch him. She sat with a half smile on her lips, her mouth faintly parted, and it seemed to her that time ground to a halt. During that altered time she could stare at him, feeling his raw, animal magnetism like a physical presence around her, feeling herself hypnotized. She could not have torn her eyes away from him if Mischa Busnetsky had come into the room at that moment arm in arm with Stalin.

As the bodyguard turned away from the door at last, Laddy felt herself slowly and deliberately uncross and recross her legs, the smooth nylon of her stockings making a sensuous slithering noise that she thought the whole world must hear.

The dark man's motion was momentarily checked, and as though his ears were directionally attuned, or he had been watching her out of the corner of his eye and had caught that subtle movement, he turned, slowly, and his sensuous gaze slid along her body from the tips of her smart black-and-white shoes, over the long, elegantly poised legs, over slanted hips, over waist and breasts and throat, to her mouth and eyes. Full face he looked even tougher, she saw, his mouth sensuous, the tanned flesh firm over hard cheekbones, the dark eyes....

The sound of the yellow pencil breaking between Laddy's hands was like a pistol shot in the silence as recognition flashed. Time abruptly returned to normal, and in another moment the man who was Mischa Busnetsky had moved to stand behind the microphones and was asking for questions.

She controlled her physical trembling by a violent effort of will, her hands clenching the two halves of her sharp pencil, her jaw tight.

Mischa Busnetsky, the man whom she hated with a cold violence she had never experienced for any other person, was now the most frighteningly attractive man she had seen in the whole course of her life. While he stood commandingly behind the microphones and answered questions from her colleagues, Laddy fought desperately against the clamor in her blood and learned to look at him with a faint smile that did not reach her eyes.

He answered questions for fifteen minutes, and every time his gaze brushed over her, Laddy steeled her own gaze to watchful indifference against the indefinable emotion in his glance. At length she began to feel threatened, as though some danger that she could not understand faced her and she might be attacked at any moment.

She was right. At the conclusion of the fifteen-minute session, as Mischa Busnetsky left the room and everyone around her burst into chatter and motion, she was suddenly aware of a uniformed man bending over her and saying softly, "Miss Penreith, would you come with me for a moment? Someone is asking to speak to you."

A phone call for her here could only be from Harry, and a grave emergency. Snatching up her notebook, her black trench coat and her handbag,

Laddy nodded to the man and moved after him without question. He led her out of the lounge and down a corridor to another door, which he opened for her to pass through into a small room furnished as an office. Then he closed the door behind her.

Leaving her alone with the dark and dangerous man who stood across the small room from her in front of a window that opened out onto a damp gray London morning and a silver jet that was landing in the distance.

For a fatal second she was rooted by surprise, and by the time she turned back toward the door he had crossed the small space to forestall her. A large brown hand closed like steel on her arm above the elbow, and she started as though she had been burned.

But immediately she brought herself under control, and standing motionless, her back to him, her head high, she said woodenly, "Let go of me."

"No," Mischa said softly, and that one word was enough to send ungovernable panic pulsing through her bloodstream.

"Let me go," she repeated, after a dizzy moment. "Or do you want me to start screaming?"

"Yes," he said, his voice grating. "Yes, I want you to start screaming. Then I would have an excuse to hit you."

Shock brought her around to confront him, but although he let her arm slide in his grip, he did not release her; face to face now, he seemed unbearably close.

She was in icy control again in a moment, and tilting her head back to look into his eyes, she said through clenched teeth, "I'm looking for an excuse to hit you, too, so take your hand away!"

For an answer he moved a hand to imprison her other arm and, with an effortless little jerk, pulled her a small step closer, so that now there were only inches between her body and his own. In spite of herself, fear quickened Laddy's breathing.

"You—" she began.

"Shut up," he said, and threaded through his tone and behind his eyes she suddenly perceived an intense burning anger.

She looked down at the large powerful hands that gripped her arms and up again at the broad chest that was so suffocatingly close, and she felt suddenly that her bones would be like matchsticks in his hands.

"What do you want from me?" she demanded hoarsely, fear giving force to her angry hatred.

A dark smile lifted the corners of his firm, sensually curved mouth. "What have you got to offer?" he asked.

Her face hardened. "To you, nothing," she said coldly. "Believe me, nothing at all!"

"I believe you," he said. "Nothing—no honor, no integrity, no justice, either. Am I right?"

She gasped as though he had in truth struck her. "*I?*" she repeated, almost speechless with anger. "*I* have no justice, no integrity? My God, I'm amazed you even took the trouble to learn those words in

English. *You* must have precious little use for them! How dare you say that to me!"

He said, his voice like a whip: "Did you think those insignificant little pieces you were writing about me would escape notice? Did you think that I would ignore those slanted half truths, those journalistic techniques that I recognize sooner than my own face? Was that your idea of integrity?"

"No," she admitted coldly. "It was my idea of getting my own back against someone I hate worse than poison." With sudden violence Laddy wrenched her arms out of his grasp and stood back from him, her eyes wide and burning up into his. "Someone who lied and cheated and used, and who never meant one word he said to me!"

His eyes blazed, and then, slowly, he smiled. "Oh, no," he said softly, holding her gaze. "Do not forget—*this* I said, and I meant it." And he bent his head and his mouth brushed the side of her throat with a white-hot flame.

She tore away in mindless panic and, whirling, reached for the handle of the door. But his instinct for speed was a hawk's. Instantly, with a wild ungoverned force, he reached out and gripped her arm and pulled her around so suddenly that her coat, notebook and bag flew from her grasp. As her back came up against the door, Mischa's hands closed tightly on her arms as before, and his body came up against hers.

Then, oddly, after that scuffling flurry of activity, there was a moment of perfect stillness and silence. She felt her heart pounding in hollow thuds like a huge, slow drum, and the whole room shook with the sound.

"You do not like to be reminded of that," he stated flatly. "Why?"

"Because I can't bear you to touch me!" she said through her teeth.

His eyes narrowed. "Yet in there, you invited me to remember," he said, his head jerking in the vague direction of the VIP lounge where the press meeting had taken place.

In astonished indignation, Laddy exclaimed, "I did no such thing!"

"Oh, yes," he said silkily, and his aura of dangerous strength seemed to send out sparks. Her heart would not stop thudding, and she wished he would stand away from her. "I did not imagine those signals, believe me."

When she realized what he meant she bit her lip. "That wasn't for you,' she muttered almost indistinguishably. But Mischa heard it. He laughed.

"It was for me," he said.

"No," she protested forcibly, for the powerful sexuality that emanated from him was nearly terrifying and she did not want him to think there was a breach in her defenses. "No, I didn't recognize—"

She had fallen into a far worse error, she perceived, and broke off, but too late.

"You didn't recognize me? You were looking like that at a stranger?" he said slowly, and an understanding of some sort dawned slowly in his eyes.

Smiling again, he said, "Do you look like that at every strange man in your path?"

"No, I do not!" she said indignantly, before she could stop herself. She was getting in deeper and deeper. "At least. . . ."

"No, you do not. And you wouldn't have smiled at me, either, if you had known who I was, would you? The icy look that followed was what you had waiting for me."

"And it's all you'll ever get from me!" she declared hotly, and struggled to escape his grasp. "I hate you!"

In answer he pulled her closer, and one arm encircled her back like a steel band, while his right hand came up and closed lightly on her neck. His thumb forced her chin up.

"You hate me?" he queried, with interest. "You hate this touch of my hand, my body?"

She felt tormented. "Yes! *Yes!*" she declared wildly. Mischa bent his head, and moving her own effortlessly with a strong negligent hand, he let his mouth trail kisses over her face, her throat, her ears.

"This is torture to you?" he asked huskily as his lips explored all the sensitive places he had discovered six long months ago, and Laddy bit her bright red lip and tried to hold onto sanity.

"Tell me," he commanded in a hoarse whisper, his mouth hovering dangerously near her own.

If he kissed her, she would go mad. "Stop it!" she cried. "Let me go!"

"I want you to tell me that this is hateful to you," he persisted, and both hands gripped her head as his body held her immobile against the door.

She closed her eyes against the sight of that sensuous, angry mouth, his searching dark eyes. "I loathe you," she said hoarsely. "When you touch me I want to die. Let go of me."

"In a moment," he said. "First I want you to experience exactly how much you hate me, so that you will be motivated to avoid it. Remember, in future, how much you hate this."

His head came down and his mouth was savage on her own, passionate, thrusting, wild, taking a pleasure from her that she had learned from him long ago was only a foretaste of what he wanted to take from her. She felt the urgency of that desire in his body then, and as an ungovernable answering clamor began in her, he lifted his mouth again.

"Remember this," he said hoarsely, "when you are tempted again to write your subtle lies about me in your newspaper, my Lady. You will do well to remember."

"What do you mean?" Laddy demanded, in a voice that shook. She was terrified of him now, of what power he might have over her.

"I mean that I have the means of punishing you and that I will use it if you try to lie about me. I will have no more of it."

"Don't you dictate to me what I can—" she began furiously.

He interrupted calmly, "But I do not dictate. I merely tell you that every time you lie about me or what I do in print, wherever you are, that night you will wish that you had not."

She gasped. "Are you threatening to *rape* me?" she choked out violently.

He half smiled at her through slitted eyes. "I have not forgotten, if you have, the way you looked at me before you recognized me. Nor am I inexperienced in the language of your body. You hate me, Lady, with your mind. But your body—that is something else, eh? No—I will not rape you. But I will make you forget that the man who touches you is the man you hate. Then I think you will not fight me."

She shivered uncontrollably. "I shall never forget that you are the man I hate," she said defiantly.

There was a short silence while her words seemed to reverberate in the room.

"Must I prove that you are wrong?" Mischa asked. "Do you in fact wish to provoke me to that?"

"Take your hands off me!" she said, spitting with a rage that disguised her panic. "Just get away from me and don't touch me ever again!"

He released her and stood back. "That is in your hands," he said, as she stood for a moment glaring at him, her breast heaving.

She said, "I can't believe I was ever so deluded as to think I loved you. You're the most hateful, vile man who ever existed."

"And you are a woman without honor," Mischa returned flatly. "Therefore, I deal with you in a manner without honor. Remember what I have said. I shall keep my word."

She stared at him as he spoke, her face losing every trace of emotion, her lips parting slightly in fear. When he finished speaking, she bent to collect her scattered belongings and, clutching them to her, wrenched open the door and stumbled out without a word.

"HARRY," Laddy said, with a note of desperation in her voice, "I'm getting awfully tired of this Busnetsky thing. Could you get someone else to cover him while he's in England?"

A fat cigarette hung out of the corner of Harry's mouth as he finished jotting a note with one hand and reached out to take the phone with the other. He dropped his pencil, took the cigarette out of his mouth, exhaled on a greeting into the phone and fixed his thoughtful gaze on Laddy, all at the same time. He seemed to be only half listening to the voice on the other end of the phone, but that was one of Harry's deceptive tricks: Laddy knew he wasn't missing anything important.

He spoke briefly into the phone, hung up and barely turning his head called out something to his deputy editor—all without removing his speculative eyes from her face.

"You know, dear girl," he said, taking a long drag on his cigarette and exhaling, "in the past few months you've been looking less and less like an underpaid, dedicated reporter and more and more like a mannequin from Harrods. If you're not careful I'll have someone in the executive offices telling me you're overpaid. Why are you so tired of Busnetsky?"

It was the kind of thing Harry could always do to her—snap something at her when he had made her unwary. But this time she counted to three and resisted the almost irresistible compulsion to rush into explanations.

"He's done everything of interest he's going to do, and I don't want to follow him around listening to him repeat himself," she said.

"He hasn't done anything on this side of the Atlantic for nearly six months," Harry pointed out. "Give him a chance. I understood this publication party tonight was for the general press. So he's bound to say something of interest, dear girl. Besides, six months ago you were begging me for that assignment, and very well you've done out of it, too. Don't abandon him on us now. The readers know you know him, they've followed your very abrupt change of attitude. They'll be curious now—they smell a vendetta."

"That's ridiculous!" Laddy exploded. "I'm not a columnist, I'm a reporter!"

Harry fixed her with an amused look. "I'm glad you said that, dear girl. I was wondering if you remembered."

She drew in an indignant breath, but Harry only

continued calmly, "Don't abandon him on us just yet. He's still news for a while, whether you know it or not." In a judgment of that nature, Harry was rarely wrong. "He'll settle into anonymity soon, and then you can forget all about him."

Laddy sank into the chair at her own desk and gazed unseeingly at the out-of-date manual typewriter in front of her that should have been replaced long ago by a modern computer terminal. Her breathing was labored and difficult, as though something were sitting on her chest. She did not want to attend the publication party tonight. She did not want to see Mischa Busnetsky again. She was terrified of him.

Woodenly she drew the afternoon edition of the *Herald* toward her and gazed down at Bill Hazzard's photo of Mischa Busnetsky.

A shock of his thick black hair fell over his right eye, and he was listening closely to someone, an amused half smile stretching one half of his wide mouth. The high white shirt collar framed his strong neck, and his broad shoulders disappeared out of the photo. He looked powerful. He looked like a conqueror. He looked like a man who kept his word. Laddy's eyes flicked to the copy under the photo.

"Looking very much more the jet-setting author than the recently released Soviet dissident and exile, Mikhail Busnetsky arrived in London today to promote sales of his latest books...."

She had switched the angle of her attack, but her

target was still his credibility, and she was a fool if she thought he wouldn't notice. Laddy glanced at her watch and sucked in her breath. Four-thirty already. The cocktail party that the publisher was throwing began at five. She would arrive early and leave early, when the place would be most crowded, but she shivered suddenly, as though something told her that such a tactic would not save her if Mischa Busnetsky had been angered by that article....

"Coming for a drink tonight, love?" John's voice broke into her reverie, and she surfaced with a little shake of her head and blinked at him.

"What? Oh, no, John, I can't. I've got to drop in on a publication party for Mischa Busnetsky tonight."

With a characteristic motion of his hand and his head, John tossed back his blond hair and stood looking down at her.

"I thought you'd done a story on him once already today."

"Yes, I did. But I still have to go to this thing tonight; I can't get out of that," she pointed out.

"Have you tried?" John asked with a hard edge to his voice.

"Tried what? To get out of it?"

"Yes."

It made her angry, though she couldn't say why.

"Yes, I did try," she said briefly, standing up. "Excuse me. I want to get there early and get away early."

"Shall I come with you, love?" John asked with

a sudden change of tactic. With her coat and bag in her hands, Laddy paused.

John had a grudge against Mischa Busnetsky. His presence might protect her from the man—or between them they might start something that would only embarrass her, since she had no doubt of Mischa's coming out on top. Besides, she, too, had a grudge against Busnetsky—and she preferred to fight her own battles.

"Thank you, John," she smiled. "But I won't be there more than half an hour. And then I'm going straight home to clean my house and do some laundry."

"How about a show tomorrow night?" John asked. "I haven't seen you all week, Laddy."

"All right. Come around seven for a drink first," she called, turning to smile at him as she walked across the newsroom to the door.

THE RECEPTION was held in a large and luxurious suite in a hotel whose windows overlooked Hyde Park, and when Laddy was shown into the large reception room shortly after five o'clock, the first person she saw in the crowded room was Pavel Nikolaivich Snegov. He saluted her across the room, and the first germ of an idea sprouted in her mind. With a smile that was friendlier than any she had previously given him, she collected a cocktail from a nearby tray and crossed to Snegov's side.

"Good afternoon," she said. "I see that your distaste for his literature has not kept you away."

Still smiling, she let her glance roam, and from this new vantage point she could now see the dark figure of Mischa Busnetsky several yards away, chatting with a number of her colleagues.

"In the West," Pavel Snegov riposted, "one learns the advantages of social pragmatism." It was said with dry self-deprecation, as though he were performing a necessary ritual, and the unexpectedness of it—it was something she had not thought Pavel Snegov capable of—made her laugh aloud. Her laughter fell into one of those sudden silences that sometimes occur in crowded rooms, and several people glanced her way. Mischa's attention, she saw, did not waver from the group around him. But she knew from the tightening of his jaw that even at that distance he knew the laughter was hers and with whom she was laughing. Laddy smiled grimly to herself, and continued in conversation with Snegov as long as she could bear before crossing casually to join the increasingly large group of media people facing Mischa Busnetsky.

They were talking to him about *To Make Kafka Live* and *Love of a Lady*, the reviews of which would be published—with luck—in the next few days. As the number of listeners increased, the questions and answers took on the more formal air of a press conference. At length someone asked, "Mr. Busnetsky, would you tell us how you managed to bring your manuscripts out of the Soviet Union with you?"

Mischa laughed. "No exile brings his manuscripts with him out of the Soviet Union," he said. "My manuscripts had been smuggled out of Russia by someone else while I was still in prison."

"You dedicated *To Make Kafka Live* to Dr. Lewis Penreith, who published some of your earlier work. Was it he who obtained the manuscripts?" another reporter asked.

Someone protested, "Lewis Penreith has been dead nearly four years."

"But it was, in fact, Dr. Penreith who obtained these two manuscripts and brought them to the West," Mischa's deep, commanding voice said, and it seemed to Laddy that there was an odd little silence, as though everyone in the room paused for breath at the same time.

"So the manuscripts have been here in the West for several years at least?" prodded Larry Hague, a reporter who was well experienced in Soviet affairs. "Why weren't the books published earlier, Mr. Busnetsky?"

"Dr. Penreith died shortly after he had obtained the manuscripts. They were not found again until several years after his death—in fact, they remained hidden until shortly before my expulsion to the West," Mischa said calmly, and by now he was the only calm one in the room.

"You call Dr. Penreith a martyr in the dedication of your book, Mr. Busnetsky, yet he was killed in a traffic accident. Do you have any comment about that?"

"A martyr is a person who dies for a cause. You

know what Dr. Penreith's cause was," Mischa replied imperturbably, and Laddy felt the blood draining from her face. How far was he going to go?

"You say he died shortly after obtaining these two manuscripts, Mr. Busnetsky?" Larry Hague calmly headed straight for deep waters. "Do you feel there was a connection between those two events?"

Mischa looked at him steadily, a glint of amusement in his eye.... So in control, Laddy thought, and so very different from the man who had had his first meeting with the Western press at Heathrow six months before.

"It is my opinion that there was a connection between Dr. Penreith's work and the manner in which he met his death," Mischa said clearly, and suddenly there was a babble of questions from ten different sources. "That is my opinion only, and I will not be more specific than that," he said, cutting through the babel.

Then a woman's voice predominated. "Can you tell us who found the manuscripts?"

For the first time, Mischa Busnetsky hesitated over the answer. His glance brushed fleetingly to Laddy, who stood ashen-faced at the outer edge of the group, staring at him in disbelief.

"I believe it was Dr. Penreith's daughter," Mischa said slowly.

It almost went by. Someone had already begun another question. But there were several people in that group who knew Laddy well enough to know who her father was. One by one, their faces frowning in perplexity, they turned to look at her, and as they did so, their neighbors also turned. Within a minute, though it seemed longer to Laddy, every head in the room had turned around, and every eye was on her.

Over that bank of curious faces, her eyes met Mischa's. He sketched her a mocking salute.

"Anything to promote sales of my latest books," he said mockingly, and now that she was the only person to see, his eyes were glittering with anger.

CHAPTER SIXTEEN

AT TEN-THIRTY that night the front doorbell rang. Laddy, stretched out in the sitting room with a book, stiffened and sat up, her heart beginning to pound. It couldn't be! He couldn't have meant it!

She moved into the hall and quietly opened the door that led from her apartment into the communal front hall. Then she stood a moment without breathing while the doorbell pealed again.

"Who is it?" she called.

"It's Margaret, dear. I've forgotten my keys," she heard, and exhaling with sudden relief, Laddy pulled open the heavy front door. Margaret smiled apologetically. "I'm sorry, Laddy, I took the wrong set of keys. I've been standing here for ten minutes ringing our bell, but you know what Ben's like—he must be sound asleep. Brr! I'm nearly frozen. Did I wake you?"

"Oh, no," Laddy smiled. "I was just reading."

They chatted in the hall for a moment and then Margaret said good-night and opened the door that led upstairs into the Smileys' flat. Moving back into the sitting room lighted by a soft lamp and fire glow, Laddy flung herself onto the sofa and picked up *To Make Kafka Live* again. Her heart was still beating with the fright she had had. . . . She must be a bundle of nerves, she thought.

The book was absorbing, whatever she thought of the man. Laddy had no idea how long she had been reading when she heard Margaret's footsteps coming down the stairs again. She glanced up and realized that the friendly fire she had built had nearly died.

There was no immediate tap on the door, and Laddy read another half page, gently torn between looking forward to a late-night cocoa and chat with Margaret and wishing to be left alone to read this remarkable treatise on totalitarian methods.

"Come on in!" she called when the knock sounded, and let the open book drop to rest on her stomach.

"Can't sleep?" she called as her hall door opened and shut. "I hope you're looking for cocoa and a nice long chat."

In the moment when she became aware of the extraordinary fact that she could hear footsteps going back up the stairs, a deep masculine voice said, "I am sorry to disappoint you, but it is not cocoa or a chat that I want." And in the shadowy doorway beyond the end of the sofa she saw the dark figure of Mischa Busnetsky.

Laddy jackknifed to a sitting position and onto her feet in one panic-stricken movement. She stood facing him with her back to the fire, her eyes wide, her breath rasping in her throat.

"What are you doing here?" she demanded.

"But you know this already. You invited me to come," Mischa answered, and in the shadows his mouth was unsmiling and his eyes never left her face.

"What?" she screeched. "Of course I didn't!"

"I had a printed invitation," he said silkily. "It was printed on the front page of the paper this afternoon."

"Did you seriously expect me to take any notice of your threats this morning?" she demanded contemptuously. "Did you think that a word from you would throw over the freedom of the press?"

He looked at her through eyes that were heavy lidded with anger. "This has nothing to do with the freedom of the press," he said in a dangerous tone. "This is between you and me."

The note in his voice sent a whisper of fear up her spine. "It is, like hell!" she shouted. "Get out of my house!"

There was a moment of tense silence between them, and suddenly, with a thrill of fear, she became aware of his size, and his power seemed to flow out and touch her. With an abrupt wild motion Laddy threw the book she was holding at his head.

Mischa caught it with one hand and, glancing at the title, laughed shortly.

"Were you waiting for me?" he asked, dropping the book nonchalantly onto the low sideboard inside the doorway as he moved into the room toward her.

Laddy could not stop herself from backing up a step, the fine silk of her long burgundy caftan brushing her legs and the carpet with a quiet whisper.

"Keep away from me!" she shouted, but somehow her voice, too, was a whisper.

"There is a way to keep me away from you," Mischa said roughly, advancing on her slowly, step by threatening step. "Tomorrow you will wish that you had followed it."

She stepped to one side of the fireplace and turned to run, intending to go around the sofa to the door, but she was brought up short by a pull on the hem of her robe. It was caught on one of the rough logs stacked by the fireplace.

The beautiful fabric snagged and came away as she jerked it, but it was too late: he had understood her intent and was now so close in the soft circle of lampglow that he could stop her escape with one slow hand.

"No," she begged him, her eyes wide with trepidation, her voice catching hoarsely in her throat.

Mischa smiled sensuously, unkindly. "How can it be 'no,'" he asked lazily, "when you are wearing the robe of the sacrificial virgin?"

She swallowed, and involuntarily her eyes followed his hands as he pulled open his coat. His trench coat was lined with a luxurious black fur, and he wore it over a black turtleneck sweater and casual but well-fitting black corduroy trousers. His eyes not leaving her, he shrugged out of the coat and threw it negligently onto the thick pile of cushions on the floor behind her. It landed on a large high cushion and splayed out over half the pile with a silken rustling that revealed the sensuous black fur of the lining.

It made the cushions suddenly seem like some barbaric warlord's bed, and Laddy found herself staring over her shoulder at the shiny silken blackness, her lips parted on a gasp of surprise.

"It is even more beautiful to the touch," Mischa suggested softly. "Like your hair."

She felt his hand on the ribbon that tied her long hair back on her neck, and she jerked her head around to evade it. But he simply tightened his grasp and brought his other hand up so that his arms encircled her head, and slowly he pulled the ribbon from her hair.

She was shaking like a leaf, hating him, hating the burning, erotic touch of his hands upon her as he brushed her hair's black cloudiness around her shoulders.

Laddy dropped her eyes shut and gritted her teeth. "Take your hands off me!" she said violently, then opened her eyes to blaze at him. "I hate you. The touch of your hand on me makes me sick!"

He smiled a cold smile, showing his teeth. "You hate me," he agreed lazily, "but before this hour is out you will ask for more than the touch of my hand on you."

"No!" she cried as panic filled her, twisting to

get away from him. But she was backed up now with her feet and ankles against the pile of cushions, and losing her balance, she fell sideways onto them.

For a brief moment she felt the silken black fur against her cheek and under her outflung palm, before a strong dark hand gripped her wrist and pulled her onto her back—and in that instant the broad heavy body of Mischa Busnetsky flung itself against hers and pressed her into the cushions. Without warning his mouth clamped passionately down on her own, forcing her head back and her lips apart in a deep, thrusting kiss that scorched through her. And suddenly, terrifyingly, a flickering flame caught in her blood and threatened to lick through all her veins.

"No," she whimpered, when his mouth released her. "Oh, please, *no!*"

He sought out the sensitive spots that six months ago he had discovered and taught her, and she closed her eyes and desperately clenched her hands against the response her body made to the heat of his mouth against her ears, her neck, her throat and the soft hollows of her shoulders.

"Oh, how I hate you!" she ground out, after his touch had made her gasp aloud. "Let me go!"

His hand slid through the low neckline of her robe and found her breast so suddenly that she gave a hoarse cry of need, and Mischa laughed deep in his throat.

"No," he whispered, his mouth tantalizing against her ear. "You do not hate me, my Lady—

not my mouth, or my hands or my body. Someone else you hate, but don't think of that now. Think only of this—" he ran his hand along the length of her shuddering body "—and this—" he tilted her head back over his arm and kissed the hollow of her throat "—and this—" His lips began to taste hers slowly, deliberately, his tongue flicking between her parted lips with tormenting lightness till she was nearly mad for the violence of his mouth on hers.

She was breathing through her mouth in little half moans of despair and desire. Then, involuntarily the cry was on her lips, and not until she heard it did she realize what he had achieved. "Yes," she begged huskily. And suddenly, realizing, she cried in horror, "No! Oh, God!" But she had remembered herself too late. In the moment when she had made that first begging cry, Mischa's rough-clad body had come down on top of her again, his legs between her own, his hands firm around her wrists.

She was tormentingly conscious of the black fur against her hands and her wrists, of the pillows giving under her back, of his thighs warm against hers—and of how deeply he was aware of her.

"No?" he asked huskily, meaningfully. "Still no?" His legs and hips slid down against her until his mouth was against her breast, caressing the swelling tip through the wine-dark silk that both covered and revealed her passionate response to him.

With agonizing slowness his hand encircled her

other breast, and his mouth found that one, too, with its heat and caress.

He touched the silk impatiently and leaned over her on one elbow. "Take this off," he commanded with a deep growl. "I want to touch you."

"No," she said, her jaw clenching against the knowledge that she wanted his mouth on her bare skin as much as he did.

"Take it off or I will tear it off," Mischa said without raising his voice, and the threat was all the more real for the quiet certainty with which he made it.

"It is the last gift my father ever brought me," she said coldly. "You took *him* from me, why not my memories, too? Go ahead and tear."

He breathed deeply, then gathered her up against his chest with one strong arm, her body frail against his, and his other hand, with gentle impatience, slid the dark silk up between them till her breasts were bared to him.

With rough possessiveness he ran his hand from her knee over the curve of thigh, hip and waist, till it closed firmly on her breast, and he bent with open mouth to kiss the firm roundness.

She wanted him. God forgive her, in every nerve and cell, in every pore of her skin, she wanted him. She wanted to feel his skin against hers, she wanted his body to find hers as it had done long ago.

She gritted her teeth, willing him to admit a need as great as her own, but he only watched her in the shadowy light with half-lidded eyes and flickered a smile each time her breath caught in her throat.

She grasped at a tiny corner of reason through the swirling sea that she drowned in and understood dimly what torment would be hers if she gave in to the icy passion that burned in him.

She understood it, and still she wanted him. She could not have moved a muscle to fight off the searching fire of his mouth, the hot caress of his rough, passionate hands, the disturbing pressure of his hard body. She could not push him away when every second was increasing her wild need of him. She must make him push her away instead—before the cry in her throat told him the truth.

"Pavel Snegov," Laddy whispered gropingly, hardly knowing what she said. "I...."

Mischa's mouth was between her breasts, and she whimpered and her hand pressed against his thick dark hair as though to hold him there forever.

"Yes?" Mischa breathed, and then he stiffened as though the name had suddenly reached him, and with the tearing pain of desolate need she knew she had won. "Pavel Snegov will want to know what valuable information you gave me tonight," she said, amazed that the noises her lips were making could produce any kind of sense. "You must tell me something that will make him happy."

Mischa rolled away from her onto his back and lay cursing softly in Russian. The agony of being left alone tore through Laddy's body like a shriek, and she bit her lip against it. The pain restored her to reason, and she sat up to pull her robe down over her aching body and dropped her head forward on her knees.

The sound of Mischa's throaty laughter behind her made her stiffen. Before she could move, his hand was in her hair and she was pulled down onto the cushions beside him as he bent over her. He smiled down into her eyes, a strange dark smile that she could not read.

"Tell the good comrade this," he said, his finger brushing her lips with an odd fierceness. "There is one thing in this world with which he could destroy me. But it is mine—and he will never touch it."

He reached over her to grasp the soft folds of his coat, and she could sense a deep silent laughter in him. He flung the coat over his arm and sat looking down at her with an expression in his eyes that again she could not understand.

"Have you learned that it will be wise to stop writing lies about me?" he asked.

"I don't write lies!" Laddy blazed, the passion he had raised in her finding an outlet at last. "I write what I see! And neither you nor anyone else is going to stop me!"

His eyes smiled with a glittering sensuality that made her breath stop.

"Good," he said huskily. "That is very good."

"What?" she whispered, confused.

"Oh, yes," he said with slow deliberation. "We have unfinished business, have we not? I will read the paper to learn when you will wish to finish it."

With an easy movement he was on his feet looking down at her.

"What a pity you cannot review my books," he said. "That would give your hatred great scope—and think how I would make you pay for it afterward."

He crossed to the hall and went out, but Laddy closed her eyes and did not watch him go. She heard the noise of the door to her flat and then of the front door while she lay shaking, clenching her hands—lay trying not to let her wild brain imagine how Mischa would make her pay for a scathing attack on one of his books.

THE SATURDAY-MORNING PAPERS went to town on what had happened at the publication party the previous evening. The circumstances of her father's death had been quickly researched and rehashed, as had his long career as a fighter in the area of human rights and as founder of the International Council on Freedom. The statements that Laddy had made after Mischa had so abruptly thrown her to the wolves were also given prominence.

She was a little startled to see how much she had said:

Miss Penreith, a staff reporter on the *London Evening Herald*, who was attending the reception on the media side, was obviously surprised when Mr. Busnetsky made his statement. But she confirmed that her father had been to Russia shortly before his death four years ago, and that she had reason to believe it was on that trip that he obtained both of the Busnetsky manuscripts being published this week. She said her father had hidden the manuscripts in a special place she was not aware of until the discovery of the manuscripts early this year. Miss Penreith said that the manuscripts, which she found in their original condition, would almost certainly have been moved to her father's publishing offices in Covent Garden within two or three days of her father's acquisition of them. But the manuscripts, *To Make Kafka Live* and *Love of a Lady*, were not found in his office. Miss Penreith would not say where the hiding place had been. Earlier this year the *London Evening Herald* published a series of articles by Miss Penreith that were the result of extensive interviews with Mr. Busnetsky. The articles, acclaimed for their in-depth study of the personality of the well-known dissident, were syndicated in newspapers and magazines around the world.

Laddy let the paper fall back onto the table and wished she had not got out of bed this morning. She leaned wearily back in her chair, pressing her eyes with thumb and forefinger, then stood up.

Outside the kitchen window a gray November day was just beginning to throw chilling rain against the glass. Laddy sighed, pulling the belt of her terry-cloth robe more securely around her, and picked up her cup and moved to the stove to refill it from the coffeepot.

She leaned against the counter, cradling the warm cup in her hands, and watched the drops of rain on the window multiply.

"You're a great one to talk about honor, Comrade Busnetsky," she muttered aloud. "That's another thing I won't forgive you for as long as I live."

The rain didn't let up all morning and by early afternoon it was getting steadily worse. With her house having been cleaned, her groceries got in and her laundry done on Friday night, there was no reason for Laddy to brave the elements, so after lunch she settled down with *Love of a Lady*. It was not a large book and she knew it was fiction; she told herself that she did not have the mental energies on such a bleak afternoon to continue *To Make Kafka Live*.

By the end of the first chapter her eyes were swimming so that she could hardly read, and when, hours later, she had finished the book, she flung it violently aside and a storm of weeping overtook her.

She was filled with a sense of desolate loss. After months of hating Mischa, she was painfully reminded of the fact that once she had loved him, that once her heart had overflowed with warmth and love. Now it was a cold black lump in her breast that for some reason kept on pumping blood to keep her alive, and she understood that Ben Smiley was right—she had survived by becoming less than human.

Love of a Lady was a prose poem, a paean of love for a woman she recognized as herself. Mischa had told her the simple truth when he said that her memory had kept him alive over the years of their separation. The book had been written over a period of nearly four years, beginning at the time of his first arrest after they had met in a roomful of paintings. It was a diary of love letters, of yearning, of promises—yet at the same time it was a novel, with a unifying core that she felt but did not quite recognize.

This was what she had lost. This was what suspicion and fear and lack of trust had destroyed. A love that had once been consuming and fearless, a love that had triumphed over every agony of body and mind....

That a man who had loved her so much could have hurt her so brutally was a contradiction almost impossible to believe. Laddy remembered the look she had seen in his eyes six months ago when he opened the manuscript she had brought him and translated the title. He had loved her then as much as the man of the book loved his lady, and instinctively she had known it. But the man in the book would have accepted far, far more from his woman than any small mistake Laddy had committed against Mischa....

What had happened to change his love? What

had occurred between the day she had given him the manuscripts and the day he had accused her of being a spy?

He had come to know her. The dreams had become a reality. That was all, nothing else.

So although the dream woman who had kept him alive had been herself, Mischa had not been able to love the real Laddy Penreith the way he had loved her image for eight years.

That was hardly surprising. The only surprising thing about it, in fact, was that this thought had never occurred to her before. All the accusations of espionage and betrayal had been a cover for the real fact—Mischa had learned that he simply did not love her.

Laddy was no longer crying. Her eyes were as dry as her heart was cold. He had not been hurt by her, he had not felt betrayed—he had been too much of a coward to tell her the truth, that was all.

She could not stop herself picking up the book again, staring down at the wine-red dust jacket spattered with infinitesimal dots of a red so dark it was almost black and at the golden lettering of words that had once been meant for her.

"Love is strong as Death." The quotation, unattributed, had a page to itself immediately before the text. Laddy sat with the page open in front of her, wondering what the source was. She had heard the quote before, but she could not now remember the context. And suddenly it seemed important to know where the line came from.

She knelt on the sofa, gazing over the back to the bookshelves that ran from floor to ceiling along the wall by the door, and let her eyes run along the lettering on the spines of the books.

She felt sure the line was taken from a love poem, but that was as far as her memory would take her—if even that much were correct. John Donne? Yes, perhaps....

Half an hour later, when the doorbell rang, she was sitting on the floor by the bookcase with a stack of poetry books beside her, still hunting down the elusive quotation but no nearer to it. As the warm tones of the bell sounded, she leaped to her feet, surprised to see that the rain had stopped and it was quite dark outside. How long had she been reading, then?

She pulled open the front door with a book of poetry closed in one hand, her finger marking the place.

"John!" she exclaimed blankly.

John Bentinck had been smiling, but now his face darkened angrily.

"When you look at me as though you've forgotten my existence it means you've been thinking of Busnetsky," he said bitterly. "Is he after you again now he's back in England?"

Laddy sucked in a startled breath.

"Don't be ridiculous!" she laughed. "If I'm absentminded it's because I'm trying to track down a quotation." She held up a volume of John Donne's poetry and stepped back from the door.

"Come on in. Where does 'Love is strong as death' come from?"

"I don't know," John said, moving inside as she closed the door. He eyed her briefly up and down, noting her worn blue jeans and scruffy sweater. "You must want to know pretty badly if it made you forget to get dressed. How long have you been looking for it?"

"Not very long. Anyway, what's the matter with the way I'm dressed?" Laddy smiled quizzically.

"Nothing, I suppose," John said after a moment. "I did get seats in the stalls, though."

Laddy made a moue of contrition.

"Good heavens, is it that late? I thought you were early!" she exclaimed. "I must have been flipping through those books longer than I thought!"

She was lying: she had totally forgotten the date she had made with John yesterday to see a show tonight.

"It's just on seven," John said.

Laddy scooped up *Love of a Lady* as she passed behind the sofa to the bookshelves and slid it onto a shelf along with the volumes of poetry she had pulled out in her search for the quotation. She indicated the bottles on the sideboard.

"Help yourself to a drink, and I'll be ready in ten minutes, no more. What are we going to see?" she said, pausing at the door.

"A friend of mine had tickets he couldn't use for *Much Ado About Nothing*," John said. "At the

Aldwych. It's supposed to be a very good production.''

"Super!" she said, and disappeared into her bedroom.

It *was* very good, with a rather stronger actress than usual playing Hero, reminding Laddy of her own pain at being falsely accused, and making her take a dislike to the weak but handsome Claudio that was almost cathartic.

"He didn't love her at all, he just wanted to make a good marriage," she said to John afterward. They were sitting over a late supper, which Laddy was attacking ravenously, having eaten nothing at all since lunch. "Would *you* throw off a woman you loved like that?" she asked, and her eyes gave away more than she knew.

John smiled softly, and reached out a hand to cover hers.

"Never, love," he said, allowing a deeper shade of meaning to color his voice. "No man who loved a woman could do that to her."

She knew it was true; yet later at her front door when John bent to kiss her good-night, she allowed his kiss but could not respond.

She hated Mischa Busnetsky, but his face still stood between her and any other man.

THE REVIEWS of Busnetsky's books in the large Sunday papers the next morning were unanimous raves. Mikhail Busnetsky was a powerful, compelling writer, and *To Make Kafka Live* was a uniquely disturbing indictment of the Soviet system of repression.

But it was obvious to everyone that Busnetsky's great talent lay in fiction. "Mr. Busnetsky has said that his political writings were made necessary by the society he lived in, but that fiction was made necessary by his soul," Laddy read. The reviewer was quoting from her published interviews with Mischa, and she could not help remembering the sunny spring day on the cliffs when he had said it to her. "If *Love of a Lady* was necessary to the author, it will become equally necessary to many readers...."

Another reviewer compared *Love of a Lady*, surprisingly, to the *Song of Solomon*: "...tremendous passion that, like the *Song of Songs*, also cloaks an inner meaning. The *Song of Songs*, a quote from which prefaces the book, is, of course, held by some to be an allegory of God's love of Israel. Future students of this work will be more than usually justified in considering the Lady of the title a metaphor for freedom...."

Thoughtfully Laddy let the paper fall. A metaphor for freedom! Was it possible? Was the deeply passionate love she had discovered last night in *Love of a Lady* directed toward freedom and not herself at all?

Well, what did she care, anyway? It was all an academic exercise. She hated Mischa Busnetsky, and whether he had once loved her or had never loved her made no difference at all—except to her pride. If she could think that Mischa had believed he loved her for a while, she would feel less of a fool for having believed him. But it made no real difference to her at all.

Well, at least she now knew the source of the quotation he had used. Laddy got up and walked into the living room to pull down a Bible from the bookshelves. She sat down and, captured by the power of the words, stopped skimming for the quotation and read the *Song of Songs* right through. She found the quotation toward the end:

> For love is strong as death; jealousy is cruel as the grave: the coals thereof are coals of fire which hath a most vehement flame.
> Many waters cannot quench love, neither can the floods drown it.

Laddy finished the Song, breathing shakily. If Solomon had indeed written this, he deserved to be famous for more than his wisdom! But whoever the writer was, she had the feeling he might have laughed in delight to hear the scholastics label this poetry an allegory of anything at all, that he would have felt that this passionate love poem was an end in itself.

With a sinking sensation in the pit of her stomach, she realized that she was hoping that Mischa Busnetsky was laughing, too, this morning—and for the same reason.

CHAPTER SEVENTEEN

FOR THE NEXT TEN DAYS Mischa Busnetsky stayed out of the pages of the *Herald* and, for the most part, out of the public eye, while Laddy and the world wrestled with some ominous developments in the Middle East. But by the end of November things had almost settled back into their normal insanity, and Laddy, who had told herself more than once during those busy days that she was glad she had heard nothing of Busnetsky and hoped she never saw so much as a press release about him again as long as she lived, gave in at last and began to phone her contacts to find out what the man was up to.

Richard Digby was out of town and his office was not familiar with Busnetsky's movements, so she rang the ICF. Nobody seemed to know where Mischa was. Finally she got in touch with an old friend of her father's who was involved in the ICF, a woman named Mary Regent.

"I don't think he's doing much of anything except settling down in England," Mrs. Regent said. "And I think he's writing another book. He's not taking any kind of lecture engagement till January at the earliest, I know that."

"Where has he gone to do his writing?" Laddy asked.

"I really don't know." The woman's voice was warm. After a few more pointless remarks, Laddy was about to hang up when Mary Regent said abruptly, as though she had just come to a decision, "You know, Miss Penreith, no one who read your interviews could seriously believe you're hostile to Mikhail Busnetsky. But a week or two ago, when he came back from America, you did make him seem rather...selfish and self-seeking. And I, for one, think you should know that all future earnings from *To Make Kafka Live* have been signed over jointly to the ICF and the Campaign Against Psychiatric Abuse."

Laddy sat up and reached for a pencil. "Really?" she queried, her voice surprised. "When did that happen?"

"Quite some time ago," Mary Regent said. "I wanted you to know for your own information."

Laddy's pencil paused in its scribbling. "For my own information? But may I publish this?"

"Oh!" The rather kindly voice sounded taken aback. "Well, I don't really know, Miss Penreith. Nothing was said about keeping it secret, but...."

"Well, if nothing was said..." Laddy suggested.

"Yes, I really don't see why it shouldn't be published," Mary Regent said, with quiet decision, and Laddy thanked her. But when she hung up the phone she was laughing. Mary Regent was either very naive or very canny, and Laddy did not think she was naive.

Laddy herself knew perfectly well that Mischa would not want this information made public. Since the publication of his interviews with her, he had given no personal information whatsoever to the media. He talked about torture, he talked about psychiatric abuse, he talked about the Russian state—but he did not talk about Mikhail Busnetsky. Laddy knew as though he had told her that this piece of information was not for publication.

She felt her blood singing with challenge as she called three other people listed in her contact book to get confirmation of the facts from them. None of them seemed concerned that she had got the information, but it only meant they did not know Mischa Busnetsky as well as she did.

And if Mischa did not like her hostile stories, he was going to like her favorable publicity even less, she told herself grimly. With an excited, nervous laugh she rolled paper into her machine and wrote up the story for the late-afternoon edition.

"Mischa Busnetsky, well-known Soviet dissident and exile who arrived in the West ill and penniless just six months ago, has donated all future earnings of his critically acclaimed book *To Make Kafka Live* to international civil rights groups. . . ."

He was waiting for her in the street when she left work that evening just before five o'clock. Laddy's heart skipped a beat as she saw him, and then it rushed into wild thumping, as though this were a meeting with a deadly enemy. As Mischa approached her across the pavement, a black London cab slid out from between two navy-and-white *Herald* delivery trucks and pulled up beside them.

Mischa took her wrist in a deceptively light grasp and opened the taxi door.

"Get in."

His voice was a low growl, and his posture was threatening, like a predatory animal. She felt that if she moved, a lightning velvet paw would crush her before she had even decided on a direction.

"What the hell do you want?" Laddy demanded in a low angry tone that she hoped disguised her nervous confusion.

"You," he said. "Get in or I'll pick you up and throw you in."

"You will not!" she declared, backing away a step—into the taxi door that stood open at her back. She was trapped.

Mischa smiled glitteringly at her, silently underlining her predicament.

"If you don't let me go right now, I'll scream," she said, as calmly as she could. "Try keeping your name out of the papers with a charge of assault on your head, Mr. Busnetsky!"

His black eyes caught her gaze; she couldn't look away.

"If you start to scream I will kiss you," he said flatly. "Here in the street in front of your colleagues. Who do you think will win then?"

"You can't kiss me forever," she said, smiling

angrily. "As soon as you stop, I'll start screaming again."

"Have you learned so little?" he asked, his voice grating tinglingly on her nerve ends. "If we start to kiss here on the street we shall be lucky if we do not end up making love in the back of the taxi. And you would not cry out until I made you do so. Get in the car."

Her knees shaking almost uncontrollably, Laddy climbed into the taxi and sat in the far corner of the seat. Mischa said something to the driver through the window and climbed in after her, and suddenly the roomy interior of the cab was too small for comfort.

Laddy shifted nervously as the cab pulled out into the rush-hour traffic and crossed her legs away from him.

Mischa smiled at her, but his smile only increased her nervousness. His anger filled the cab—she could taste it when she breathed.

"Where are you taking me?" she demanded, so hoarsely she could hardly be heard.

"To a place where we can talk," Mischa said shortly. "And we will talk when we get there."

In the rush-hour traffic the drive was tortuously slow, and the panic and anticipation his silent presence caused in her was just becoming unbearable when the cab stopped in front of a large white terraced house in Queen's Gate, not far south of Kensington Gardens. Laddy stepped out of the cab and blinked at the expensive house in the near darkness.

"Where are we?" she asked coldly when Mischa had paid the driver. He took her arm firmly to lead her up the wide white steps to a black-and-brass door.

He unlocked the front door without speaking, then the vestibule door and ushered her into a well-lighted black-and-white-tiled hallway where a marble staircase curved up to another floor. There was only one door on the main floor, and he unlocked that and waited for her to enter.

"We are in my home," he said finally, as he closed the door behind them.

The apartment covered the whole of the main floor; it was huge. She stood in the center of the enormous, well-furnished front room and simply stared.

"*Yours?*" she repeated, gazing up at the high ceiling, which actually had a mural painted on it, like some baroque cathedral. "What *do* you do for money?"

"You are mercenary minded," he said dryly. "Paperback rights for *Love of a Lady* have now been negotiated. You may publish that piece of information, if you must. But I do not care to see any mention of this place in the pages of your newspaper."

He took off her coat and his own and threw them onto the sofa, the casual action belied by a nervous tension, in his body and in the air, that she could almost touch. Involuntarily she shivered, as though his hand had brushed her back.

He moved over to a well-stocked drinks table and lifted a crystal decanter.

"Cold?" he asked. "Would you like sherry, or do you prefer, perhaps, whiskey?"

"Sherry," Laddy whispered. She did not want a drink, but there was wisdom in saving her energy to fight more important battles. She watched him pour her drink, her tension increasing in direct proportion to his studied calm. Crossing the few feet of space between them, Mischa handed her a glass and raised his own to her. Laddy took the heavy glass but did not drink.

"Would you mind telling me what I'm doing here?" she demanded finally, moving away from him as though to look at the furnishings.

Mischa lowered his glass and gazed at her, his dark eyes unreadable.

"Do you not know?" he asked, his deep, rough voice dragging out the last vowel on a sensuous note that brushed alarmingly up her spine and made her shiver again.

"No, I don't know!" she said hotly. "But if it's because of the article this afternoon about your book royalties, let me remind you of the way you threw me to the wolves awhile ago, and of the fact—"

He interrupted her with smooth anger.

"But this was a very friendly article you wrote today. Why should this cause me to be angry?"

"Because you think you're above everything, that's why, because I made you—" She broke off in surprise as a most extraordinary expression entered his eyes, as if a light had just come on in his brain. His gaze, suddenly very black and intent, riveted her own.

"In fact," he said slowly, "this article, like all the others, was written to make me angry."

"No, it wasn't!" she protested sharply. "Whatever I write is *news*, without regard to—and stop pretending it didn't make you angry, because it did! You think you ought to be untouchable. That's why I'm here right now!"

She stopped speaking because he was laughing, a delighted, husky, caressing laugh.

"But this is not why I have brought you here," he said, smiling deeply at her. "You are here because I want you."

"What are you talking about?" she demanded shrilly. "You want me for what?"

The look in his eyes froze her into immobility, and she stared at him in angry fear.

"No!" she cried, flinging up her hand instinctively, without conscious intent. He understood, however, and moved aside, and the beautiful crystal glass she had been holding shattered into bits against the marble fireplace. In the next second Mischa's own glass was on the table, and his powerful dark body was moving across the room to her. Laddy tore her startled eyes away from the shards of glass and turned to run to the door.

He let her battle frantically with the impossible lock for several seconds, standing watching her from a two-foot distance as she jerked uselessly on the door.

"There is a bolt above your head," he said at last, and as her hand snapped up and turned it, the length of his body was against her back and his broad fingers closed ruthlessly over the slim white hand on the bolt and forced it down.

"Do not fight me, my Lady," he whispered dangerously, his lips moving erotically against her ear as he spoke, his voice sending waves of melting heat through her body.

"I hate you," she moaned into the door panels, her teeth clenched against the passion his nearness was arousing. "I hate you, damn you! Why can't you leave me alone?"

For an answer he pulled her around to face him, pressed her body tightly against his and with one hand on her throat forced her head back to look into her eyes.

"I do not leave you alone for the same reason you do not stop trying to anger me with what you write. This reason—" His mouth closed on hers with a gentle urgency that made her head swim. She had no balance and she clutched at him, knowing she would fall if he let her go.

When his searching mouth abandoned her lips to rain light kisses over her cheeks and eyes, her face lifted to his mouth involuntarily, like a flower to spring rain. His large arms wrapped tightly around her then as though he would never let her go, and she felt an unbearable ache that she had not known for months stab her heart.

"There is another reason," Mischa whispered, suddenly no longer kissing but only holding her, and Laddy opened her eyes.

He was looking down at her, his face grave and unsmiling.

"I love you, Lady," he said.

Laddy recoiled as though he had struck her.

"What?" she demanded, her voice rising to an incredulous squeak. Her hands pushed frantically against him, and her body strained back against the pressure of his masculine arms.

"I love you."

"Don't say that! I can't bear— *Let me go!*" she cried wildly, twisting and turning as she fought to be free, so that her long hair flung out, blinding both of them.

Mischa's arms shook her impatiently.

"Lady, stop this! What—"

"Let me go!" she cried again, and the unmistakable note of panic was in her voice.

When suddenly his arms no longer enclosed her, she was off balance, and she staggered. His broad right hand caught her arm above the elbow in a tight steadying grip, and Laddy drew herself up straight, then looked from his hand on her arm to his face with cold disgust. She stepped back, and Mischa's hand dropped from her. She breathed shakily, trying to control the dry painful shudders that shook her slim frame.

"You love me?" she said in contemptuous horror, when she could speak. "You *love* me? And when did that happen? When did you discover *that*?'' Her voice was shrill in the large room, as though it echoed back from the ceiling and windows.

"I have always loved you," Mischa said, and she sucked in her breath with an involuntary hiss.

"You never loved me. You don't know what the word means."

"I taught you what it means," Mischa said, in a calm measured voice that betrayed no emotion.

"You taught me *sex*!" she blazed. "*Sex*—not love! I taught myself love—more the fool me. I taught myself to love a man who.... But it was a myth. The man I loved never existed. And I didn't have to teach myself to hate the man you really are! That came naturally. I hate you and I'll always hate you, and when you use the word love to me it makes my flesh creep!"

He stood watching her for a long moment of silence. "Why?" he asked at last.

Laddy snorted in angry derision.

"Why?" she repeated. "You—all right, I'll tell you why: when you were in the States, in that clinic, I wrote you a letter. Did you know about that letter?"

"Lady, I—"

"Just answer my question!" she said, flinging up a hand to stop his protest. "Did you know?"

"Yes. I knew," Mischa said, and his voice, strangely, was gentle, and his eyes looked at her as though he understood much more than her words.

"I knew you knew. I never doubted that you

knew," Laddy said in a brittle voice. "There's your first why. Second—John Bentinck wrote you a letter explaining how those interviews got in the *Herald*, explaining that I had nothing to do with it. Did you get that letter?"

"Yes, I got it," Mischa said.

She faced him across a three-foot space, her back rigid, her head flung up with proud strength to meet his eyes.

"And you believed what he said, didn't you?" she demanded.

Mischa looked at her a moment before replying, "I believed him."

"So you knew. Long before I wrote you, you knew the truth. But still you let a total stranger answer my letter. You let me suffer that. And now you tell me you've always loved me. Tell me, did you love me while Marsha Miller was answering my letter for you?"

She was cold—exultantly cold, like a distant star, with a shell of ice around her brain. She looked at Mischa Busnetsky and knew that he could never hurt her again if she lived for a thousand years.

"Yes," he said. "I loved you then."

Her laugh pealed out like icy chimes. "Well, if that's your idea of love, I suppose I must be grateful that you've never hated me!" Laddy said brightly.

"Lady—" he began, still in that same oddly gentle voice, but she interrupted him.

"No, wait! We haven't had the sixty-four-thousand-dollar question yet! Did you actually ever believe at any time either that I was giving information to Pavel Snegov or that I had anything to do with betraying your whereabouts to the media?''

Mischa's eyes still watched her steadily, his face tight and unmoving.

"Not for any significant length of time, no," he said impassively.

"Thank you," Laddy said huskily. "You've confirmed what I've always known. If you don't understand why I hate you, you should. As for your having always loved me—well, once you told me that you did not and never had loved me. And either you were lying then, or you're lying now. You'll forgive me if I tend to think that today you are a liar."

She moved over to the sofa and picked up her black leather coat and put it on. With unhurried motions she tied the belt tightly around her waist and pulled the wide collar and lapels up around her neck and cheeks. Then she faced Mischa, a cold half smile on her lips, nothing in her eyes.

"You destroyed me, Mischa," she said flatly. "I'm only half human, thanks to you. You have no right now to pretend it never happened, no right to try to get me back into the bed you once threw me out of." She paused. "And no right to tell me that what you feel for me is love."

"No," he said quietly. "I am sorry. I will not tell you so again."

She did not move so much as an eyelash as she

stared at him. Then she crossed to the door and opened it.

"I hope to God I never see you again as long as I live," she whispered, her voice evincing emotion for the first time.

Mischa's jaw tightened. "This I cannot promise," he said.

She went out without a word.

CHAPTER EIGHTEEN

IT WAS THE COLDEST WINTER Laddy could remember. The heating bills for the house were enormous, and everyone was edgy with the cold and the possibility of oil shortages. The *Herald* began to remember the frightful winter of 1963 and wonder if another one was on its way. With a large segment of the population now dependent on central heating in their homes, the prospects were not comforting.

On a Saturday just before Christmas the fourth anniversary of her father's death passed, and Laddy sat over her breakfast coffee with two sweaters on and gazed out at the swirling snowflakes that blew coldly over the stiff, naked twigs and branches in the blackened garden. She had lost more weight, and she felt too thin for such a cold winter.

She would spend Christmas as she had each year for three years: in Richmond, with the large bustling family of a friend from college days who now worked in a publishing house. Today was the last day she would have any time for Christmas shopping, and her list was long. She had always enjoyed Christmas shopping, but today she knew that it would be a task. The thought of the crowds on Oxford Street—or even in Highgate Village—made her weary before she began. But to go to Richmond without gifts was unthinkable.

HER CHRISTMAS passed pleasantly, with her friend Miranda bringing home yet another new boyfriend for her family's approval and the young man turning out to be an instant success with all members of the Christmas party.

"Should I marry him, do you think?" Miranda's reflection in the dressing-table mirror laughed and made a wry face at her and Laddy smiled back. It was late on Christmas night, and tomorrow Laddy would go back to London. The house was silent around the bedroom that had been Miranda's since childhood and that now the two girls were sharing.

"Do you love him?" asked Laddy.

"Darling, of course I love him!" Miranda laughed, and stroked the brush through her red gold hair. "I love *all* my men—you know I do."

Laddy closed her eyes for a moment of painful envy of the lighthearted, nearly callous ease of Miranda's affections.

"You're not very well, are you, darling?" Miranda's voice broke in on her thoughts, and Laddy opened her eyes to see that her friend had swung around on the seat and was regarding her with an air of concern.

"Of course I'm well," Laddy returned easily.

"You don't look at all well, my Lad," Miranda shook her brush admonishingly at her. "It's all this cold weather. You need to get away somewhere warm before you collapse.''

"I can't afford to get away somewhere warm." Laddy forced a laugh. "Do you know how much that house is going to cost me to run this winter?"

"Couldn't you afford to get away to Corfu even if the parents let you have the flat?" Miranda asked. Laddy smiled, shaking her head. It was typical of Miranda to make a show of concern, but Laddy knew better than to count on the offer. She had learned long ago that Miranda was a friend for the good times. She was charming and good fun— but far too self-absorbed to wish to understand anything outside her own immediate, rather shallow emotional ken.

"Not even then, I'm afraid," Laddy said, suddenly wishing that Miranda were the sort of friend she could tell about Mischa Busnetsky with some hope of being understood. Miranda's heart had been broken a score of times. Surely she knew a way to cope? "Anyway, it wouldn't help," she said. "Wherever I go, I'm taking myself along. You can't escape yourself."

"Well, you should try to get away *some*where, darling, even if you have to borrow to do it," Miranda said, returning to her reflection with the happy satisfaction of someone who has settled a troublesome problem with selfless concern. "Because you look awful."

She was right, Laddy thought a few days later as she looked out again over the Highgate garden that seemed more dreary and infertile with every day that passed. She ought to get out of London, where the dirt and the traffic made the winter even more desolate. She had a week's holiday still to come, and though she would not go into debt for a holiday abroad this year, she could at least get into the country—the Lake District or Cornwall. At least there would be no tourists at this time of year.

Or Wales.

"I THINK you arrived just in time," Brigit said, standing at the window of Mairi Davies's bright kitchen and eyeing the lowering sky with concern. "The air's felt odd all day. We're in for something, but I don't know what."

"Snow," Alun Davies said succinctly, just that moment coming in the door. He moved over to the ancient black cook stove to warm his hands. "Georgy is predicting a very bad storm." Georgy was an old man who had been a sailor and whose weather forecasts were reputedly more accurate than the BBC's.

Brigit looked worried. "Would you like to stay here, Laddy?" she asked. "We can get one of the guest rooms ready in no time, you know."

Laddy shook her head and smiled as Rhodri burst smiling into the warm room with a rush of words, complaining strenuously about the cold. He divested himself of coat and boots in record time and rushed over to Laddy's side.

"We put coal out back in the old animal shelter

for you," he informed her. "Enough for half the winter, I think. And wood, too—Alun and I, and.... We did not want you to freeze, you know."

Laddy hugged him. "Thank you very much. It's nice of you to look after me like that. I wasn't expecting—"

"Well, if it snows the way Georgy says, you will need it, you know."

Brigit interrupted. "Surely you would rather stay with us, Laddy—at least till we see how bad this is going to be?"

It was the wise thing to do, and yet she wanted to be alone in that little cottage, away from everyone—even from the warmth of this family.

"What?" demanded Rhodri indignantly. "After all the work Alun and I have done? No, no, you want to go, don't you, Laddy? Besides, there is a surprise there for you—but I am not to tell you what it is."

"Yes, I do want to go," she said. "And I ought to go now and get settled in before it gets dark." She stood up, thanking them for taking the trouble to make the cottage ready for her, and took the key Brigit had had waiting for her on Helen Digby's instructions.

Everyone trooped out to the car to see her off.

"Have you got enough supplies?" Brigit asked, stooping to the car window.

"Yes, I stocked up in Fishguard," Laddy said. "I won't need to come in for anything except the papers."

"If we don't hear from you, we'll send Rhodri over to check on you," Brigit said. "I hope you've brought something to read."

Laddy laughed and waved and drove off into a wind that was already stronger than it had been half an hour ago. She glanced up at the black sky and wondered at the wisdom of what she was doing.

Helen had been enthusiastic when she had asked about the possibility of a week in the cottage. Wales was beautiful in the winter, she had said. Of course Laddy must go. Helen had only been sorry that she and Richard would both be in town till February.

Laddy pulled her red car up to the white gate and looked at the sky again, feeling the unfamiliar nip in the air. Was that the snow that Georgy smelled? She almost hoped it would be snow. If those clouds carried rain, she could almost believe that Trefelin would be washed off the hillsides and into the valley.

She made three trips across the wintry meadow, her arms full of suitcases and provisions that she left at the door. There was smoke from her chimney, which the wind immediately dispersed: Rhodri and Alun had made her a fire. That must be Rhodri's surprise, the reason he had wanted her to come: the house would already be warm and welcoming.

She didn't need the key; they had left the door unlocked. Laddy quickly set the bags inside the kitchen and with a shivery "Brr!" closed the door on the cold weather and tried to warm her nose with an equally cold hand.

Leaving the shopping bags to sink down against one another on the floor, she picked up her cases and headed for the bedroom to take off her coat and change her clothes.

She got no farther than the door of the sitting room. There, with a startled yelp, she dropped her cases and stared, her face a mask of incredulous dismay.

Sitting on the sofa in front of a roaring fire, large and dark and looking very much in charge of the situation, was Mikhail Alexandrovich Busnetsky.

He had the sofa drawn up before the fire, his long broad arms stretched over the back on either side of him, one ankle resting on a knee. A posture of possession, and Laddy noted it and gritted her teeth. He was wearing a thick navy turtleneck that molded his muscular body and worn blue jeans, and with his thick dark hair curling down over his collar and across his forehead he looked like a sailor or a gypsy.

A lock of hair fell from his high forehead as their eyes met, and for a split second Laddy saw his face as though for the first time. She saw a face of enormous intelligence, upon which were etched the knowledge of pain and suffering, and indomitable courage. She saw the face of a man who had fought against enormous odds. She saw....

She saw Mischa Busnetsky, whom she hated, in a place that was filled with memories of him, in the last place in the world that she wanted or expected to see him.

"What are you doing here?" Laddy demanded, when she could speak.

"I am here to write a book," he said. "What are you doing here?"

Laddy began to take off her coat. It seemed ludicrous to stand in the doorway staring at him as though he represented some kind of physical danger.

"I'm here to think, and I doubt if I'll do very much with you sitting there. I presume you are *not* planning to write your book in this cottage?" she said sarcastically, as she busied herself with her coat and scarf.

"The idea is not without appeal, but I am established in my own," he said regretfully, as though she had invited him to stay with her.

"Good," she said, ignoring that. "Would you mind returning there?"

"And not even thanks for this warm fire?"

Laddy looked at him. It was a long time since Mischa had joked with her. "Do I owe the thanks to you or to Rhodri?" she asked.

"We laid it together. But I lighted it," Mischa said, with a gravely confiding air.

"And you told him not to tell me you were here," she said, suddenly understanding that Mischa was the surprise the boy had spoken of.

Mischa shrugged a very Russian shrug. "I didn't want you to break an ankle in your haste to see me," he said, wresting an unwilling laugh from her.

"Of course not," she agreed dryly. "Would

you—" She hesitated. She had almost said, "Would you go now?", but the sight of the first few snowflakes swirling against the window stopped her. Suddenly the idea of being alone on a snowy evening on a lonely cliff was not nearly so attractive as the thought of company—even if that company was Mischa Busnetsky.

So she changed it to, "Would you excuse me? I want to change," and tried not to flinch when he stood and crossed to pick up her cases.

He set the suitcases on the bed while Laddy hovered nervously by the wardrobe. Somehow he seemed to dwarf the room as he stood for a moment looking down at her.

"Am I invited to tea?" he asked, his eyes smiling at her as though nothing terrible had ever passed between them. As though the last eight months hadn't happened.

"Uh, I...uh, yes, why not? I had a cup of tea with Brigit, but I'm certainly hungry enough to eat something. I'll just get out of these—" She was babbling; she could hear the flustered panic in her voice and broke off.

"You have been driving all day," he said. "Relax—take a hot shower. I am capable of making a meal."

"All right," she said. "But, Mischa...."

In the doorway he halted and turned to look at her inquiringly. "Yes?"

"Don't..." she lowered her eyelids "...don't think because I want company that I...I've changed my mind about...."

"I shall not forget your feelings for me," Mischa said. "You need not be afraid of me, Lady."

There was a short pause.

"Thank you," she said.

She came out of the shower feeling warm and clean, but not relaxed, to find Mischa in the very efficient process of creating a meal. In her warm red toweling robe, she paused for a moment, the tiles cool beneath her bare feet.

"What are we eating?" she asked.

"Omelet," said Mischa. "Call me when you are two minutes from being ready."

"All right," she agreed, feeling somehow nervous.

"Lady."

She was on her way out of the kitchen when his quiet voice halted her. Her heart beat loudly for a second and then quieted. Wordlessly she turned and looked at him.

Mischa moved over to stand in front of her, lifting his large comforting hands to hold her shoulders. His eyes smiled down at her with a friendly warmth.

"Just for these few days of being neighbors, shall we try to forget everything—all the passion, the violent emotions—and try to be friendly with one another? I don't like to see you flinching from me as though I might strike you at any moment without warning. You have nothing to fear from me—not love, not hate. I will not hurt you again. Can you believe this, try to believe this, while we are here?"

She closed her eyes, suddenly wanting to believe

it more than anything in the world. For no matter how much she hated Mischa Busnetsky, she knew in a moment of blinding clarity that he would always have the power to hurt her. If only she could believe that he would never use that power....

For the first time in months Laddy felt the hard shell ease around her heart. She looked at him and swallowed. "If I believed you and you...you hurt me again...it would kill me this time," she said, not understanding how much she was confessing to him.

"Yes," he said softly. "So I will be very careful with you."

She wanted to trust him more than she wanted breath. They could never be lovers, as she had once believed they would, going through time together—but Mischa had been more than a lover. He had been a friend who understood everything she thought and was.... "We could try to be friends," Laddy said, and her heart began to beat as though she had leaped a dangerous chasm.

Mischa bent down with a gentle smile on his lips. "Hello, friend," he said, so softly it was almost a whisper, and kissed her lightly on each cheek. Involuntarily she kissed him back, her mouth brushing the firm flesh of his cheek with a satisfied sigh. She might be a fool, but it would be worse than foolish to continue to freeze her emotions because a man who had believed he loved her had not known how to tell her that he had made a mistake. She had to forgive him, to try to become human again, so that one day she could love someone else....

When they had eaten the delicious meal he had prepared, Mischa banked the fire and they sat down together on the sofa and talked and listened to the fire and the silence and the snow....

When he reached out to pull her gently onto his shoulder, she rested her face against the hard muscles of his chest and breathed in the scent of wool and of the man with undisguised pleasure.

"I feel as though nothing could ever hurt me again," she murmured drowsily, hardly knowing she said it.

"Never, when I am by," the deep voice said over her head, and she knew he was a friend and she could say anything to him.

"Will we still be friends when Marsha Miller is around?" she asked, her voice muffled against him.

She counted one beat of time, and then he said, "She is not going to be around. Why did you think she would be?"

"Aren't you going to marry her?" she asked, because she couldn't quite answer that.

"No," said Mischa. But he did not order her off the subject, so she pressed.

"She's very beautiful, isn't she?"

"Very," Mischa said.

"How did you meet her?"

"Her mother organized the sponsoring of one of my lectures. Marsha attached herself to me."

"Did she?" For some reason Laddy found that funny. "And didn't you have any say in the matter?

Or couldn't you turn away anyone as beautiful as her?''

"I couldn't turn away anyone who reminded me so strongly of you," Mischa said quietly.

"Oh!" Laddy stiffened and tried to sit up, but he held her where she was.

"Don't panic," he said. "You asked and I told you. Is the information so dangerous?"

If it wasn't, why was her heart beating so erratically, as though she had barely escaped a fall into a bottomless chasm?

"No," she said hesitantly, and then more strongly, *"No."* She could ask him for explanations here where they were locked away from the world, where nothing mattered.

"You couldn't turn away someone who *looked* like me, and yet...."

"Yes?" he asked gently, and she heard in his voice that he wanted her to ask, he wanted to tell her and again she drew back in fear. Again his warm arm held her. "I have finished with hurting you," Mischa said. "What I say now can have no power to hurt you, Lady." But she was not so sure.

"In America I tried to do what was impossible: I tried to forget you. I thought about health and good food and the rules of squash games, and I tried to forget you. I believed I could succeed, I believed I *was* succeeding—sometimes half a day would pass without my thinking of you, although in prison you had been with me constantly.

"Marsha Miller had hair like yours," he said,

"and your long legs, but I told myself that meant nothing. Then your letter came, sent on by the clinic. I saw your writing on the envelope and I knew that I had not forgotten you at all and that if I read the letter, I would never be free of you.

"I was already receiving fan letters because of your newspaper interview. I put your letter with them, and when Marsha offered to answer such letters for me I thanked her."

As he spoke she felt a painful twist deep inside and bit her lip at this proof that a man she hated could still hurt her with words.

"Free of me?" she repeated steadily. "Is that what you wanted?"

Mischa looked at her long and steadily. "My love, I loved you so much. So much more than I thought possible, so much that the book I wrote for you was only a shadow. You could have led me to hell and I would have followed with a smile on my face.

"On the night your friend kissed you and on the morning the reporters came I realized that though I had survived the betrayal of so many friends and strangers and fellow fighters, I would not survive if *you* betrayed me."

"But I would never—" She had begun to protest as though the last eight months had not been, and hearing her own words, she broke off suddenly.

"No," he agreed. "No matter how much I accused you, how much I tried to make myself believe, I knew you would not. But I was afraid to believe it, afraid to believe in your love, knowing how much power you would have over me.''

''You had the same power over me,'' she whispered.

''Do you understand what it is like to be in prison?'' he asked her gently. ''To be completely powerless, entirely at the mercy of every whim of every guard and civil servant and bureaucrat who crosses your path? Can you understand this? For ten years, since I began my battle with the Soviet state, I had had only one weapon against them—my will. My refusal to accept their falsehoods.''

''God,'' she whispered.

''And then there you were, without any power of wire fences or walls or dogs, with only love, and my love for you, to use against me. And I saw that I had no weapon at all against you, that there was nothing I would not do for you.''

''But you were wrong, weren't you?'' she said in quiet bitterness. ''Your love was not as strong as you thought.'' Mischa looked down into her face for a long moment as though reading what lay behind her eyes. Then he breathed deeply in decision and leaned forward to knock his pipe against the grate.

''I think it's time I went home,'' he said. ''It is late and my fire must have gone out hours ago.''

Laddy stood up and shivered as the colder air of the room beyond the fire reached her.

''It's *cold* in here,'' she exclaimed. ''The temperature must have dropped since this afternoon.''

"Not only the temperature," said Mischa, at the window looking out. "Look at this."

There was nothing to see except a blinding white swirl and, whenever it momentarily ceased, white as far as the eye could reach.

"But this is *Pembrokeshire*," Laddy protested, as though the snow had better disappear, and Mischa laughed at her.

"Obviously the weather should be taught a lesson," he said, pulling on the boots he had left by the fire. "But I am not sure how this should be done." They walked to the kitchen door, and he lifted a hand to her cheek.

"No coat?" she asked.

"In my own cottage," he said. "I did not need it this afternoon."

"Your cottage will be freezing if the fire's out," she said, not understanding why suddenly she could not bear to be left alone. "Do you want to light a fire and come back here to wait until the place is warmer?"

He smiled, his dark eyes warm. "Do you not understand that I do not want to leave at all?" he asked. "That is why it is time to go, my Lady."

She swallowed convulsively. "Oh. Well, then I.... Good night, Mischa."

"Good night, Lady. Don't let your fire go out. Perhaps you had better make your bed on the sofa."

"Yes," she said.

Snow and freezing air boiled into the room for a

moment, and the wind shook the cottage like a giant hand. She heard Mischa laugh into the wind, and then the door slammed and she was alone in the cottage, safely shut away from the wind and the storm...and Mischa Busnetksy.

CHAPTER NINETEEN

THE SNOW HAD FALLEN steadily all night and was still falling when she got up in the morning, though the wind had died. The thick blanket of snow transformed the countryside so that the view from the cottage windows was new and unfamiliar.

She had made up her bed on the sofa, because if she did not keep the fire going she would freeze, and in any case the bedroom was too cold. But she had not fallen asleep without effort. Round and round in her head she had kept hearing Mischa's voice saying, "I would not survive if you betrayed me...."

Mischa arrived just as she was filling the kettle, carrying two large bundles and covered with snow from head to foot. He stood inside her door looking like the abominable snowman, and Laddy began to laugh. Suddenly her heart leaped, as though it was not snow but sunlight that he had brought into the little cottage with him.

"Now I know what they mean by 'large as life,'" she said, trying to brush him down with a tea towel and laughing so hard she drove snow into his eyes and down his collar. "You can't imagine what you look like!'' she gurgled, as with a laughing muttered oath Mischa wrested the towel from her helpless grip.

"If you get any more snow down my neck," he growled threateningly, "I will see what *you* look like when you have climbed out of a snowdrift."

"Did you fall in a *snowdrift*?" she asked delightedly. "Is that what happened? And you the great expert from Siberia!"

Mischa looked at her with a threatening smile. "How would you like to be hugged by the expert from Siberia?" he asked, making a sudden advance.

Laddy leaped back with a shriek, and Mischa laughed.

"All right," Laddy said, mustering her dignity. "Do it yourself. I'll make the coffee. What's this?" she demanded, stooping over one of the bundles. It was a bed sheet full of various objects, which rolled out in all directions as she opened it.

"Food," Mischa said, stamping the last of the snow from his legs and boots. "All my supplies, in fact. The other bundle is my clothing. I am moving in."

Laddy looked down at the pile of brightly colored packages.

"Why?" she asked.

He said, "Because the snow is not going to stop. Because the temperature is still dropping. It will be effort enough to keep one house warm. And because we might need each other."

"I might need you, you mean," Laddy said. "I'm sure you can handle anything. I can't imagine a situation in which you would need me."

"Don't be too sure," Mischa said.

The snow fell steadily all day, creating utter silence and a brightness that seemed to cut the little cottage off from the world. Mischa and Laddy filled cardboard boxes with coal and stacked them in the kitchen and brought in as much of the wood as they could find space for. They turned on the oven of the electric stove and opened it to warm the kitchen when they needed it, and they kept the fire well fueled all day.

They sat on the sofa in front of the fire most of the day, playing chess on a set Mischa had unearthed from the back of a kitchen cupboard, or cards, or simply talking.

More than once Laddy sighed with contentment. *If only the outside world could never intrude on this,* she thought. *If only we never had to let them in, I could be happy like this. I would never remember.... If the outside world had not intruded eight months ago, Mischa might never have learned that he didn't love me, and I would never have had to learn to hate him.*

She tried to curb these thoughts when they occurred, but she knew that somehow, when the snow melted and the world came back, she was going to discover that she had let herself in for even more hurting....

"Would you like some Ovaltine?" she asked that

night when they had listened to the eleven o'clock news on her little radio and learned that all of southwestern Britain lay under the same incredible blanket of snow. Ovaltine seemed so unbelievably domestic that she laughed aloud.

"That sounds as though we've been married twenty-eight years," she explained at Mischa's questioning look. "But what could warm you better on a night like this?"

Mischa underlined the question with a smile. "I can think of things," he said. "But I will take the Ovaltine, thank you."

She hummed along with the radio as she watched for the milk to heat without scalding, and filled two large thick mugs with the creamy beverage. She laid them on a tray with a plate of cookies and the radio and boogied in time to the music as she carried the offering back into the sitting room.

Then she stopped dead and gaped.

The sofa, which had been comfortably near the fire, had been pushed back, and in its place on the floor was the double mattress from her bed, piled with blankets and comforters—and two pillows.

Mischa was adding coal to the fire, and she advanced to the edge of the mattress.

"What is this?" she asked, but her voice was not as calm as she tried to make it.

Mischa glanced around casually, as though he had not detected any trace of panic in her tone. "It is where we are going to sleep tonight," he said. "We will need each other's heat and all the blankets if we are not going to freeze."

"I'm not sleeping in the same bed with you," Laddy said bluntly.

"Why not?" Mischa asked in surprise, as though there could be no reason. This had the effect of flustering her. She dropped her eyes from his inquiring gaze.

"Because. . . I won't, that's all."

"Yes, you will," Mischa said flatly. "I'm not going to spend a cold night for an unintelligent whim. I've had enough years of cold nights to last me a lifetime."

"I'm not—"

"You will sleep with me on the same mattress and under the same blankets," Mischa said harshly. "If one of us were to get a chill and become ill—even only with a bad cold—what then?" He sat down on the mattress, reached for a mug and smiled up at her. "Now, let's drink our domestic Ovaltine and go to bed. If we have been married twenty-eight years, no doubt we can pass a night now and then without making love, if that is what worries you."

It was exactly what worried her, and when he smiled at her like that she could almost forget. . . .

"No," he said quietly, seeing remembrance come into her eyes. "No, you have promised to forget that for now. We are friends, Lady. That is all."

She changed in the bathroom into warm flannelette pajamas, which had long stripes emphasizing her tall thinness. Mischa looked up at her from where he crouched at the fire, stoking it.

"Do you always wear these unfeminine night things?" he asked curiously.

"Yes, I do," she said woodenly. Mischa smiled at her again.

"If you were my woman, you would not wish to wear such a garment to bed, even when alone," he said smilingly, as though this were an academic subject of dispassionate curiosity. "Who is your man that he inspires in you no joy in your beautiful body?"

"Guess," she said sarcastically.

"The man who taught you that love was pain," Mischa said quietly.

"That's right," Laddy said brightly. "So let's get into the bed that is going to be colder than you think, in spite of the blankets and the human warmth—shall we?"

While Mischa showered and changed, she turned out the lights, with the exception of one lamp, which she brought down to the floor beside the mattress. Then she crawled between the icy sheets and lay propped on an elbow, looking into the fire that was only a glow under the heap of new coals Mischa had piled on.

He came into the living room with his hair damp, wearing a pair of soft white trousers with elastic at the waist and legs that looked like part of a jogging or warm-up outfit. Above them his chest and arms, unbelievably brown against the white, were naked.

Laddy sucked in her breath.

"Can't you wear pajamas like everybody else?" she asked testily. "Do you have to come to bed half-naked?"

His feet were brown, bony and muscled, with fine dark hairs curling on his ankles under the white elasticized cuffs, and they gripped the floor as if they owned it.

"I do not own pajamas," he said mildly. "I do not wear them. This—" he indicated the woolly trousers "—is a concession to your modesty."

"Why on earth don't you own pajamas?" she asked in irritated discomfort, and his face crinkled into laughter as, fists on hips, he gazed down at her. He looked like a Persian prince or a genie out of a golden lamp.

"Because they are an unnecessary restriction of freedom," he said, kneeling down to throw back the blankets. "And I want to be free."

He crawled in beside her, smelling damp and masculine, and eased his long body between the sheets with that sensuous enjoyment of a soft bed that she had noticed once before, on a bed of grass.

"Ahh!" he breathed, his broad biceps flexing as he folded his arms under his head. "I expect whoever invented the spring mattress died a millionaire. Did he?"

She couldn't help laughing at this.

"How on earth would I know?"

"Is he not a famous hero?" Mischa asked. "The Americans have made heroes of so many—surely they have not let this one pass unsung?"

"Next time I talk to an American contact I'll ask him for you, shall I?" she laughed.

"Thank you," he said, and she realized with a

sinking heart that that had sounded as though she would be seeing him again.

"Lady," he said gently, reaching an arm toward her, "come here. Don't be afraid of me—I want to talk to you."

She could not resist the tone in his voice. Wordlessly she slid to his side under the blankets and, under the pressure of his hand and arm, rested her head against his shoulder in his gentle embrace.

"How warm you are against me," he breathed. "Lady, my Lady—don't be afraid of me tonight," he whispered as she tensed. "I will not try to make love to you, my love, much as I want to."

"Why not?" she whispered, her stomach suddenly filled with a wild fluttering.

"Because you hate me, and because I love you," Mischa said. "And because I want you to love me when we make love again."

Her jaw clenched against his chest at his first mention of love, and he felt it.

"Mischa, I will never love you," she said quietly. "Don't think it."

He absorbed that in silence. "You loved me once," he said at last.

"More fool me."

He leaned up over her, his hand stroking her arm from shoulder to elbow, and she shivered.

"You tremble when I touch you, Lady. You tremble with desire," he said. "Do you think this means nothing?"

"It means you're very attractive and I'm attracted to you," Laddy said flatly.

"That is all?" She looked wordlessly at him, letting him read the answer in her eyes. "And how many other attractive men create this response in you? How many men have loved you since I left you in the spring?" he grated harshly.

Her eyes widened in fear, and she twisted her face away. Mischa caught her chin and turned her head back, looking deep into her eyes.

"Say it!" he commanded. "One? Two?" He paused. She made no sign. "Three?"

"No, of course not!" she exploded.

He breathed, "Of course not? A woman like you—passionate as I know you are, beautiful, intelligent, loving—do you tell me that no man has touched you since I went away?"

"That's right," she said, angrily, unable to lie.

He took a deep breath. "Yet you tell yourself that you want me only because I am physically attractive?"

"Well, I meant it's a purely physical attraction," she muttered.

"What foolish things are taught about love," he said after a moment. "I cannot believe that you yourself believe this."

"I don't see why not!" she flared. "You feel a physical attraction for me, too, Mischa, I know that much!"

He laughed gently, laying his broad hand against her cheek and temple. "Of course I do, my dearest love. But this is because I love you."

She felt shakily near tears for a moment and bit her lip.

"You've got a funny way of showing it," she said dully. "I'll never believe again that you love me, Mischa. You can't convince me you know what love is."

"I will show you, and I will convince you," he said quietly. "I will give you all the time you need, Lady. Because I know that you love me. Under the pain and hatred I made for you, there is still love. I know it!" he whispered, holding her to him and brushing her brow with his lips.

"No," she said stonily, closing her eyes against the look in his—a look of love that was never going to fool her again.

"Don't think about it now," he said. "Go to sleep against me as though we have been married twenty-eight years—as, one day, if we live, we will be. Go to sleep, my love. Sleep on this: that I have loved you since before the dawn of time, and I always will."

LADDY WAS STRUGGLING through snow up to her thighs, blinded by driving flakes, her whole body frozen. The brightly white sun reflected glaringly from the endless white around her, and she knew she was utterly alone. The loneliness was an ache inside her, and in her dream she thought, *I have felt this way before.*

There was a small house ahead of her suddenly, and she recognized it as her childhood home in Vancouver, somehow different, and here in the middle of nowhere. There was smoke coming from the

chimney, and the door was open. Her struggle
ceased, and she was inside the door, where a fire
burned in a stone fireplace, and someone was sitting
in a chair in front of it. Warmth seeped through her,
and the lonely feeling stopped. "I'm home!" she
said aloud, and the sound of her voice woke her.

She was curled up against Mischa and his arms
surrounded her. He was watching her as she woke,
his face lighted by the glow of the fire. Lifting his
head from the pillow a little, he smiled.

"You had kicked off the blankets," he whispered. "When I warmed you, you said, 'I'm
home.'" And his arms tightened around her.

In her sleep-and-dream-fuddled state, it seemed
the most natural thing in the world, and as his
mouth came down on hers she delighted in the
unique, familiar fire that burned slowly through her
being.

He lifted his mouth from hers and looked at her.
"You are so beautiful," he said. This time his slow
kiss deepened, probed, and his tongue sought out
the soft recesses of her mouth with an intensity that
made her tremble. As he raised his chest to draw her
under him, the blankets fell away from his naked
back, and drowsy with sleep and love, Laddy lifted
her arms to stroke the warm taut skin. But the contact of those firm rippling muscles touched something deep within her, and she tightened her arms
around his back as though she would never let him
go—as though she would break him, but knowing
he could never be broken.

"Mischa," she breathed, when he lifted his mouth again, and it was a passionate whisper that told him everything.

His large powerful hands held her head, and she felt his mouth trace the line of her neck down to her shoulder, and shuddered at the response of the thousand nerves that suddenly seemed to be clustered there.

She could hear the stars, she could touch the silence of the snow, she could see infinity. Every sense was attuned, and her heart was molten gold in her breast.

Mischa's hand trembled as he unbuttoned her pajama top, and the knowledge of how she was affecting him tore at her and she wanted to be in his arms forever, to go through time in this one moment.

When at last he pulled her pajama jacket open, she saw his eyes close for a moment, and he said hoarsely, "Lady, Lady, I have waited so long for you!" Looking into her eyes then, he placed one large strong hand, rough with passion, on her breast, and he smiled at her when she gasped in response. "You see," he said, and she saw what she had always known, that his touch moved her to passion.

She replied, "Yes."

It was a whisper, and his hand moved over her body with a strength that was almost painful. "Tell me!" he demanded, knowing she could hardly speak.

"Yes," she said, and this time the whisper was a moan of desire, and again he closed his eyes.

"Yes," he said.

He moved under the blankets, and then he was lying full-length on her body, their legs touching and she could feel the heat and strength of his powerful thighs along the inside of her own.

This touch immobilized her like a sudden blow, and her arms fell away from him, curving over the pillow above her head; his hands grasped her wrists and held them there. His broad chest seemed terrifyingly large; he towered over her, from a distance of six inches. She yearned now to touch him, to run her hands and mouth over his skin, but when she tried to move, she could not.

Never in her life had she felt so completely in anyone's power. Physically and mentally she was his. If the cottage had burned down around them she could not have moved until he gave the word.

He would not let her move to touch him: he held her wrists and bent his head to kiss her neck, her shoulders, her breasts until she cried out. She gazed at him, willing him to kiss her mouth, waiting the agonizing time it took him to lower his mouth to her own, waiting for the deep thrusting kiss that, when it finally came, made her want to weep in ecstasy.

Unable to respond with her hands, she moved her long legs against his longer ones, frantic by now to touch him, to move him, to possess him completely. With a sudden movement, he jerked his legs against hers, pushing them farther apart and raised his head to see in her eyes the power he had over her.

But she had power over him, too. His eyes blazed

with it, and his hands trembled so that she felt it in her wrists where he still held her.

Mischa released one wrist to reach down and slide his hand over her pajamaed leg. "Nightclothes," he said softly. "Did I not tell you that nightclothes are a restriction of freedom?" His hand moved up to the elastic at her waist, and she felt his rough touch on the skin of her hip.

"Mischa," she begged, and raised her free hand to the mat of black hair on his chest.

"No, not yet," he said, and his voice was suddenly hoarse. He grasped her wrist and held it again immobile, looking into her eyes. "First I am waiting to hear you tell me that you love me." And in the moment he spoke Laddy knew that it was true. The cold pain that had enveloped her heart was gone; she knew that this passion was love, and it swamped her.

It was as it had been eight long months ago: her heart threatening to burst within her, filling her with warmth and life. She had never hated him, her hatred had been pain and betrayal—

The eight months of pain and betrayal and memory came flooding back into her brain in a rush, and she felt as though she were awakening from a drugged state. And she knew again, as though she had forgotten, that this was the man who had left her, who had coldly rejected her when she had wept and pleaded for his love; that this was the man who had more power to hurt her than any other human being.

And whatever he said, he did not love her.

"I don't love you, I hate you," she said, in a cold little voice. "Let me go."

Mischa's eyes darkened with pain, and his hold on her wrists tightened convulsively.

"You love me," he said hoarsely.

"No!" she cried.

"This is only physical attraction?" he demanded. "This is only lust?"

"I hate that word," she ground out. "And I hate you. And that's all this is—a hateful feeling for a man I hate."

"All right," he said with dangerous calm. "I am a fool not to take this half loaf when it is offered me. I want you and you want me. So be it."

She felt the keening "No!" rising in her throat, but she had no time to utter it. His mouth was urgent upon hers, forcing the word back into her throat with such passion that her own answering passion made her unable to speak it.

He tore off her clothing and kicked off his own, and they lay naked on the sheet in the flickering firelight. She lay under the touch of his hands and his body, unable to protest against the bitter pleasure he was giving her, unable to stop her body rising to meet the first sweet, painful thrust of his.

He knew it, and his jaw clenched at her hoarse cry, not knowing how nearly it was a cry of love.

"If this is what you love," he said, his voice anguished, "let me see how much I can give you."

He set out then to drown her in pleasure. His

hands, alive with passion, made her cry out, and his mouth made her weep. The crescendo built and built till she lived on the edge of rapture, but he kept her from release. She could not hide her responses from his intimate knowledge of her... and he would smile, and wait, and begin again.

"I love you," he rasped at last. "Do you hear me, my Lady, my love? I love you. If you take this from me now you take a gift of love."

And then what began in her would not be stopped, and when her hands gripped him and her head arched back on a high pleading cry, he answered her cry, and the golden heat coursed through her blood, her nerves, her brain... and her heart.

"I love you," Laddy cried, knowing it for truth, her heart at last renouncing fear and pain. She loved him, no matter what the price. She could not hide from love anymore. "Mischa, I love you," she said again, feeling tears in her eyes and on her cheeks.

His body surged against her, and in one motion he gathered her up against him, shuddering and trembling and whispering over and over: "Love me, oh my Lady, love me...."

CHAPTER TWENTY

TREFELIN WAS a collection of oddly-shaped bumps under a thick white blanket that stretched from the cliff top to the horizon of low encircling hills. Smoke was rising from fluffy white chimneys as if from strange subterranean dwellings. The sun, bright in a blue sky, sparkled blindingly from the dark icy sea and the diamond crystals of white snow.

"Good morning!" chirruped the little mound of snow at the door that seemed to have Rhodri's eyes and voice. "Have you seen the snow, both of you?"

"How could we not?" Mischa asked him, chuckling, his strong white teeth clenched on his pipe, while Laddy burst into laughter.

"Have you been in an avalanche?" she demanded. "Rhodri, you look like an igloo!"

"Yes, they have igloos in Canada, don't they?" Rhodri said with interest, futilely trying to brush off the worst of the snow before coming in. "Did you live in one when you were little, Lady?" Although he called her Laddy in any other company, when the three of them were alone he had taken to pronouncing her name as Mischa did. His thin smiling face was pink with exertion, and his dark eyes were glowing with his joy at seeing both of them; Laddy loved him.

She had to laugh. "An *igloo*?" she repeated. "Rhodri, where I lived we never even got snow at Christmas. Speak to Mischa, here. He's the one who knows his snow."

"Be careful," Mischa said menacingly, "or you will soon know it as well as Rhodri."

Giving up on the task of trying to stamp off his burden of snow while standing almost thigh deep in the stuff, Rhodri entered the kitchen like a confident puppy, sure of his welcome whatever his condition. Laughing, they stepped back and watched him close the door. Then he jumped up and down in one place, and it was slowly revealed that he wore a white jacket.

"I thought that was all snow," Laddy said.

"Well, there *was* quite a bit, wasn't there?" Rhodri said, looking with interested pride at the circle of snow on the floor around his feet. "I like it, you know. I have never seen *real* snow before. It is very white, isn't it, when it is thick? Perhaps when I am older I shall live in Canada. Brigit sent you a loaf of freshly baked bread, but I do not think it is as warm as it was," he chattered, holding out a white plastic-wrapped object. "And I am to be sure you are both all right."

Laughing helplessly, Laddy took the bread from him. "Take off your coat," she said. "Have breakfast with us."

"I am not allowed to, no matter how much you ask," Rhodri said sadly. "I am to go home for breakfast, Brigit says. Mairi, too." He looked from one to the other. "Brigit wants to know if you are finally going to get married," he said matter-of-factly. "She said I was not to ask, but I wish to know, too, and I knew you would not mind if I said so."

The bread was still faintly warm, and its fresh smell filled her nostrils as Laddy carefully unwrapped the thick brown loaf.

"We are certainly getting married," Mischa's voice said behind her.

With a satisfied, "Good," Rhodri turned to the door. "There is a cathedral in St. David's," he said. "You had better get married there." And with this settled to his satisfaction, he pulled open the door and set out back along the shadowed path of his footprints that was the only mark on the dazzling whiteness.

Laddy and Mischa stood in the doorway, looking down toward the village and breathing deeply in the cold, crackling winter air.

"All that snow," breathed Laddy. "Just like my dream."

Mischa's arm tightened around her. "You are home safe now, my Lady. I won't let you go again."

She nuzzled the thick white wool of his sweater under her cheek. "Please don't ever let me go," she said.

As Rhodri's thin figure receded in the distance they drew back inside and closed the door, shivering as the icy air that had crept through their clothes finally attacked the warmth of their skin. The kettle was just coming to a boil on the stove: a cozy, homey sound, and Laddy sighed with deep contentment.

"We're going to be stuck here for a while, I think," she said.

"Good," said Mischa, with masculine satisfaction.

"You can write your novel, as you planned," she protested. "It's all right for you. What will I do?"

"I did not plan on writing a novel," said Mischa. "I planned on teaching you to love me. And I have not finished yet. You will have enough to occupy you, my Lady. And when the snow clears we will go into St. David's and get married."

She drew a finger down his cheek, and his mouth turned in to her palm. "Liar," she accused, laughing. Mischa caught her hand and held it to his lips, and she closed her eyes. "How could you plan to...be with me when you didn't know I'd be here?"

He chuckled deep in his throat. "Do you not know that Helen telephoned me in Crete a week ago when you asked her for the use of this cottage?"

"What?"

"I had been waiting since that night at my apartment to get you alone for long enough to make you listen to me. Helen and Richard kept me informed of your movements so that—"

"And what were you doing in Crete?" she demanded skeptically.

"Looking at a boat I thought I might kidnap you on if I bought it," he said, "and staying away from the constant temptation to make late visits to your flat."

He was stroking her hair tenderly, and she could feel his touch as though her hair were alive with nerves. She closed her eyes as he bent his head to her lips, and for a long moment in the bright kitchen there was silence, except for the high whistling of the kettle.

"Were you awfully angry about those articles I was writing? They weren't really so bad, were they?" Laddy asked later as they ate a leisurely breakfast.

"I don't know," Mischa smiled. "They gave me a good excuse to think that my violent feelings toward you were only righteous anger."

"Aha!" she said. "And when did you know they were not?"

"The night I came to your flat. You talked about being in league with Pavel Snegov—and suddenly everything fell into place in my mind."

"What everything is that?" Laddy inquired after a moment, concentrating on her futile struggles with the lid of a new jar of marmalade. He took the jar from her, and under his broad palm she heard the snap of air invading the vacuum.

"I saw what a fool I was to worry about the future when I could have love in the present. I knew that there was no connection between you and Pavel Snegov and never would be, that you would never betray me. But even if you did, I knew that I would always love you more than life—and if *you* led me to hell, what reason was there not to go?''

Her face went white, and she gazed at him with wide, vulnerable eyes.

"Do you really love me like that?" she whispered, feeling as though her breath had ceased to function.

"Do you not know it?" Mischa asked.

"No...I...I...no."

He set down his coffee cup and came round to pull her from her chair. "What did you think?" he asked, almost angrily, his eyes searching her face. She stared up at him, not able to answer, and with a muttered exclamation he pulled her to his chest. "But what else could you think, after I had hurt you so much?"

He breathed shakily, "My love, did you not understand that when I told you to tell Snegov that there was one thing in the world with which I could be destroyed, I was speaking of you?"

There was a deep and utter silence as she absorbed it, and then he sought her lips in a kiss.

"You laughed that night as though—" She broke off.

"I laughed because I felt the way Newton did when the apple hit him on the head. I laughed because I understood. I did not know then how deep your pain was. I thought you were only angry.

I thought you would write another article about me and I would teach you that your anger came from love and not hate.'' He kissed her again and let her go, and she sat down and shakily drank her coffee.

"And the next article was a friendly story about the royalties.'' Sitting, Mischa laughed and shook his head. "Until you told me that you thought it, too, would anger me, I was afraid you had given up. That you really did not want to see me again. I thought I would show you the apartment and tell you not to write about it and see what you did then. But this was unnecessary—the friendly article, too, was meant to anger me. I believed then that I could make you remember you loved me. But when you showed me how much I had hurt you, I knew that if by some miracle I could teach you to love me again, it would not be that night. Such a thing would take a long time, and patience. And I knew I must wait for the right time...."

"What sort of right time?''

"When I could get you alone for a few days.''

"So when I asked Helen for the cottage, I gave you the perfect opportunity.''

"Not perfect—I was not sure whether our memories here would make you remember love or pain. But I could not wait any longer.'' And he smiled slowly at her.

"But when I saw you, I might have run away,'' Laddy said. "How could you know there would be a snowstorm to keep me here? Or did you get friendly with the snow god while you were in

Siberia?'' Her voice lifted in horrified mock accusa-
tion. "Is this storm some kind of personal favor to
you?"

He laughed with her, pulling her to her feet.
"Snow or no snow, you would not have got away
from me easily," he said.

"How would you have stopped me?" she asked
indignantly, and Mischa laughed, his teeth white
against his face.

"I would have incapacitated your car, for one,"
he said.

"I could still have gone to stay at Mairi
Davies's," she pointed out.

He said softly, "I would have gone to bring you
back, Lady. And you would have come with me if I
had to carry you kicking through the streets. I did
not want to wait any longer."

"Mmm," Laddy murmured lovingly into his
throat, and he led her into the sitting room to the
sofa that had been restored to its position in front
of the fire.

"Why did we put the bed away, I wonder?" Mischa asked teasingly. "That was shortsighted."

She laughed and put her arms around his neck.
"I love you," she said urgently. "Oh, I love you so
much!"

"Thank God," he said huskily, his mouth hovering over hers. "I love you, Lady. I was afraid I
would never hear you say that again. When I discovered that my real freedom was your love, only to
learn that I had lost you—"

He held her tightly to him, and she had never been safer than she was in this moment. She raised her lips to him like a hungry supplicant.

"Mischa," she moaned, as he kissed her.

He drew back his head a little to say, "I like to taste my name on your lips. Say it again."

"Mischa. I love you, Mischa, Mischa..." she chanted, until his possessive mouth made her mute.

SUPERROMANCE

Longer, exciting, sensual and dramatic!

Fascinating love stories that will hold
you in their magical spell till the last page
is turned!

Now's your chance to discover the earlier
books in this exciting series. Choose from
the great selection on the following page!

Choose from this list of great
SUPERROMANCES!

SUPERROMANCE

Complete and mail this coupon today!
